SOLDIERS OF SAEDO
COLLECTION 1

BOOKS 1 - 4

CALLA ZAE

PROSE & CONCEPTS

CONTENTS

SOLDIERS OF SAEDO

COLLECTION 1

BOOKS 1-4

USA TODAY BESTSELLING AUTHOR

CALLA ZAE

COPYRIGHT

An Alien Dare:

Ebook ISBN: 978-1-952820-09-0

Audio ISBN: 978-1-952820-13-7

An Alien Storm:

Ebook ISBN: 978-1-952820-11-3

Audio ISBN: 978-1-952820-12-0

Paperback ISBN: 978-1-952820-17-5

For those yearning for a new beginning.

.

.

.

"Your life does not get better by chance. It gets better by change."
– Jim Rohn

ALARUS GALAXY MAP
PLANET CELERON

AN ALIEN RESCUE

SOLDIERS OF SAEDO 1

USA TODAY BESTSELLING AUTHOR

CALLA ZAE

AN ALIEN RESCUE #1: BLURB

"You weren't the only one who was rescued. We saved each other."

Emma is on vacation with her six siblings to ring in the New Year with everything auspicious and nothing to do with broken relationships, disappointments, and heartache. But what she got was an alien abduction.

Raeko, a beautiful green star-being, rescues her from horrific beasts that want her to reproduce for them. His protection and honesty stirs her heart in a way that echoes the love she has always wanted.

Is he Emma's New Year's gift? Or is he another male who's going to bruise her heart?

CONTENTS

ONE

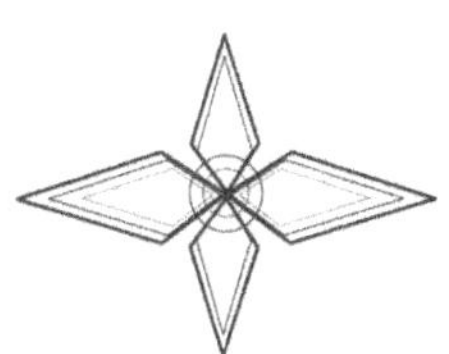

The energy of New Year's Eve placed a smile on Emma's face as she rushed into a crowded restaurant to celebrate with her six younger sisters. They all needed a new beginning and vowed that this New Year would be the start of a new life. A life that gave them a purpose. A life that offered their hearts more happiness than pain and disappointment.

Emma cursed under her breath for being late. This was unlike her punctual self. But she had to take care of the sudden headache that forced her to remain in bed a while longer.

She straightened her sequined dress, tucked a loose strand of brown chin-length hair behind her ear, and wandered out to the private patio decorated with holiday lights. Out on the sandy beach, her sisters' laughter echoed against the crashing waves.

Emma removed her Christian Louboutin shoes, left them on the patio, and stepped onto the white, warm sand, heading toward her siblings. "Sorry, I'm late. We can start our ritual now."

"Don't worry about it. We're on vacation." Sasha flicked her long, brown hair that had recently gotten beautiful golden highlights.

"This is our year. I can feel it." Emma inhaled a deep breath of fresh air. "Let's change up our ritual this year. Instead of waiting a few more hours until midnight to reveal our wishes to the Universe, let's say them now. Keep the wish a secret until it's fulfilled. It's like a baby that needs nurturing."

With hands pressed together like a prayer, the seven sisters closed their eyes and spoke to the Universe, asking for whatever their hearts desired. Though the restaurant boomed with celebration, they were cocooned in their own world outside.

Seven sisters with seven wishes sent out loving energies from their hearts to the Universe that heard everything.

When they were done, they all looked at each other in the eye, sealing the ritual.

Emma felt a rush of warmth in her heart, confirming that she was ready for a new beginning. She erased her broken six-month relationship from her mind and looked toward the future.

Emma took out her phone. "Time for selfies. We didn't get to go anywhere last year, so we need all the pictures to mark this moment. This is a turning point year for all of us."

Sasha spread her arms wide. "Call in what you want, babes! Forget all the jerks in our lives."

As a nurse, Emma was used to taking care of others. When it came to her own needs, men always failed miserably. Maybe she demanded too much. But demanding respect, honesty, and love wasn't an out-of-this-world request.

She had cleared her slate for all possibilities this New Year. She recalled her wish from earlier. *I deserve a man who loves and respects me. I deserve an honest man.*

Emma plopped down on the sand, closed her eyes, and inhaled the salt air.

"We have two more days to enjoy this lovely, warm weather. Let's bask in it." Sasha gave Emma a one-arm hug. "I know you don't hear this from me often, but thank you for dealing with my mood swings and taking care of us..."

Emma opened her eyes when she couldn't hear the rest of her sister's comments or the crashing waves. She tried to turn, but she couldn't move her body.

Why was she so drowsy? She hadn't drank any cocktails. Before she could contemplate further, her body thudded to the ground and sand kissed her cheek. The last image her eyes captured was a massive silhouetted figure with a wagging tail.

Emma opened her eyes to wild, growling sounds. Fear bubbled up her spine when she couldn't move her hands. They were tied behind her back. What the hell?

Her back leaned against the cool slate wall.

Sasha's head drooped on Emma's shoulder. Her sisters were all unconscious.

"Sasha?" Emma whispered and nudged her sister. "Vanessa, Inga, Rita, Isabelle, Nina...?"

No one responded. Fear had never crippled her like this before. Emma's lips trembled. "God, please help us."

Who had kidnapped them?

She glanced around the spacious room made of stones. A wide window with tinted glass was on the opposite side of where she sat. A metal door was the only way out, only feet from the window. Who was watching them from the other side of that panel?

Scary, raucous sounds that had woken her boomed from the other side of the metal door. When the door kicked opened, her heart stopped. She gasped at the horror that walked in. Three monsters with brown skin, large horns coming from their foreheads, and thick, scaly tails strode toward her. Each one had two sets of eyes on the side and a wide mouth with fangs still caked with flesh or whatever it was.

One beast opened its mouth. What came out were noises that sounded like a dying car engine. Their speech was the loud clanking noise that had woken her.

Was this a dream? It had to be. This strange situation, this terrifying image was too surreal for it to be reality. She shifted and a few sequins fell off from the ripped seam of her cocktail dress.

The lead beast eyed her exposed thigh and moved closer. It grinned and gray saliva drooled from its mouth. The other beasts licked their worm-like lips as they gazed at her sisters.

Emma had to find a way out. How would she escape? Why wasn't she screaming?

Shock had locked logic into a dark corner of her mind. She found it again when the beast pushed its face close to hers. Its rancid breath made her gag. She opened her mouth, and screamed for her life.

The beast backed away and stared at her. Its friends paused and flared their nostrils. Their gazes turned to her siblings as if they were dinner.

In that moment, her sisters woke. *Thank God.*

Terror filled their eyes, and the room erupted with female screams.

One beast roared and silenced the room. Her sisters gawked and froze in fear.

A boom shattered the air and the ground trembled beneath her as the wall exploded. Debris covered her in sharp, itchy shards of stone. She turned to her sisters who appeared to be okay, covered in dust as she was.

Another explosion broke down the rest of the wall, ripping off limbs from the beasts. Daylight from the outside streamed in, broken by three green men in black armor. They rushed through the debris and untied Emma and her sisters. The green beings assisted her sisters out of the room.

One of the men, a green being with short, brown hair and the bluest eyes Emma had ever seen cut the ties from her hands. With a gentleness she didn't expect, he lifted her and carried her from the room like she was a feather. He said something, but she didn't understand it. She kept staring at this beautiful green being. A smirk curved on his lips, and her stomach fluttered.

Why would her stomach flutter at a moment like this? How could she be enjoying this when she should be worrying about her life and the lives of her sisters? Why wasn't she afraid of this stranger?

So many questions bombarded her. She didn't have time to contemplate them all when his body jerked, and he let out a painful cry. More blasts popped in the air. She slid to her feet as he shielded her with his body while shooting back at the enemies. Ten brown beasts charged forward with massive guns.

Her savior shouted something to the other green men who ushered her sisters into a silver—

Emma blinked and gawked at the silver dome with metallic wings that swung up like doors on a Lamborghini. The massive spaceship was five times the size of her house.

"Where are you taking them?" Emma started toward her sisters, but the green man held her back. He released husky sounds, but she didn't understand. "What?"

The spaceship took off and disappeared in a flash.

"Wait! No!" A hundred horrible images popped into her mind. Where were these men taking her sisters? Why weren't they waiting for her and this green man?

She tried to yank herself free from this green being who shielded her from the vicious monsters. She stopped fighting. If they both died, she wouldn't be able to see her sisters. She needed this man alive to help her find them. Caution tickled her mind. For all she knew, he could be another kidnapper. She ran behind him, trying her best to keep up.

Emma couldn't run fast as rocks and twigs poked her bare feet, and she stopped for breath. She was no marathon runner. The man who had saved her picked her up, tossed her over his shoulder, and fled. Shock and fear prevented any protest from firing out of her mouth.

The blur of motion made her dizzy. A dark shadow fell over them, and the smell of wet soil and rotten leaves filled her nose. When he slowed down and placed her on her feet, Emma wobbled for equilibrium. She peered around, suddenly aware of her location. They were in a forest of trees with wide trunks and fan-like leaves. Fog snaked around them.

He muttered something, and, again, she didn't understand a word.

Emma gestured with her hands. "I don't understand you." She looked up at the sky, and the two suns beamed down at her. Holy hell, two suns?

She'd contemplate that later. Right now, she had more important things to worry about. "Where are my sisters?"

He surveyed the area and when nothing came after them, he turned back to her. He reached into the pocket of his black metal armor and pulled out a small silver device. He gave it to her, pointing to his ears.

Maybe it was an earbud? She placed the device inside her ear, and the metal surface cooled her skin. Energy hummed, and the humming traveled into her ear and beyond. Something clicked in her mind as a wave of energy warmed her ears, her face, and then her entire head.

"Can you hear me?" He tapped his ears. "Can you under-stand me?"

Awe and surprise overcame her. She nodded at the comprehension. "Yes, I can. You understand English?"

"I understand all human languages." His husky voice sent a thrill down her spine.

"What is this thing in my ear?"

"A language translator."

That innovative device could assist nurses and doctors. She wanted one for Earth.

Blasts boomed in the distance. "Can you keep up with me?" he asked. "The Ulkrins will catch up if we don't get going. My brothers will meet us on the other side of this forest."

Purple blood seeped through the fabric over his bicep. She had forgotten he had been hit while carrying her to safety. "Are you okay?"

"I'm fine. Just a minor wound. What's your name?"

"Emma, and yours?"

"Raeko." He clutched her hand, and they ran together. "I can answer all your questions later."

Two Ulkrins appeared to their right. One threw a massive arm at Raeko and missed while the other beast eyed Emma. He moved closer, taunting her. She picked up a sharp rock and prepared to defend herself.

Back to back with Emma, Raeko blocked the attack, gripped the Ulkrin's arm, and twisted it. Bones cracked, and Emma winced from the sounds. From her job, she had witnessed horrible, bloody things and heard gut-wrenching noises, but this surreal experience brought on a new level of fear and violence.

Emma wanted to help, but she didn't know what she could do.

Raeko aimed his blaster at the beast's face and blew it apart. Emma ducked to avoid the flying flesh. With rage, the other Ulkrin rushed toward them, blasting wildly, a furious expression on his face. Like earlier, Raeko shielded her as they moved away, using the wide tree trunks for cover.

They ran toward a small opening in the side of a hill. Raeko pushed her inside and away from him as he whirled around, blasting at the Ulkrin, hitting him several times in the chest. The beast dropped to his knees and roared in pain. The Ulkrin whipped out something from his claw. Raeko grabbed her hand and fled further back into the dark cave, avoiding the explosion. Rocks crumbled, the ground shook, and boulders blocked the cave entrance. The opening that might be their only way out.

That knowledge sent a new wave of terror through her. "How are we going to escape?"

Raeko pressed something on the plate of his chest armor and a beam of light glowed from within. He pulled a device from his armor, tapped it, and a virtual screen appeared, revealing a map. "There's an opening on the other side of this tunnel, just past a pool of water. My brothers will meet us there."

"How will they know where we are?"

"I just sent out a signal. They can track me." He placed the tablet back on his arm and pointed to the ground, lighting a path for them to walk. The luminescence from his light cast a glow over his face. He was a beautiful man with a strong jawline she wanted to trace with her fingers.

Blue eyes stared at her with concern. "Are you okay?"

"Physically, I'm okay. Mentally? I'm not sure. I never expected to be kidnapped on New Year's Eve, running for my life from monsters. What are the Ulkrins? Are there more like them out there?"

"They're star-beings known to abduct females to reproduce. There are many decent star races who do not believe in that. I'm one of them."

Emma didn't know how to respond to his comment. The

possibility of meeting an alien had never crossed her mind. She met his gaze. "So aliens are real..."

"I prefer the term star-beings." He smiled, and the laugh lines around his mouth deepened, sending another flurry of nerves through her stomach. "What kind of star-being are you?"

"We're Saedos. Saedo is a province on planet Celeron. I'm one of the Soldiers of Saedo, tasked with protecting the villagers." He led her deeper into the tunnel, and the beam of light brightened, adjusting to the darkness.

Emma had known she wasn't on Earth when she saw those two suns, but his confirmation brought on a reality that scared her. "Do you know where my sisters are?"

"My soldier-brothers probably took them back to Saedo. We picked up on Ulkrin energy and knew we had hostages to rescue. Don't worry, your sisters will be safe with my brothers." He brushed a hand over Emma's cheek, and his blue eyes glowed. "You'll reunite with them soon."

"Your eyes..." She pointed. "They illuminate?"

He glanced away for a second. Was that a sliver of shyness she just witnessed? When he met her gaze again, the blue irises shifted through various colors. "Only when I'm attracted to a female."

This muscular soldier who stood well over six feet tall and who had killed a number of monstrous beasts with ease had just revealed his vulnerability to her.

Her heart raced at his honesty and gentle touch. She appreciated the truth more than he could ever know. None of her previous boyfriends had shown her this much of themselves.

Heat warmed her cheeks. "Thank you for saving me and my sisters."

Raeko tipped her chin up to look at him. "I've never met a female who could make my entire body tremble. If only you could hear my *corra* beating in my chest. That's what we call the 'heart' here."

"You're very honest. I like it." She recalled her wish to the Universe and was afraid that it was teasing her. "Do you know a lot about humans?"

He lifted a shoulder. "I have nothing to hide. I know enough about humans. I've met a few before. If there's a chance, I'd like to explore this powerful attraction between us, Emma."

Her name sounded like a gem on his lips, but her past had taught her to proceed with caution. She couldn't ignore the way her heart hammered every time he looked at her. She wasn't ready to share that yet.

"I'm open to possibilities," she said.

"That sounds good to me. Let's get you out of here."

He held her hand as they walked in silence. The simplicity of it gave her comfort in the darkness.

With no monsters chasing her and a moment to catch her breath, Emma concentrated on her surroundings. She inhaled a breath and focused on her body's reaction. She felt nothing was off. Her inhale and exhale came easily, so the oxygen level was good. She didn't wobble when she walked, so her equilibrium was fine. She glanced around and found only dirt and rocks.

Raeko stopped when something hissed in the distance. He gripped his blaster and pushed her behind him.

An animal the size of a bear with eight legs and two heads stalked forward, crouched low as if preparing to lurch at them. Each head had three eyes. Sharp fangs glinted in Raeko's light beam. Two tongues uncurled themselves and stretched out, tasting the air.

The animal leaped at them. Raeko sent a blast into one head and another into its body. It shrieked. The other head spat out gooey web-like things that landed on the hem of Emma's dress. Smoke emerged as the goo ate through the fabric. *Shit.*

Raeko gripped a section of her dress and ripped off the part stained with goo. Goo also fell on parts of his armor.

He destroyed the animal with a series of blasts. He grabbed a flat rock and scraped off the slime from his chest and legs. "These creatures have a poisonous secretion. We need to wash off all residue. There's a pool somewhere in here. I'd carry you, but—"

"Don't worry about it. You're all covered with the nasty stuff. I can walk in bare feet." She limped as sharp stones jabbed her feet and tried her best not to whine. There was nothing either of them could do.

They made two right turns and heard dripping water. Steam emerged from the pool, and daylight streamed in from an opening above the pool.

Raeko dipped his hand into the clear water. "It's a hot spring. Even better." He splashed water onto his armor and pants, cleaning off the monster's secretion. Then he stripped off his armor, and it clanked to the ground. The undershirt clung to his muscles. Desire rushed to Emma's core, tightening her thighs.

What the hell was wrong with her? This green man with wide shoulders was unraveling her in so many ways. This instant attraction was unfamiliar to her. Everything she had done prior to meeting him was careful and practical. With him, she wanted the unexpected. To jump in without thinking first.

"The heat from the pool will kill the germs." He gestured her over. "You should cleanse yourself. You can go first. I'll...be over there."

"Over there" was a mere fifteen feet.

Emma kept the smile to herself. "Thank you. Why didn't the secretion ruin your armor? Your undershirt and pants appear fine too."

"They're made from a Norakian alloy called fortisium. It's

very strong. We're friends with the Norakians from planet Terrakado."

Relief settled in her. "Do you need me to look at the cut on your bicep? I'm a nurse. But I've never treated anyone other than humans."

"Thank you, but it's only a minor abrasion. It'll heal on its own. It just needs time. The hot spring will soothe it."

She eyed his muscular body, skimming across his chest, down his abdomen to his toned legs, and back up to his shoulders. She reached up, and her fingers traced the smooth surface of the gorgeous green skin. She couldn't help herself. "Is the anatomy of a star-being similar to a human being?"

Laugh lines bracketed his mouth. "Exactly what part are you asking about?"

Embarrassment flushed her face, and heat shot down her neck. "That's not what I meant. If I were to treat you or any star-being, I'd want to know if you have the same stuff. You know, organs like the heart, lungs, and so forth. I don't want to hurt you by accident."

He chuckled. "I know what you meant. You have a way of forming interesting images in my mind. I like them."

Oh, God. What kind of images did he see?

"I'm a humanoid, so we have some similarities. I have a corra, lungs, and other organs like you. Some are larger than yours. I have blood running through my body. I have needs just like you." His gaze intensified and made her forget what she was about to say. "We hurt and we bleed. We think and we feel emotions. Like you, our corras allow us to love beyond measure." He swallowed and the veins on his neck pulsed. "You're the most beautiful female I've ever met."

Her heart skipped. "Is this how you talk to all the women around you?"

"No, only you."

"Why?"

The corners of his lips quirked. "Because you make me want things, and we don't even know each other. That's powerful." He leaned in and the warmth of his breath sent tingles down her body. "You make me want."

"No one is stopping you." She sucked in a breath when she realized what had escaped her mouth.

Victory flickered in his eyes. His lips brushed over hers, and she welcomed his mouth. The gentle kiss sent a jolt through her body and fired up her blood. His arms wrapped around her waist, pulling her closer. Her hands caressed his neck and dug into his hair. When she moaned, he slid his tongue into her mouth, and she melted.

He smelled of leather and wood smoldering over a campfire, so manly. His taste was an explosion of delicious desires overwhelming her.

He broke the kiss and smiled. "I want you, but not right now. There could be other dangerous animals in this dark tunnel. We need to get back to the village."

Emma nodded and tried to regain her sanity.

Raeko kept his word and gave her privacy to take a quick dip in the hot spring. Her body welcomed the heat from the water. When she was cleansed, she pulled on her ripped cocktail dress. Her feet stepped on dirt and pebbles and wished she had a pair of comfortable sneakers.

He stood at the edge of the pool. "I'll be fast. You should stay around here while I wash. I don't want you out of my sight. If something appears, I can help you."

"But..."

"I don't mind."

Emma could have sworn she saw a smile bloom on his face when he turned to jump into the water. The odd thing was she didn't feel awkward sitting there with an invitation to watch him. She half turned to give him some privacy. There was a casualness, a comfort between them that normally existed only between people in a long-term relationship. This instant connection intrigued her.

Could God be answering her wish? Could this be the man of her dreams?

Emma had to trust her heart. Right now, she couldn't hear her heart clearly. Too much emotion and uncertainty stirred in her. First, she needed to know if her sisters were safe. That was the most important thing. She was the older sister, and no matter where she was, that maternal aspect always kicked in.

She wouldn't let any male come between her and her family. Any man who became a wedge wasn't worth it.

A loud explosion shook the ground, and Raeko jumped out of the pool and got dressed. She launched into his body, and his arms closed around her.

"My soldier brothers are here." Raeko lifted her off her feet and carried her to safety.

THREE

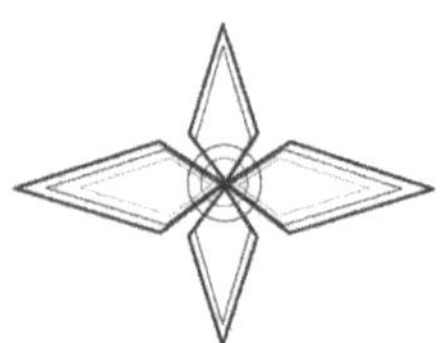

Nerves churned in Emma's stomach as she sat beside Raeko inside an oblong-shaped shuttle bus with massive wheels. Computer screens lined one wall and weapons covered another. Four soldiers dressed in the same armor as Raeko sat across from him, giving him updates on the Ulkrins. She discovered he was the leader of their group.

"We killed dozens of them. They won't lurk around Saedo territory anymore."

"Good. How are Emma's sisters?" Raeko asked.

"They're safe." The solider named Maeson, the one with brown hair that went past his ears, turned to her. "They're worried about you, Emma."

"I'm worried about them too. Thank you for saving us."

Raeko placed his hand on her thigh, covering the ripped seam of her dress. A kind and possessive gesture that did interesting things to her insides.

"These are my soldier brothers: Osayik, Arkon, and Jarzell."

They smiled and nodded at her, and she returned the gesture to the gorgeous star-beings. But only the one sitting next to her stirred her heart.

For the next twenty minutes, Emma stared out of the shuttle bus and admired the lovely environment. Enormous trees with green and purple fan-like leaves lined both sides of the paved road. The sky was bright blue, similar to that on Earth. They turned down a large road with buildings and houses made of stones. Some were multi-leveled, and others appeared to be long ranches.

The shuttle bus stopped in front of a large building. Emma spotted her sisters outside the front door. Raeko opened the door, and Emma fled to her sisters and embraced each one as if they were young kids, but she didn't care.

"Are you all right? Did you get hurt?"

"We're fine, *Mom*. What about you?" Sasha gave her a once over. "You need new clothes and shoes."

Emma glanced at her siblings. They all wore new tops and pants. Each ensemble suited the wearer's personality.

"They gave us a selection to pick from. The fabrication here is top-notch." Inga ran her hands down her shiny jumpsuit.

"Which one of those stunning star-beings is your hero?" Rita asked.

"Probably the one with the pretty woman fawning over him," Sasha said.

Emma whipped her head around as a beautiful female star-being in a fitted dress touched Raeko's face with affection. She examined the cut on his bicep with care and pushed him down to a chair. She sprayed something over the cut. Something she said made him smile.

Emma's heart cleaved in two at the sight. She should have been the one to tend to his wound. She should have been the reason to put a smile on his face. Had it only been a dream when he kissed her in the tunnel?

She thought they had something special. *You're the most beautiful female I've ever met. You make me want.*

His words rang in her ears. She'd believed him. Oh, why had she allowed her heart to open again? She should have known better.

Sadness drained her of energy, and dizziness overcame her. Bones seemed to disappear from her body.

"Are you okay?" Sasha gripped Emma's arm to stabilize her.

"Yeah, I just need to lie down and get out of this dress."

FOUR

After thirty minutes under a hot shower to clear her head, Emma got dressed in a soft, loose top and stretchy jeans. Her sisters were right about the wide selection of clothing and the innovative fabrications. The tunic she wore was made from a fabric with high-tech properties that adjusted to her body's temperature. She chose pants that looked like jeans and stepped into a pair of ankle boots that molded to the size of her feet.

The technology on this planet baffled her. She wished Earth had a quarter of the technology available on Saedo. The shower she'd just experienced was like a cosmic spa that sprayed on fragrant liquids, molding and massaging her skin until it was soft as butter. She'd experienced the best exfoliation of her life.

The soldiers invited all of them to dinner, where they would discuss the next step. They had already been told that they could return to Earth, but that wouldn't happen for another few weeks. They had to wait to get a larger spaceship capable of the long journey to Earth.

Emma joined her sisters outside, where several large tents stood like giant domes. At a glance, there were about fifty soldiers and thirty females. Ten of the females were also decked in soldier armor.

Sasha glanced around the area, searching for someone.

"What are you looking for?" Emma asked.

"Nothing. Just admiring the place. I mean, we're on a planet that's not in books on Earth. NASA hasn't even talked about it. I want to make sure I don't forget anything that's happened. Everything feels like a dream."

Emma recognized the curious spark in Sasha's eyes and knew her sister wasn't telling her the whole truth. Emma didn't press on because there were private things better left unsaid. She had some of her own.

"Did everyone receive a language translator?" Emma gestured to her ear.

Sasha nodded. "We did."

Emma's heart pounded when she met Raeko's eyes as he stood by a tent. He didn't have on his armor. Instead, he wore a dark top that showed off his athletic body. Leather pants completed a stunning physique that screamed sexy.

Sasha leaned in and whispered, "I want a man to look at me the way he's looking at you."

Emma's thighs clenched, and she looked away.

Raeko came up to them and greeted Sasha. Sasha took off to join the other girls, shooting a grin at Emma.

"I heard you weren't feeling well. Are you feeling better now?" he asked.

"I'm fine, thank you for asking." Emma strode past him, trying to catch up to Sasha.

"Wait a minute," Raeko called after her.

Emma ignored him and kept going. She didn't get far when a hand snaked around her wrist and stopped her. She turned to meet his gaze. "What?"

Concern filled his eyes. "What happened? Did I do something wrong?"

"Why are you here? You already have a woman by your side. Why are you bothering me?" Emma glared at him.

"What are you talking about?"

She scowled. "I saw you with her earlier. She treated your wound. The wound you didn't let me touch. Don't lie to me. I hate lying men."

His eyebrows pinched together. A second later, an enormous smile spread across his face. "You mean that female over there?"

Emma turned to the female carrying a large tray of food to a table. "Yes."

With a hand on each shoulder, Raeko swerved her around to face him. "That's Neesa, my *sister*."

Emma froze. "Oh." Irritation, disappointment, and sadness slid off her body like an erosion.

"We need to talk."

"We do."

Raeko led her away from the tents and toward a stone house that was closer to the woods. Ribbons of mist flowed around the trees, making the scenery mystical. She stared at the mist woven with hints of color.

"There's color in the mist." Emma pointed the waves flowing around the trees. "There's more yellow vapors around this stone house."

"Yes, colorful mists are one of Saedo's beauty. The yellow fog likes me." He opened the door. "This is my house. Come in."

Emma stepped inside and the heels of her boots knocked on the wooden floors. Fearing she had scraped the floor, she lifted her feet.

"Don't worry about my floors. They're sturdy and have

regenerative properties." He pointed to the scrape that repaired itself.

"Wow."

A soft blue covered the walls. One large black couch sat against a wall. She walked past a room filled with computers and other machines. The house appeared clean, and she could smell the food on the table. Her stomach growled.

"It's been waiting for you," he said.

"You want to eat with me?"

"Yes. I even cleaned the house just for you." Raeko grinned. "Neesa saw me cleaning and checked to see if I was sick."

Emma laughed. "Does she live here, too?"

"No, she has her own place not too far from here." Raeko brushed a hand down Emma's cheek. "I want to share everything with you. I'm sorry I didn't introduce you to Neesa earlier. She's protective of her little brother."

Emma understood that well. She had six siblings whom she loved dearly. She should go and join them, but she didn't want to leave him.

"It's my fault. I should have asked you instead of assuming—"

His lips crushed down on hers. Electricity fired up inside her, blood roaring with need. Her mind tumbled into a whirlwind of bliss. She gripped his shirt to stabilize herself as his tongue stroked and teased. Heat pooled in her core. She wrapped her arms around him, pulling him closer. He was already flush against her, but she wanted more. Passion erupted inside of her and she didn't know how to control it. Perhaps it wasn't to be controlled.

As the oldest sibling, Emma always had control. That discipline helped her take care of her sisters. But in this moment, discipline and control were not in her hands.

How could this man she just met elicit so much passion from her?

Emma had never wanted a man this much before. She moaned out a protest when he broke the kiss.

He framed her face with his hands and skimmed his fingers along her cheeks. "I want you, right now. Let me have you." Need coated his every word. "I can still taste you from our first kiss in the tunnel." He licked his bottom lip.

"I want you, too."

They stripped and landed on his couch.

Raeko kissed her until her mind blurred. Her heart pounded against his, and his arousal swelled against her belly. She moaned out her pleasure as his mouth skimmed her neck.

"I want to touch you, taste you." He nibbled her skin, and she shivered when he licked a wicked trail over her shoulder and then teased her nipple.

She cried out in satisfaction as her nails dug into his back. She arched, offering him all of her as his mouth took turns feasting on her breasts. His mouth went lower and lower, waking every nerve in her body.

His hand cupped her center, and his eyes gleamed. "You're mine."

Emma met his gaze and told him the truth. She had given him her heart. "I'm yours. And you're mine."

He pushed a finger into her, and she cried out his name as her body throbbed in desperation. She closed her eyes, giving into desires and emotions. Her hands explored the lean, taught muscles that belonged to her. Yes, this star-being was hers.

Her eyes flipped open, and her body jerked when his mouth replaced his finger. The sensation was deliciously unbearable. His tongue tantalized her until her legs went limp.

"I love the taste of you."

She almost came when she met his gaze from between her

thighs. A beautiful green man was loving her in ways she had never been treasured before.

She opened wider, welcoming him. He rose up from between her thighs, and the bulk of him drew her gaze. She wanted the glorious length of him inside her, even though his size might be too large for her. She didn't care.

Raeko slid into her and lowered himself so they were face to face. He slid in deeper and deeper, and her body accommodated him with ease. "You're perfect."

His slow thrusts heightened all her senses. She sobbed out his name, and he gripped her hips. The irises in his eyes became electric. "Come with me."

She bit her lip and nodded.

As if her confirmation fueled his blood, his next powerful thrusts had her gripping the couch for balance. Their eyes locked as they lost themselves in each other.

Fully spent, they stayed connected for a few moments before he rolled over and gathered her up beside him on the wide couch. She snuggled into him.

Emma touched his face. "That was the best sex I've ever had."

"Me too." He kissed her forehead. "Will you stay here with me?"

"I can stay the night. We must sleep on a bed, though. This couch won't make for a comfortable sleep."

Raeko sat up. "That's not what I meant."

Emma knew what he meant, but she wanted to see his reaction. She placed a gentle hand on his back and drew little hearts with her fingers on his skin. He probably had no idea what she was doing, and that was fine. The gesture was more for her. This green star-being had inspired her to believe in love again. His honesty had charmed her from the beginning.

I deserve a man who loves and respects me. I deserve an honest man.

The Universe heard her.

"I've been thinking about us." Emma said, her heart swelling with emotions. "You're everything I've ever wanted. I've never felt this way with anyone this quickly. This proves that we have chemistry. More than anything, I want to be with you. I want to see where this relationships goes. So let's give it a chance."

He beamed. "If you had said no, I'd have followed you back to Earth."

She laughed. "You would? That's a nice thought, but people on Earth would want to study you. They wouldn't leave you alone, and that's not the life I want. Besides, you have better technology here."

"This will be your home now." He rose and walked around, comfortable in his nakedness. "How will your sisters react?"

Emma wondered about that too. All her sisters lived in the New England area. Though they were adults now, could she just leave them?

She didn't know how they'd react to her decision to stay in Saedo. But the heart knew things she could not explain.

"I'll tell them tomorrow. Come here."

Raeko padded over, a crooked smile forming on his face. He stood in front of her in all his glory.

She took him in her hands and stroked. "I'm familiar with human anatomy, but I've developed a fascination with that of a star-being." She looked up at him. The colors in his eyes intensified to a powerful blue that flashed through every color in the spectrum. "I'm going to have to examine you closely. A nurse is the best caretaker, after all."

He sucked in a breath. "Show me..."

That night Emma showed Raeko her talents that had him begging for more.

Inside the large conference room center, Emma sat on a couch and faced her six siblings. "I'm in love with Raeko."

Vanessa and Isabella exchanged smiles.

"It shows." Vanessa came over and plopped down beside Emma, giving her a big squeeze.

Isabelle did the same. "About time."

"Did he have anything to do with you almost fainting on me?" Nina asked.

Emma nodded. "I thought he was with someone. That someone turned out to be his sister, Neesa."

"That explains your moodiness yesterday." Sasha smirked.

Rita said, "If he makes you happy, then we're happy."

"And if he makes you cry, he'll know the full fury of the Nelson girls." Inga lifted a fist.

Nina cracked her elegant knuckles. "Nobody messes with a Nelson sister, not even a star-being."

Tears welled in Emma's eyes as her siblings took turns suffocating her with hugs.

After they settled down, Emma said, "I'm giving this a chance. I'm going to stay in Saedo. They have a spaceship that can take you back to Earth in a few weeks." Her chest tightened at the thought of never seeing her sisters again.

Inga rose from the couch. "That's good news because, while you were missing dinner yesterday, we decided we like it here."

"We gifted ourselves that trip to call in a new life," Rita reminded them. "To set an auspicious intention that will attract what we want. We all wanted a new beginning for the New Year. God delivered. We're staying."

Sasha got up and wrapped an arm around Inga. "We're all fond of these handsome men."

Emma glanced at her sisters. "Really? Do tell."

SIX

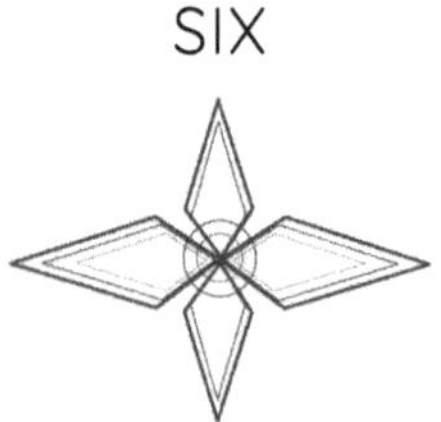

Emma and Raeko sat on a large rock that overlooked a glassy lake that reflected the rays of two suns. "They're happy for us. They want to stay."

She kept the part about her sisters being attracted to his soldier-brothers to herself. That was something that should be revealed in its own time.

Raeko took Emma's hand. "I'll take great care of you."

"I know you will."

He snapped his fingers and a robotic table rolled over. From under the table, he removed a blanket and spread it on the ground. He patted the spot next to him. "Come sit down."

"You prepared a picnic?"

"Before you came into my life, I didn't know what love was. Now that I know, it's made me want to jump up and celebrate everything." He took out two blue, cupcake-looking pastries and placed them on two plates.

"What are those?"

"Oh, you'll love these. These cupcakes are part of the Delta Delicacies infused with Venusian stardust. I'm sure you know that Venus is the planet of love. So these treats are perfect for us." He opened a box of pink sticks. "These are popular Saedo fries. They're made from vegetables." He took one out from a bag and placed it on the lower tray of the table.

Emma studied it. "It's a pink potato."

"They're fat-free. They'll cleanse your human system."

"What? I've got to try that." Emma took a pink stick, shoved it into her mouth, and tasted irresistible salt and spice. "Heaven. I'm eating heaven."

"You did last night." His eyes glittered. "I did, too."

Emma rolled her eyes. "The male species is the same everywhere."

He laughed, then his expression turned serious. "I know the Ulkrins ruined your New Year's celebration. We can make that up now."

"When is your New Year? Do you follow a calendar like us? How about seasons? Do you have those?"

"Our New Year is called Shenna. We're in Shenna 4044. Our new solar cycle is determined when the two suns make a celestial alignment on the eastern horizon, which is July 19th. We have twelve months like you. Our seasons are Shed, Suma, Auctum, and Nixum." He tapped the metal plate on his shoulder, and a virtual map floated in front of her. "Planet Celeron has a circumbinary orbit around the two suns."

Fascination hooked her as she stared at the rotation. "How old are you?"

"Two hundred and fifty solar-cycles. Time is different here because our planet is on a different dimensional matrix than Earth. Time on Earth is slower because it's denser there. How old are you?"

"Thirty-three." She smiled. "I'm attracted to older men. They have things to show me, teach me."

"You're teaching and showing me unfamiliar things, too. We'll learn from each other." He poured blue liquid from a shiny bottle into two elegant glasses and offered one to her. "A tribute to happy things. To lovely beginnings."

Warmth spread through her heart, and tears streamed down her face. Her life had completely changed in a short time. Meeting Raeko was her renewal. This was her rebirth.

Her heart was born again with him, and she was grateful for this gift.

She looked up at the sky, thanked the Heavens in her mind, and faced him. "To love and joy."

He kissed her tears away. "To us."

"You saved my life, you saved my heart, you saved my soul."

Raeko smiled. "You weren't the only one who was rescued. We saved each other." Ribbons of yellow mist circled them like an embrace.

Emma gave him a soft kiss as she filled their plates with sweet pastries and colorful fruits, reflecting on the new life that awaited them.

AN ALIEN CRUSH

SOLDIERS OF SAEDO 2

USA TODAY BESTSELLING AUTHOR

CALLA ZAE

AN ALIEN CRUSH #2: BLURB

"A promise is sacred to me, and I had to fulfill it so I could woo you appropriately."

When a heroic star-being saves Sasha from horrific beasts, she develops a crush on him, sparking hope in her heart. But then he disappears. Taking matters into her own hands, Sasha tracks him down.

Maeson, a remarkable soldier who values his word, is attracted to Sasha, but a promise keeps him from her. In order to return to her, he must first fulfill his obligation to someone else and stop a dire threat from destroying them both.

Can Maeson offer Sasha what she needs? Or will he crush her heart?

CONTENTS

ONE

Sasha squinted from the brightness of the two suns beaming down on her as she strode to her job as a stylist at the Hair Spectrum, in the Province of Saedo. She pulled on her sunglasses, and the flexible frame molded comfortably around her face.

Laughter boomed in the air. She glanced across the street, where children with green skin and colorful hair played outside. They chased the white mist, circling around them. She had never seen fog move or act this way before. The mist in Saedo was like a living thing that coexisted with these star-beings who had become her friends and neighbors. Living on planet Celeron had allowed her to see and experience life beyond her comprehension.

But the journey here didn't start out pleasant. Her body chilled from the memory on New Year's Eve. Sasha and her sisters were celebrating and sending out wishes to the Universe when Ulkrin monsters abducted them, wanting them to reproduce for their kind. But the soldiers of Saedo rescued them. Emma fell in love with Raeko, one of the soldiers. The Nelson sisters chose to stick together and start a new life in this beautiful province.

As Sasha walked, ribbons of mist circled her legs and traveled up her waist. Smiling in awe, she passed a hand through them. The mist shouldn't be visible when the weather was warm, bright, and sunny. She thought fog was created when cold air passed over warm moisture, causing water droplets to evaporate and therefore forming fog. At least that was what her former boyfriend had told her. He was a meteorologist who treated women like the typical New England forecast: something different every day.

Sasha had been his "sunshine" for an entire year, along with three other women. When she dumped him, threw out his clothes along with his video games, he called her Hurricane Ass, amongst other horrible names. But that name remained with her because he had stabbed her vulnerable point. She had been working hard at the gym, trying to tone up. She wasn't overweight, but she wasn't slim like some of her sisters. Sasha had curves, and they made her feel like a real woman.

Despite the pain, his verbal assault had strengthened her character. She vowed to never settle for anyone who didn't accept her for who she was, curves and all.

Anyway, that was the dark past. It was just a storm that had come and gone, teaching her a powerful lesson: that she didn't need a man to survive any inclement weather.

"Why are you swirling around me?" Sasha asked the fog. Her hand dipped into the stream of clouds that had a hint of blue.

"Have a good day, Sasha!" A little girl with poofy hair and two adorable horns waved from across the street with her mom. Sasha had cut and styled her family's hair last week.

"You too!" The wave hiked up her tunic. She immediately pulled it down, making sure it covered her butt.

Sasha had lived here in Saedo for a little over a month, and she was still captivated by the acceptance of the villagers. The

Province of Saedo had several villages, but she lived in the main Saedo Village. It was more like a large suburb, and the Village Center was like downtown.

Besides being close to her sisters, Sasha had another reason for staying in Saedo. The reason—the one that had her heart creating its own internal storm—was Maeson, the soldier who had saved her from those monstrous Ulkrins.

An image of the green star-being with a lovely mop of brown, shaggy hair popped into her vision and made her smile. He had a well-defined face with mesmerizing purple eyes. She remembered looking into them when he had examined her after the rescue. She had fantasized about those purple portals looking at her with passion.

Maeson did look at her that way for a couple of days before he took off without explanation. A few days later, he sent her a message to her crystal ring, which was a communication device similar to a smart phone.

I hope you're doing well.

Two days later, she received a bouquet of star-shaped flowers from him. They exchanged several sweet messages before the contact stopped completely. The last message she received from him was, *I miss you.*

He didn't reply to any of her messages. The whole ordeal confused and hurt her. She thought they had "something." Was it just her imagination? Or did he find someone else and she didn't matter anymore?

Despite that, her feelings remained the same for him. She allowed herself to feel it because passion was important in life. If a man lacked passion—the spirit to life—then he was better off with someone else. A man with passion was a man with fire in his heart. That kind of light exuded in his personality and in his work. She admired and respected a man who valued his word and kept it.

She hadn't met one yet.

Maeson had gripped her heart, choking it of rationality. No man had ever taken up so much of her brain space. The longing rewired her brain and body in ways she couldn't explain. Since when had she fallen so hard for a man?

Since never.

But Maeson didn't know that. Or did he? Even if he did, none of it mattered if he didn't accept her for who she was. She hadn't forgotten the promise to herself.

In the meantime, she'd continue indulging in fantasies of him. That gave her time to sort out her mess. A woman needed solid ground to know where she stood. And right now, Sasha was standing at the center of Maeson's spell, or whatever it was.

She hadn't seen him for weeks. Where did he go? Was he avoiding her? Was he okay?

Sasha Nelson, you're infatuated with a man who doesn't care.

It wasn't an infatuation, more like an alien crush, or rather a star-being crush. This powerful emotion overwhelmed her senses, making her yearn for something that could very well be an illusion. Still, she allowed herself to feel it.

I deserve a man who values and keeps his word and loves me as if I'm his dream come true.

That was the wish she had tossed out to the Universe right before the abduction.

Wish or no wish, she knew a relationship with no reciprocation was doomed. And right now, things weren't looking positive for her, but did she care? Nope. Sasha preferred the nontraditional route—the path that was guided by her intuition—and that reflected in the hair styles she offered to her clients.

"Sasha, you did a marvelous job with Janni's hair. The asymmetrical angles frame her face beautifully." Moxi, a female star-being with wild orange hair, stopped picking vegetables from her garden and grinned. "I need to call the Hair Spectrum and set up an appointment with you. You've been a significant addition to that eclectic team."

"Thank you. I'll be there whenever you're ready." Sasha smiled as her hand went to her right ear, where the language translator was inserted. She was grateful for the innovative device that allowed her to speak and understand the universal language.

"Why don't you use the personal rider to get to work? It'll be faster."

"I enjoy walking. It's a good workout." Sasha flexed her arm muscles. Her tunic rode up her body again. She pulled the hem down, covering her butt. She had been shedding weight ever since she started walking and eating Saedo foods, and she wasn't even trying to lose weight. The food here was delicious and less fattening than most dishes on Earth.

Did she miss her life on Earth? She missed the familiarity of things, but her heart was anchored here. Her heart wanted something here that wasn't available on Earth. Maybe it was just a momentary fascination and nothing more. Still, it gave her hope.

Maeson had sent a spark into her a month ago. That spark had grown into a wildfire that needed to be addressed before it scorched her from the inside out.

Sasha wanted to know exactly what Maeson thought of her. Did he like her? Did he want to start a relationship with her? The unknown was worse because it created awful scenarios in her mind. She had to put a stop to this uncertainty. At thirty-one years old, she'd learned to face her issues head on. It was the best way to find closure. To do that, she had to track him down.

She shouldn't let him irritate her. She had work to do. She had clients to take care of.

Squaring her shoulders, she entered the salon when the

automatic glass doors slid open and passed by four star-beings in the waiting area.

Sasha beamed and beckoned at Ivian, the wife of the village chief, Mozar. Ivian had a vertical third eye that was blue, where the other two were brown like Sasha's. Because Ivian often attended numerous planetary meetings with her husband, she had chosen Sasha to be her hair stylist. Sasha didn't mind because the chief's wife always paid extra. Hair stylists in Saedo also depended on tips for a comfortable living.

"Where are you going now?" Sasha gathered the long blue hair that was dip-dyed orange just last week. The procedure took twenty minutes with a high-tech coloring machine that didn't damage any hair strands nor produce any toxic fumes. Humans on Earth would definitely benefit from this technology.

"Mozar and I are attending a banquet in the Province of Finntoro. I have to look presentable."

"Of course you do. I've got something fancy for you. Everyone won't be able to take their eyes away from *Ivian of Saedo*." Sasha emphasized her importance and reclined the chair back. She waved at a robotic sink, and it rolled over instantly. "Let's give these gorgeous locks a wash."

On the other side of the room, someone said, "Grandma Ova really wants a haircut, but she injured her legs. She can't travel. I feel so bad for her."

"Is that why I haven't seen her herbal soup at the Galactic Galleria?" Ivian asked with eyes closed. "Grandma Ova's herbal soups are the best in the village. She gives away a lot of her leftovers to anyone who can't afford it."

That was one of Sasha's favorite discoveries in this village. Not only was it healthy, it was delicious and filling.

The star-being who was having her neon pink hair trimmed said, "I heard her home was damaged. Maeson has been helping her and her grandson rebuild it."

Sasha's eyebrows quirked at Maeson's name. So that was where he had spent his time.

Sasha wrapped Ivian's hair in a towel, pushed the chair upright, and directed the robotic sink to dump out the dirty water in the bathroom.

Ivian spoke to the star-being. "She could have a droid cut her hair."

"She prefers a living being. I do too. It's more personable."

An idea popped into Sasha's mind. She could assist Grandma Ova. She often gave free haircuts to children and the elders as gratitude for accepting her and her sisters in Saedo. Besides, she wanted to see what Maeson was up to. "I have some time. I can swing by today."

When Sasha finished tucking sparkly rhinestones into Ivian's twisty updo, she went home and got into her personal rider, which was like a compact car on Earth with modern designs. She pulled up the virtual map and tapped Grandma Ova's destination. She palmed her dashboard, and music from the popular Zeta Meida Band boomed from the speakers. Humming along, she took her rider down a paved backroad surrounded by colorful berry bushes.

She tapped her fingers on the steering wheel as the sunlight from the two suns glistened on her blue crystal ring. She preferred wearing the smart ring that was also waterproof because it was attached to her. She didn't have to remember where she put it, and she didn't need to charge it often. The solar light charged the crystal every time she went outside.

The blue gem glowed, signifying an incoming call from her younger sister.

Inga's beautiful face popped up on the screen. "Hey, Emma's testing out a new dish tonight. She and Vanessa took some cooking class at the Culinary Arts and Beyond. You coming?"

That sounded delightful, but she was occupied. She was on a mission for her heart. She could always hang out with her sisters later. Right now, she had questions for someone. "No, I'm busy tonight. I volunteered to give Grandma Ova a haircut."

"Oh, okay. Yeah, I heard she was injured. By the way, my hair needs a touchup when you have time. I'm showcasing my fashion collection in a few weeks. I need to look presentable." Inga twirled a lock of blonde hair with her finger.

"I don't know anyone more presentable than you, Inga. You're gorgeous, and you don't need me to do anything. But yes, we can set up a time."

"You're the best! Gotta go. The male models will arrive soon. I need to get clothing racks ready for the fittings. Love you."

Inga hung up as a grand house—three times larger than the house she had on Earth—came into view. It sat on a sloped land with no other house nearby, surrounded by trees and berry bushes. To the side, a field of pink grass swayed like they were greeting her.

Sasha stopped her personal rider and stared at the breathtaking view. She didn't know why, but she was expecting to see an old home. The house that stood in front of her was modern, with a two-level living space. The roof glowed from the solar energy being collected through the solar-discs that spun around. The magnificent veranda reminded her of the southern homes in the United States. Marble columns and gorgeous stones covered the front facade. The curb appeal consisted of a lovely walkway made of solar stones and adorable flowers strategically placed, which made the home welcoming.

Sasha parked in the side lot. She got out, and a male star-being with curly blue hair rushed from the house to greet her. He had light green skin, long legs, and a youthful smile.

"Hi, I'm Timmon. My grandma's expecting you. She got a

call from her friends at the Hair Spectrum. They told her you were coming to give her a haircut. Thank you for doing this. It'll thrill her. She deserves it."

"I'm Sasha. I'm happy to help. I love your grandmother's soups."

"Me too." Timmon rubbed his trimmed belly. "My stomach used to be bigger, but ever since I won a scholarship to attend the Intergalactic University, it's been shrinking. I don't get to eat as much there unlike when I'm home."

Sasha remembered her college days when she studied business and didn't enjoy it one bit. She wanted a little more creativity, so when she graduated, she followed her dream. However, her degree helped her manage her own business for a while.

"What are you studying? Where is this university?"

"I'm studying *everything* that's available. Courses about humans, Earth, other galaxies, mystic codes, cosmic creatures, energy fields, and so many other things. I could stay there for another hundred solar cycles and still wouldn't be able to learn everything. The Intergalactic Library is enormous. I get to meet other beings from all over the galaxies. It's pretty cool."

That sounded incredible. "What's your age?"

"Nineteen solar cycles. Let me guess your age. Earth years are a bit different." He narrowed his blue eyes. "Twenty-nine?"

"Close, but no. I'm thirty-one. My sister, Inga, is twenty-nine."

"I met your other sister, Rita. She works at the Village Library."

"She does," Sasha said. "I've borrowed books from there to learn about Saedo."

"I have a lot of books you can borrow. They're in the living room. Grandma Ova doesn't read them anymore. Just take whatever you want." He waved a hand. "Follow me. Let me give you a quick tour."

"Thank you. That's very nice of you. You have a gorgeous home."

"It didn't always look like this. It was actually falling apart six months ago, but Maeson and his robots have been helping us rebuild. I was stuck at school when Grandma got injured, so I couldn't come back right away. I'm here now, but I have to go back in two weeks, so I'm trying to help Maeson as much as I can. He's really good at building."

Timmon took her along a large herbal garden. A sweet scent went up her nose. "What is that fragrance?"

He pointed to a tall bush with scalloped-edge leaves. "These are astorays. They smell like flowers. They're a medicinal herb that prevents corra diseases in the elders. I'm taking a galactic herbal class. I want to start a large garden of herbs to help maintain Grandma's good health." He placed a hand to his chest. "She says that astorays also lower cholesterol. She uses them in her soups."

"Oh, right, that's where I recognized the aroma." Sasha glanced at Timmon and wished more young children cared like him. The world would be a better place. "Your grandmother must be proud of you."

"She is. She tells me that all the time. When my parents died, she took me in. I'm grateful for her."

Sasha understood that gratitude well. Emma, her oldest sister, had taken on the responsibility of parenting six younger siblings when their parents died. Sasha was grateful to Emma for keeping them together.

Banging sounds snapped Sasha's attention to an impressive gazebo. Her heart thudded when she spotted a shirtless Maeson securing a wooden panel to the interior wall with some handheld equipment. She sucked in a breath at the sight of his strong shoulders, wishing she could trace her fingers along that sturdy plane. The muscles in his arms tightened her loins and triggered something in her core. He wore a pair of high-tech denim that enhanced his ass spectacularly.

Sasha blinked and remembered the other reason she was here. She should inquire about Grandma Ova, but her mouth couldn't form anything coherent.

"Hi, Maeson!" Timmon waved and rushed over. "The gazebo looks fabulous. You work fast. It's basically done."

"I have something I need to do when this is done." Maeson whirled around and placed the equipment down on the counter.

Maeson met her eyes, and he stepped out of the gazebo. In the sunlight, his brown hair glistened like copper. It was longer than she remembered. He had it tied back with a leather strap, making a short tail on his back.

"Hi." Surprise and joy beamed on his face. Two drops of sweat slid down the side of his neck, and she wanted to wipe them for him. His sweat-drenched chest glistened like diamonds. A leather belt hung loosely on his hips. Her eyes focused on the well-defined abs that sped up her heart rate. She'd never seen anything sexier than this green man.

Timmon glanced at Sasha and then at Maeson. "You know each other?"

"Yes, we do." Maeson's gaze stayed on hers, and her body felt every second of that voltage that had nothing to do with the two suns.

Emotions rolled over her in waves of passion, disappointment, and uncertainty. After wondering and worrying about him for over a month, she didn't know how to react to his sudden appearance.

What should she say? How should she act? She had envisioned a hundred ways to express her concerns, but they all disappeared when he looked at her. The heat in his eyes scorched all her reason.

She recognized when a man was attracted to her. But why did this man not act on his desire?

"Do you mind if I go back inside to help Grandma Ova get ready?" Timmon asked. "Where do you want her? Is the back deck okay? She enjoys looking at her garden."

"Anywhere is fine. I have all my supplies."

"Great. I'll see you soon." Timmon strode back toward the house.

Purple eyes searched her face. "How are you?"

"You'd know if you replied to my messages." The words came out cold and short.

He blinked and smiled. "I was occupied. But I really wanted to."

From what Timmon mentioned, Maeson had been helping Grandma Ova, so Sasha shouldn't be angry with him. It would be selfish of her. Despite that, she wished he had made the effort to contact her if he "really wanted to."

"Words don't mean anything to me. Actions do."

He flinched and didn't say anything.

Sasha made her way around the gazebo. He reached for her arm, holding her inches from him. Her stomach somersaulted at his touch. The scent of sweat and male snuck up her nose, and had her eyes meeting him.

"I've been thinking about you. I haven't stopped since I met you, and I promised myself that after this gazebo is done, I'd come find you."

"Why did you disappear without saying anything? You sent me messages and flowers, and then everything stopped. Why? What happened?" she demanded. "I thought we had something special."

His hand skimmed down her arm, meeting her fingers. "We do."

"Then why did you leave?"

"I left abruptly because Grandma Ova got injured, and I wanted to check on her because Timmon wasn't home. Her old house was wrecked. Anyway, I had postponed the house construction when I joined the team to rescue you and your sisters from the Ulkrins. I was attracted to you, who wouldn't be?" He played with a lock of her hair. "I wanted to stay and get to know you, but I had to finish a project. I sent you messages while I was here, but the more I got to know you, the harder it became for me to focus."

Emotions swelled in her chest, and she didn't know what to say.

"So I stopped. It was the most difficult thing I had to do. A promise is sacred to me, and I had to fulfill it so I could woo you appropriately."

Sasha laughed. "What does that mean? Is that a Saedo way of flirting?"

"It's my way of seducing you." Desire and playfulness glittered in his eyes. "I want to pursue you. Cherish you, so you can think of no other man but me. So you have no excuse to run away from me."

"Why would I run away from you?"

"Because if I tell you all the things I've imagined doing to you, you'd find me... inappropriate. And that might frighten you."

Joy coupled with friskiness bloomed inside of her as she tried to envision the inappropriate things.

Courage and curiosity urged her on. She stepped closer and the blue mist swirled around their waists like ribbons tying them together. "Define 'inappropriate.'"

Mischief filled his eyes as he dipped his head and claimed her mouth, sucking her bottom lip. Then his lips skimmed over to her ear. "Something that'll make your blood roar and beg for more. Something not for the public to see, but only just for us to savor." He drew back and looked at her. "Does that satisfy you?"

Dazed by the wild imagination in her mind, she muttered, "I love your definition."

Maeson laughed, and the deep sound of his voice sank into her heart and claimed a spot.

"Grandma Ova is ready for you." Timmon's voice popped the magical bubble around them.

"I'll be right over." Sasha threaded her hands into Maeson's hair. "Let me give you a trim."

That smile again. It twisted her stomach into delicious knots.

"I've been growing it out so I could have an excuse to have you cut it."

"It seems like you've been planning a lot of things."

"When you want something, you make a plan to ensure you get it. I didn't want to mess it up."

He hooked her with that statement.

"Well, I guess you need to get back to work. I'll find you later."

TWO

Grandma Ova had light green skin, white hair, and amber eyes that could melt an iceberg. She sat in a robotic wheelchair that didn't look like anything Sasha had seen on Earth. The cushioned armrests and leg support molded to her body like soft foam.

"Lift me four inches," Grandma Ova spoke to the robotic face that popped up on a small screen on her armrest. The wheels made a sound, locking themselves to the ground.

Sasha moved to stand behind Grandma. "Are you comfortable?"

"Yes, thank you." Grandma Ova leaned back into the cushion. "Also, thank you for being so thoughtful and coming all this way. I really appreciate it."

Sasha examined the long, wavy white hair that had grown past the old star-being's shoulders. "It's no bother at all. You give free food to the villagers who need it. This is my way of helping out our community. The villagers miss you."

Grandma Ova tapped a wrinkled hand to her legs. "I miss them too. These legs need to strengthen up fast so I can resume my daily routine. I can't sit around all day. It's driving me nuts. I have things I want to do."

From her supply bag, Sasha took out the energy blade scissors, a stylist cape that tailored to the body, and the flying robotic hair-collector that moved around her hands, collecting excess hair while she cut. She wished she had this innovative device when she was on Earth; it would have saved her a lot of time.

With her ring, Sasha snapped a photo of Grandma Ova with her current hair and changed the style on the virtual screen. "Do you like this look? This will frame your face adorably."

"Make me adorable." She smiled. "How are your sisters doing? I haven't visited the Village Center to welcome them."

"They're doing well. Thank you for asking. Emma and Raeko are in love. You can see it in their eyes. I'm so happy for them."

"Love is the most potent energy in existence. The entire Cosmos functions on this frequency. So the more love you emit, the more vibrant your environment becomes. Speaking of energy, there's a shift in Saedo. I can't tell if it's good or bad. Or both." She blew out a sigh. "Maybe it's just my body playing tricks on me. I haven't been myself since the tree fell on my legs."

"How did that happen?"

"A freak accident. I guess it was a dead tree that only needed a slight push from the wind to do the trick."

Sasha looked up at the tall trees. They seemed sturdy to her. "You mentioned a shift. Do you see energy?"

"I used to see it with clarity. My old eyes aren't doing too well these days, but I'm not replacing them with mechanical eyes. These were given to me by my parents, and I'm keeping them regardless of how worn they are."

Sasha recalled reading that star-beings age differently. She couldn't remember all the details. All she knew was that star-beings had long life spans.

"How old are you, if you don't mind me asking?"

"One thousand three hundred solar cycles."

Holy shit. Sasha's mouth dropped open, and her hands froze, forcing the robotic hair-collector to hover in one spot in front of Grandma Ova's face. It took Sasha a few seconds to absorb the magnificence of life on this astounding planet.

"Do you know how old Maeson is?"

"Two hundred and fifty-two solar cycles." When Sasha stayed silent, Grandma said, "Physical age isn't important. Look at the soul. That's where it's crucial. That tells how mature or immature someone is. Don't compare a star-being's age to that of a human being. We live in different dimensions, and time is a tricky thing."

When Sasha resumed the trimming, she said, "You're the *hottest* grandmother I've ever seen."

Grandma Ova snorted out a laugh that shook her shoulders. "I'm glad you and your sisters are here. You've added a lovely energy to Saedo."

Maeson, Timmon, and the robotic assistant hauled some equipment past the deck and into a large shed. Maeson shot Sasha a look that made her stomach flutter with excitement. Then he waved at Grandma Ova.

"He's exceptional with his hands and with his corra. Once he sets his mind on something, he gets it done, and he gets it done right. That's admirable. Some individuals quit after a while, especially when it gets tough, but not him. He sees it through. He's like a brother to Timmon. I don't know what I'd have done if he hadn't been around to help me." She gestured to her extensive land.

Sasha said nothing. She was having a tough time trying to

calm her racing heart. Had he been fascinated with her all this time? Making plans to be with her? The idea was shocking, yet everything he had told her and everything she had witnessed proved to be true. He was here rebuilding a house and a gazebo, rushing to get them done so he could come back to her.

It didn't matter how big or trivial the job was, the fact that he had made a promise and kept it, reigned supreme in her heart.

Sasha focused on adding gel that straightened out Grandma Ova's waves and styled it into a classic hairdo that curved around her heart-shaped face.

"There, you look adorable." Sasha gave her a handheld mirror to check.

"I love it! Thank you. My head feels ten pounds lighter." She returned the mirror. "You're very talented."

"Thank you."

"He really likes you. He told me about you."

Curiosity spiked as Sasha placed all her tools back into the supply bag, zipping it up. She didn't know Grandma Ova well, but there was a warmth about her that made you want to tell her things.

"What did he say?"

"That you're the one."

Sasha chuckled at the nonsense. Maeson didn't know her well enough to be certain of that. Yes, he was attracted to her. She saw that in his eyes. But what Grandma Ova was referring to was something more. That "more" took time, passion, and devotion that required more than a simple attraction, a crush.

"That's crazy talk. He doesn't know me."

Grandma Ova placed a hand over her chest. "The corra knows things. It's a miraculous organ that doesn't give any explanation."

Sasha had thought she "knew" things in the past, and those

assumptions had left a massive bruise on her heart. Despite that, she knew when her heart was urging her on. This unknown force was the same force that had driven her here to look for Maeson. So yes, the heart knew things that were beyond comprehension.

"Energy knows energy. Resonance is important, and I can sense your energy resonates with his. Like anything, if you take care of it, it will grow. Just look at my marvelous garden. I've put so much love into it, and it shows."

Sasha liked Grandma Ova's perspective. "You can call me whenever you need another trim or in need of a fancy updo. I'll swing by. It's no problem at all. Besides, I love the view here."

"Let me give you some credits for this amazing haircut that shaved a hundred solar cycles off my face."

"No, no, it's my gift to you." Sasha held up a hand. "This is the least I can do to show you how much I appreciate your amazing soup. I've had nothing better, even on Earth."

Grandma Ova's face beamed. "Well, I want to give you something. Stay a few days, enjoy the view here, and you can have as much soup as you'd like. It's on the house." She gripped Sasha's hand. "If you say no, you'll break an elderly woman's corra, and I already have injuries." She pointed to her legs. "I might never recover from another."

Sasha shook her head, unable to resist the star-being's charm. "How can anyone say no to you?"

"Smart girl. Now, go get what you want."

Sasha's cheeks burned. "I don't know what you—"

"I've lived a long time, Sasha. I *know* things, I *see* things." She smiled. "I know how you feel for Maeson. I can see his smile—his energy—is brighter because you're here. He's like a son to me, and I'm protective of him. I like you, and that's why I'm urging you on. See you at dinner." The wheelchair rolled toward the side door and into the house.

Sasha pulled up the virtual screen and checked her work schedule. She could afford to take a few days off. She had no appointments until next week.

A growling sounded near the tall trees, and when she turned, an adorable blue bunny with two tails dashed out of the bushes, running toward the gazebo. What other animals lived in these woods?

Sasha took Grandma Ova's advice and went after her dream: Maeson.

THREE

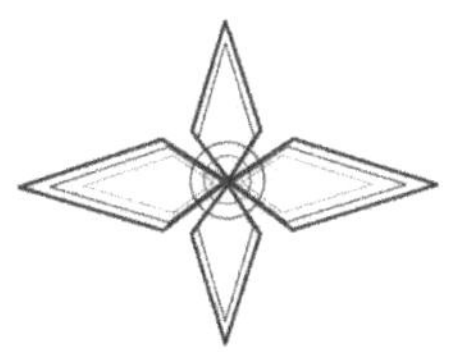

After dinner, Timmon returned to his room to study for some virtual math exam.

Grandma Ova offered Sasha a set of soft pajamas. "I always have extra sets here. They're new and soft. Don't worry, the fabric will adjust to your size. There are new toiletries in the bathroom. Use whatever you like." Then she showed Sasha the guest room—which was next to Maeson's.

Grandma Ova looked up at him. "I heard the gazebo's finished. You work fast."

He lifted a shoulder. "When you have something important to do, you need to get it done quickly." He stood beside Sasha, wearing a casual shirt and high-tech denim and smelling like a spicy blend of woods.

"What's more important than my gazebo?" Grandma Ova demanded.

"Absolutely nothing." He patted her shoulder.

"Liar, but I'll forgive you this time. I'm heading to bed. I'll see you both tomorrow." Grandma Ova wheeled her chair down the hallway.

Maeson grabbed Sasha's hand and led her out of the house. "I want to show you something. Something important to me."

Outside, the warm breeze caressed Sasha's skin while the crickets played a soothing lullaby. The stars were so clear they winked at her. She could also see silhouettes of asteroids or whatever they were floating about in the distance.

He took her to the gazebo. "It's stunning." She walked around the architecture. It was three times the normal size of a gazebo, with a circular counter for outdoor cooking and a lovely seating area that had netting to keep the bugs out. The roof had several solar discs that lit up the ceiling with soft lighting.

"You built this?"

Pride beamed on his face. "From a sketch to the finished product. The old one was destroyed when the tree fell on it."

"The same tree that fell on Grandma Ova's legs? The same tree that damaged the house?"

His eyes glittered. "You're catching on, but no, not the same tree. The previous gazebo and house were constructed with poor quality materials. I'll tell you about that later."

Nodding, Sasha reviewed the extraordinary craftsmanship, the etchings on the wood panels, the texture of the metallic columns, the stone layout on the floor, and all the labor that went into this work of art.

"You brought magic to life," Sasha said.

"I thought of you every day I was building it. Every panel I secured, every stone I laid out, every solar disc I attached, was one step closer to you. I had to finish it so I could start something with you. Having you here to witness its completion is like a dream come true. You're my dream come true. I want to build a solid relationship with you."

His genuine words stopped her heart, and a flood of emotions welled up, making it hard for her to breathe. No one had ever said anything so beautiful to her.

Sasha had come all the way here to find him, to demand answers as to why he hadn't come to see her. And he tossed these precious words at her that annihilated the barrier around her heart. Tears streamed down her face, and his fingers caught them.

"I don't know what to say."

"Your tears have said enough." He pulled her in and kissed her gently, then deeply.

She fell into his embrace, loving the way his protective arms wrapped around her. She drew back to look at him and was lost in his purple eyes. Each speckle had a slightly different hue. They moved around like liquid colors, and her core quivered.

Was it possible to get aroused from simply looking into a man's eyes? Well, this green star-being was doing exactly that to her.

He smirked as his eyes dragged over her body, waking every nerve ending. If he could do this to her body with just one look, she desperately wanted to know how her body would react with skin-to-skin contact.

Maeson's eyes turned to mischief, as if he read her every thought. His arousal thickened against her body. Her heart pounded with urgent need. She lifted a hand to his chest and felt the frantic pounding of his heart.

"My corra beats for you," he said, pulling her onto his lap as he sat on the bench outside of the gazebo.

He crushed his mouth to hers, kissing her hard. Frustration and need fueled the kiss. His mouth took and tantalized, while his tongue teased and tormented.

She responded with the same hunger. He changed the rhythm and softened the kiss. A seductive growl escaped his mouth. He drew back, looked at her as his hand stroked down the column of her neck, and then cupped her breast through the silk top. She let out a satisfying moan as her back arched, offering him whatever he wanted. His hand roamed across her stomach and slid over her hips to settle on her buttocks.

Hurricane Ass echoed in her mind, and she stiffened.

"What's wrong?" Maeson asked, not moving his hands.

Sasha didn't know what to say. Embarrassment overwhelmed her, and she cursed herself for not being strong enough to wipe away those words from her memory.

His eyes stayed on hers. "Do you trust me?"

"Yes," she whispered.

"Then trust me with your fears. What's bothering you? Did someone hurt you here? Did someone spank you?" He kneaded her buttocks gently and grinned.

His comment and his silly expression pushed the darkness away. "No one spanked me. The only person who ever did was my mother when I misbehaved as a kid."

"Then why did you flinch at my touch?"

Communication was important in a relationship. She looked into those caring eyes and said, "My previous boyfriend didn't like my ass. He said it was too big, too full, too curvy. He gave it an unforgettable name that stayed with me." The admission released a heaviness she didn't know she was carrying.

His eyes steeled, but his hands remained steady on her ass. "Is he dead?" The calm in his voice would make most men run.

"No."

"He should be." One hand tipped up her chin. "Listen to me: I love your ass, and I have a name for it too. I have names for many parts of your body. They were part of my imagination when you weren't around."

She narrowed her eyes in amusement, wondering what those names could be. If his intention was to make her laugh and to forget the sting of the past, he achieved it.

"What names?"

Smiling, Maeson's purple eyes darkened as he leaned into

her ear. His hand brushed across her hardened nipples. "I love these double stars. They wink at me when I think of you naked."

Sasha let out a delightful laugh that shook her body. "Stars? Really? You're crazy. No one has ever compared my body to heavenly things."

"Then you've been surrounding yourself with the unimaginative individuals." His hands went back to her buttocks, kneading them. "The moon is most beautiful when it's full, and I've wanted Sasha's Full Moon for a long time."

Oh. My. Goodness. She stifled the laugh, but struggled miserably. With his skillful hands and the sexy mouth that spewed dirty humor, he had her completely enchanted. These cheesy—yet adorable—lines dripped, melted, and comforted her like a slice of pizza. The laugh broke through her restraints. It came out loud and unladylike, and she didn't give a damn. The vivid image of her ass—from now on to be known as Sasha's Full Moon—would forever live in her mind like an unexpected guest she had come to love.

"You've made me look at myself in a whole new light. Pun intended." Joy erupted inside her and destroyed the hurricane in a flash.

"Humor aside, I meant it." The intensity of his eyes revealed a truth—a passion—she hadn't seen before. "I love your body, every aspect of it. I accept all of you. I love the curves, the dips, the softness." His hands wandered and demonstrated. "You don't know how many nights I've spent wondering what your body would feel like under my hands, on my lips." He lowered his mouth to hers.

Warmth bloomed inside her and opened her heart even wider. His lips demanded, and she met him need for need.

When they broke for breath, she whispered against his lips, "I guess we've been busy fantasizing about each other."

An eyebrow arched. "You've fantasized about me?"

Sasha nodded. "Too many times."

A crooked smile appeared. "Then let's play out our imaginations. Let's make them real."

A growl interrupted the moment, and Maeson let out a vehement curse as he whirled toward the sound. A creature with two bulging eyes emerged from the dark woods. It growled again, and she recognized it from earlier when the blue bunny ran away. Maybe it was escaping from this terrifying monster. It looked like a bear with a long, spiky tail. Its massive claws glinted like knives. The claws swiped at a tree, and the tree thudded to the ground. It struck another tree, and that one collapsed away from the house.

Fear spiked as Sasha glanced at the beast and then the house —the house where Grandma Ova and Timmon were sleeping. "It's going to destroy the house!"

"No, it won't," Maeson hissed.

Maeson grabbed Sasha and moved her inside the gazebo. He pressed a button on the wall, and thick glass panels came up from the foundation, protecting every opening. He snatched a silver gun from a drawer and stepped outside. Then he secured the door to the gazebo, locking her in.

"Maeson! Come back here!" She pounded on the glass panel. "What are you doing? It's too dangerous. It's going to hurt you."

"Stay in there. It's safer for you." Maeson ran away from the gazebo as he blasted the creature, hitting its leg.

Snarling, the creature didn't go after Maeson. Instead, it looked at Sasha and charged at her. Its body slammed against the glass panel and bounced back. Sasha screamed, tripped on something, and fell to the floor. The glass didn't budge or break. She scooted away and pushed herself up.

Maeson aimed several more shots at the creature. Blood

oozed from its body, and part of its face and skull were destroyed, leaving only one eye open to glare at them.

Beating its tail furiously, the creature let out a vicious howl, like it was calling out to something. Then it jumped at the tall trees, pushing several down toward the house. A wide net of energy appeared, catching the fallen trees and preventing them from damaging the house. One tree fell in the opposite direction and crushed Sasha's personal rider.

"No!" Sasha shouted.

Maeson continued to battle the creature. Though blood trickled from various parts of its body, the creature didn't appear weakened. It slashed at his leg with its spiky tail.

Sasha's heart dropped. "Maeson! Are you okay?"

The creature prowled closer, snarling. Maeson whipped something out at the beast, and a balloon of smoke exploded. He twisted away from the creature and shot again. The creature snapped its tail at Maeson's arm. The force sent his gun thudding onto the ground.

She had to do something. She couldn't just hide in here while Maeson died trying to protect her. Fear crawled up her body, but she kept her focus on Maeson. He needed her right now, and she needed him too. The thought of him dying was more frightening than that horrific creature.

Frantic, Sasha searched for a button or something that could unlock the door. She also needed a weapon. She found a few cabinets, but they were all locked. "Shit!"

Out of frustration, she slapped at a wall and accidentally hit a knob that blended to the wall. The door opened, and she rushed out to Maeson. Blood soaked his leg.

"Are you all right?"

"It's not safe here. Go back inside. You'll be safe in there."

"Then come with me." She helped him up. The creature moved closer, eyeing her. She grabbed a rock on the ground and whipped it at him. It slammed right into its head. All those years playing softball in high school paid off.

Maeson sent a blast into the animal's other eye. The animal wailed and thrashed, swiping its claws vehemently at the open air. With two eyes out, the creature slowed its movements as it sniffed its way around. Sasha had to keep it away from Maeson. She remembered she had something in her personal rider that could be a weapon. She climbed over the fallen tree and reached for her hair supply bag. The blades of her scissors were sharp enough to be a weapon.

With a high leap, the creature charged at her. Maeson sent a series of blasts toward it. Sasha's heart hammered as she gripped her scissors and pitched it right into its chest. "Layer cut, five minutes!"

The scissors punctured its skin and began cutting.

The three energy blades responded to her command, snipping and ripping flesh, organs, and bones. She shivered from the awful sound. The creature wailed and collapsed as the blades destroyed its body.

Sasha froze at the horror. When Maeson limped over, she smiled. "You're okay..." Her vision blurred, and she passed out in his arms.

FOUR

Sasha woke to sunshine and sweet fragrance. She turned to a bouquet of pink flowers.

"How are you feeling?" Maeson sat down beside her, looking well-rested.

She sat up, looking at his leg. "How's your wound?"

He patted his thigh. "It's just a minor scar now. Grandma Ova has the best herbal medicine. Thank you for saving me." He took her hand and kissed it. "For saving all of us."

"You did most of the work." Sasha couldn't believe she actually killed the awful thing with her scissors.

"But it was your scissors that took him down. You should've seen the mess."

"Where are my scissors? I'm going to need some new ones for the salon. I'll save that pair for something else." She wasn't sure what yet.

"Timmon took Grandma Ova to get you a new personal rider. They'll be back soon."

"What? Why? She doesn't need to. What about her legs? She can't travel far."

"She insisted, and she's stubborn. No one says no to her. I

called one of my brothers to help. Osayik is taking her and Timmon in the spacecraft. Timmon will drive the personal rider back. It's a gift for killing the beast that hurt her legs and destroyed her gazebo and home."

Sasha's eyebrows lifted. "She knew it was the beast all along?"

"We all did, but we didn't want to alarm anyone. That's an Ulkrin creature. It should be in the Province of Agarrek, with the rest of the Ulkrin clan, not here. The Chief is looking into how it got here."

"You weren't here just renovating and building, were you?"

"No, I had to make sure the creature didn't get out to the Village Center. I have something precious there." The purple eyes deepened. "My soldier-brothers and I went looking for it in the woods, but we couldn't locate it. While I waited for it to return, I rebuilt the house and the gazebo, using upgraded materials. They're strong enough to withstand extreme damage. We established an energy net to catch any fallen trees within the vicinity of the house." Maeson ran a knuckle down her cheek.

Sasha loved the gentle way he touched her.

"I called your sisters and told them what happened. I reassured them you're not injured. I'm sure you have messages from them on your smart ring. You're staying here with me for another week before you head back to work."

She'd check her messages later. "What? I can't take that much time off. I have scheduled appointments. Besides, I'm fine, really."

"Your appointments have been rescheduled with no issues. Everyone wants the best for you. I know you're physically well, but it's good to rest. Let your mind purge the unnecessary stuff. What you've experienced was traumatic. I don't want it triggering any memories you've harbored from the abduction. Plus, I'm being selfish." His expression was almost probing. "I want to spend more time with you here, away from the Village Center, away from everyone." He paused a moment, and then said, "I have something important to show you."

His logic and the way he looked at her broke through her cautionary wall. Like the trees from last night, she had fallen hard, thudding all the way into his lap.

When Sasha came out here looking for Maeson because she needed answers, he gave her more than she expected. Not only did he give her all the answers, he also gave her back self-respect and self-worth. Qualities she had buried because a man didn't like how she looked.

Everything changed last night when their lives were endangered. That moment confirmed that life was too short. That things could change in an instant. She had to make every second count.

Sighing, she surrendered to his suggestions. "How long was I out? It seems like you got a lot planned and accomplished."

"Over twenty-four hours."

"No way!" She had never slept that much before. Apparently, her body needed the rest.

A ribbon of blue fog swirled around him and flowed over to her. "I see blue mist around you. Sometimes I see it around me too. Does everyone have it around them?"

"No," said Grandma Ova from the doorway. She wheeled herself in with Timmon by her side. "When you meet your starmate—your forever mate—the mist will reveal the color of love to them and also follow them. The specific color binds their souls. That's the lore of Saedo mist."

Sasha slid a glance over to Maeson, who shrugged. "I've never heard of it. I've always seen mist around me. Sometimes, I see it around others too, but they're all white. The only colorful fog I see comes from the trees, plants, and water."

"A star-being's color is shown to his mate. It's resonance of energy." Grandma Ova turned to Maeson. "Your soul's color is the one *you* see all the time. What color is it?"

"Blue."

She swerved to Sasha. "And you see what color?"

A blue ribbon floated around Sasha, and she waved a hand through it. "Blue."

He was her starmate, her forever mate. He didn't have to say it; the spark in his eyes matched the spark in her heart.

Grandma Ova clapped her hands together. "This is divine news. I've been waiting for this."

"Waiting for what?" Timmon asked.

"A beautiful change. You young kids won't understand. Anyway, it's not important right now. We have something that's more critical." Grandma Ova jerked a chin at Timmon. "Show her."

Timmon splashed an image of a gunmetal personal rider, an upgrade to her older one. "It's all yours. This one is exceptionally fast, and it can lift you to higher elevations, but not as high as a spacecraft or spaceship."

Sasha gawked at her new gadget car. "You didn't have to." She had planned on using the credits she had saved to purchase a new one at a later time.

"Yes, we did. You killed that evil creature for us. You deserve the moon."

Maeson cleared his throat and went to pour himself a glass of water. But not before she saw the grin on his face.

She would never look at the moon without thinking about the name he had given her ass. It was their private code that bonded them together, and she couldn't wait to offer him the moon.

FIVE

Three days later, Maeson led her to an open field where the soil had been prepared and two robotic machines with massive claws stood inactive nearby.

"Are you building something?" Sasha stepped on the soil, the color more orange than the brown dirt on Earth.

His boot patted the orange sand that glistened in the sun. "I just added compacted sand to this area. Did you know that sand has textures good for irrigation without shifting the foundation?" He walked around the flat land with a mesmerizing view. "The textured fragments will catch against one another and lock into place like puzzle pieces. It adds another layer of stability."

Perplexed by the sudden education on sand, Sasha looked at him. "I'm glad you find sand interesting."

Maeson turned to her, and his purple eyes sparkled with a sudden seriousness. "Grandma Ova gifted me this plot of land. She has acres and acres and no time to tend to them. I'm building a second home here." He clutched her hand. "And I'd like for you to accompany me."

"What do you mean? I'm not a construction worker."

He laughed. "I've never felt like this before. It's terrifying and beautiful at the same time." He tapped his chest. "My corra is yours. I think it's time we give us a real chance."

Sasha's heart quickened, and her lips trembled, unable to speak.

"We can come here when we need a break from the activity and noise of the Village Center. Or we can make this our permanent home. The drive to work isn't far, especially with your new personal rider. I want you to be a part of this new beginning with me." Maeson looked at her like she was his dream come true.

That thought brought back the wish she had tossed out into the Universe not too long ago.

I deserve a man who values and keeps his word and loves me as if I'm his dream come true.

Closing her eyes, Sasha thanked the Universe for this gift of a man. When she opened them, she threw her arms around him. "You've made me the luckiest girl in all the galaxies." His actions validated what he felt for her. Extreme happiness brought out her frisky side. "Let's mark this place."

"I'm not sure—"

"You know what I mean." She kissed him hard.

Maeson scooped her up and brought her to an area where the pink grass came up to his waist. "I'm having my way with you." His gaze stayed on hers, and she loved feeling secure in his powerful arms.

Anticipation and desire coursed through her. "A dream come true."

Chuckling, he lowered her to the ground. An unexpected soft bedding of grass cushioned her back. The land was her foundation, and the sky was her ceiling. Maeson was her anchor to this reality.

"I've fantasized about having you out here." His lips brushed against her ears. She bent her neck to the side, giving him access to her throat. She moaned when he took it, nibbling to her mouth. "I'm going to cherish you. Love you."

Sasha's heart swelled as he kissed her senseless and sent her pulse racing. He had shown her the meaning of dedication, passion, and the value of his words. A man who viewed a promise like a sacred mantra was her kind of man.

She believed his words, and emotions rose in her. "Same here."

This outdoor way of lovemaking liberated her, allowing her to bare her emotions to the Universe. They were both on their knees, facing each other. She removed her clothing and then his. He smiled when his boots thumped somewhere. Her eyes wandered every inch of his body. Physical labor had earned him marvelous muscles that made her mouth water. His manhood was a glorious sight, all ready for her.

"Do you like what you see?" he muttered, while his hands skimmed down her arms.

She shivered slightly from the cool breeze and from his touch. She was about to answer him, but gasped when his mouth closed over her nipple, sending fire straight to her core. She moaned and arched her back, offering him all of her. She watched as he feasted on her breasts, kissing, nipping, licking and sucking every inch of her exposed skin.

Maeson's purple eyes darkened to naughtiness. His hand slid down to her center and his fingers did wicked things to her. His mouth found hers, and his urgency played out with his tongue. Heat warred with heat. Passion tangled with passion.

"Maeson…" she murmured against his lips.

"This is better than I imagined." Maeson nipped at her bottom lip. "If dreams had a flavor, it would be you."

He owned her with those words. "You're my dream come true."

Sasha's heart raced as he lifted her butt with both hands,

kneading them. He studied her exposed center like a gem. Embarrassment spiked, and she pushed her thighs together. He gently urged them apart. "This is mine." His voice low and firm.

Maeson's lips settled onto her core, and her vision blurred. *Holy shit.* Desire swirled through her, whipping her from side to side. Sensations roared as she gripped at the pink grass to stabilize herself. She didn't know her body could feel this way, this alive.

With heavy-lidded eyes, he lifted his face and licked his lips. Magnificently aroused, his manhood aimed straight at her. He reached for his denim, which lay on the side, and pulled out a bottle of Safe-Sex Spray. She knew what it was from conversations she'd overheard in the salon. He sprayed the length of him with a translucent layer of protection that added an interesting texture to his surface.

She examined the bumpy texture with her fingers. "Interesting..."

"It's time I claim Sasha's Full Moon."

Sasha let out a small laugh. "It's already yours." She got onto her hands and knees—a playful position she had imagined trying with him—and arched her back, giving him what he wanted. He shifted behind her and caressed her with his hands.

When he filled her, a song of completion rang in her ears. She welcomed his powerful thrusts as he went deeper and deeper into her, sweeping her away to a place where there was nothing but the two of them. Pleasure exploded, rippling through her body.

He bent over, and his sweat-drenched skin kissed her back. He nibbled her ear as he intensified his thrusts. She moved in rhythm with him, coaxing him until he reached an orgasm that ricocheted his body against hers. Her name tore from his lips. "Sasha..."

They collapsed into each other's arms and remained there

while the blue sky and the field of pink grass were their audience.

After a few minutes, he popped up on his elbow. "Repeat? You said you have several positions to show me."

Sasha laughed, rolled on top of him, and demonstrated how she liked to take control.

SIX

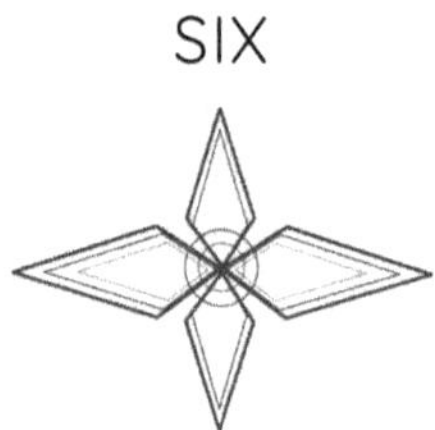

A week later, Sasha went to check on the foundation of her new home. It would be her permanent home with Maeson. She would commute to work and visit her sisters in the Village Center. They were happy for her and couldn't wait for the housewarming invitation.

With a joyful heart, Sasha inhaled a breath of fresh air as she went to search for her star-being, her lover, who had just returned home from an urgent meeting with his soldier-brothers and the Village Chief regarding the Ulkrin creature.

Her ring glowed with a message from Inga. "Hey, I need a huge favor from you. Please say yes. Please, please." Inga pressed her palms together in prayer.

Concern bubbled in Sasha. "What is it?"

"I have a fashion show next week, but the three male models who initially agreed to do it were just sent on assignment. I'm in dire need of three replacements." Her eyes twinkled. "Can you please ask Maeson if he'd help me? I've already asked Emma about Raeko, and he said yes."

Relief slid away from Sasha, replaced by amusement. "You're still missing one model if Maeson agrees."

"I know." Inga sighed. "Maybe Maeson can ask his brothers if any of them would like to help me out?"

Maeson had a nice build that would make any outfit look fantastic, but she didn't know if he'd be interested. As if he sensed she was talking about him, he appeared fifty feet away and strode over to her. She liked his casual and confident walk. He'd make an exceptional model.

"Please," Inga said when Sasha didn't reply. "This is my first fashion show here. It's important to me."

"I'll try, but I can't promise anything, okay?"

"Okay, thank you. I've got to go now. I have a fabric vendor coming in a few minutes. Chat later." Inga hung up.

"Who were you talking to?" Maeson pulled her in for a kiss.

She ran a hand through his shaggy hair, admiring the trim and golden highlights that brought out his eyes. "Inga just called, asking for your help."

He furrowed his eyebrows. "My help? What does she need?"

Sasha described the situation to him, and he roared with laughter. "I don't know if I can help her, but for you, I'll try."

"Thank you. It means a lot to me. My sisters have helped me when I needed them." Sasha went on her tiptoes and kissed him. "I'm ready for a tour of our future house."

"There's not much to see, but okay."

Blue mist swirled around them as Maeson took her hand and led her to their future home. Beside the stone foundation, a single flower grew with a blue bud that hadn't bloomed yet. Sasha pointed it to Maeson as blue vapors ribboned around it.

"It's a gift from the land to us," Maeson said.

With gratitude, Sasha glanced around her, appreciating the beauty of what life offered. She'd never imagined finding love on another planet, but here she was, falling deeper and deeper into love with a magnificent star-being. The old adage that anything was possible was true. Her life was the perfect example of the heart manifesting phenomenal possibilities.

AN ALIEN DARE

SOLDIERS OF SAEDO 3

USA TODAY BESTSELLING AUTHOR

CALLA ZAE

AN ALIEN DARE #3: BLURB

"I love challenges, and you're the most captivating challenge to cross my path. I will unravel you."

Though excited to showcase her first galactic fashion show, Inga is stressed because she's desperate for one more model. A stunning star-being with the perfect body emerges, but his ego irritates her. Annoyed, she dares him to model for her, not expecting a challenge to her heart.

Osayik, an outstanding soldier with no interest in "strutting" down some runway—whatever that means—can't resist a challenge. Fascinated by Inga, he wants to know what lies beneath the beauty.

Does he dare listen to his heart? Or will pride get in his way?

CONTENTS

ONE

Stress flashed and anxiety flickered as Inga attached the gemstones to her marvelous gown inside her design studio. The exquisite gown hung on the dress form made of liquid foam that mimicked the body and flesh, making it easy for her to pin and prick. Like the dress, Inga was revealing her soul, her creations, to the world. The blue dress was one of many ensembles she would showcase at her first fashion show in the Province of Saedo on planet Celeron. Though excitement and anticipation sparked in her, fear and failure frayed her nerves.

What if these star-beings didn't like her styles? What if they thought her designs were dull compared to their out-of-this-world creations? After all, Saedo fashion had top-notch fabrics that allowed for fantastic innovations. Access to these cutting-edge materials was a designer's dream come true, and Inga immersed herself in that wonder.

She glanced down at her dark denim pants made from high-tech fabric with properties that toned and sculpted her butt and thighs every time she moved. She burned extra calories without even thinking about it. How outstanding was that? She paid a lot of credits for it, but the results were well worth it. Her soft blouse had tiny spores of lotion embedded within the fabric that moisturized her skin when the room got too dry. She could design a whole line of gadget clothing with these technologies. She loved clothes that were functional and stylish.

A headache flared, but she ignored it. She had too much to do. She walked around the dress form, adding another gemstone to the neckline of the dress, and tripped over a pile of fabric she forgot to put away, knocking over the container of gemstones. Colors glistened as they covered her floor.

"Shit!" She placed the gemstone fastener down on the table and sat down on the floor, staring at the sea of sparkles. She glanced around her studio, which was adjacent to her office. Two dress forms, three racks of clothing, piles of fabrics, and containers of sequins, studs, and zippers covered her pattern-making table, couch, and coffee table. This was the chaotic image of what went on behind the scenes before every fashion show she ever had on Earth. She'd learn it wasn't that different here.

She rubbed the tight muscles around her neck, straightened her back, and released a heavy sigh. Then she gathered up the spilled gemstones, secured the lid, and pushed it aside. She needed a break from working on that dress. She glanced at the other dress form, which held a special jacket that didn't need to meet anyone's expectations. This was her baby. This was for her.

Inga designed a personalized gadget jacket, part of her Ingavex collection made of the smart-vex fabric. This innovative fabric gave the wearer a layer of protection from the high-voltage circuitry that was embedded on the exterior surface of the material. She had worked with an engineering group of star-beings and paid a lot of credits for it. This jacket was a secret project she had worked on for a while. She wasn't ready to share her baby yet. Working on it was a cathartic way of releasing stress, like writing in her diary. She could let go of the need to be perfect, rest her mind, and play with it.

Letting go was one of the reasons she was living here in Saedo instead of Earth.

There was nothing that held her on Earth. Her job as a dress buyer sucked her energy. Her passion was in designing, not buying. She hoped to have her own collection one day. But because of the shrinking economy, she took whatever job she could find. Her unhappiness with her career and the fact that her ex-boyfriend, Eric, was the merchandise director for the company, hadn't given her much hope. In fact, she lost all hope in relationships because of him.

Every time she sat in the same meeting with him, a reminder bubbled in her. The way he waved her off, cutting off her comments like she had nothing important to say. The way he dragged her around a roomful of important people and showed her off like she was some damn trinket flashed in her mind like a sad movie on repeat. He had considered her an accessory, something inanimate, something he could easily replace. *Asshole.*

Just because she liked to reward herself with clothes, jewelry, and shoes didn't mean that those things *defined* her. She wasn't an accessory. She wasn't replaceable.

She was extraordinary, and if he couldn't see that, she was better off without him.

"You need to redefine your standards, Inga." Talking to herself while she worked was part of the healing process too. "Never lower your standards for any man. Especially the good-looking ones."

How had she failed at connecting with men? Her relationships had been superficial, and like all superficial things, they didn't last. When the new season arrived, they became last year's fashion.

Was it just bad luck that had her choosing men who didn't want to see what lay in her soul? She wanted someone she could share stimulating conversations with, someone who understood her as an artist and as an individual who had more to offer. She wanted a man who could look at artwork and comprehend the internal process it took to bring the masterpiece to life. Even if he didn't understand it, as long as he *wanted* to, she could *show* him.

That was the missing link. Where was that person who *desired* to know her? She yearned for the deep, magical connection. More magical than any princess ball gown or glass slipper.

The dreamy Inga believed that kind of man was waiting for her somewhere, but the practical Inga knew that man didn't exist. If he did, he was probably taken. Good things didn't wait around for her. So, she indulged herself.

"Life is too short to wonder and wait," Inga convinced herself. "I'm twenty-nine years old, I need to make myself happy, otherwise, I'd be waiting forever." She didn't like the angle of the collar on her jacket and used a fabric pen to mark the new shape. "Life is all about redesigning when things didn't look good, right jacket?"

She didn't expect the jacket to reply, but as an artist, sometimes she wondered what her creations thought of her. If she could see through their eyes, what would they see? A lonely, creative, and ambitious woman?

Right now, this woman needed more coffee if she wanted to finish that dress today. On her way to retrieve her coffee, she walked by the window. The plant she had purchased last week to help keep the air clean inside her apartment was dead. She yanked the dried plant from the soil and tossed it into the trash. She made a mental note to buy some herbal seeds to plant in the soil, to reuse the pot instead of letting soil go to waste. Maybe she could buy an indoor tree that produces a lovely fragrance.

There was nothing wrong with pampering herself when she worked hard. If she didn't treat herself to things that brought her joy, then *what* was the point in living?

She was done with men looking at her like a Rolex, something to add to their ensemble, making them presentable to their peers. They thought she was an accessory at dinner parties and nothing more.

I'm not a damn trinket.

She hated how Eric used to demand what she did or didn't wear. How did she allow these outrageous demands to go on for as long as they did? Her hope that he would see her as more than a pretty bauble vanished when he cheated on her.

So on New Year's Eve, Inga and her six sisters had tossed out their wishes to the Universe. The Universe had delivered wishes to her sisters Emma and Sasha. Both had fallen in love with two extraordinary soldiers of Saedo, the rescuers who had saved them from an abduction from the horrendous monsters called Ulkrins. Inga had stayed in Saedo because that was what sisters do. They were her only family, and she couldn't imagine life on another planet, unable to see them.

Inga's own wish from that fateful night echoed in her mind. *I deserve a man who sees and understands my heart. A man who values me like a gem to his soul and not a gem on his ring.*

Her smart bracelet vibrated, and an image of Sasha popped onto the virtual screen. "Hey! Are you bringing the outfits for Maeson to try on tonight? To make sure they fit him before the big day? There's going to be a lot of yummy food."

Inga glanced at the rack of clothes that desperately needed organization. The weight of her to-do list suffocated her. She had planned on skipping tonight's dinner to attack the list, but she didn't want to disappoint Sasha's joyful face. Besides, Maeson was doing her a favor by modeling.

"Yes, I am. I'll be there soon."

"Great. Maeson asked a couple of his brothers to stop by as well. You might find another model."

That issue glared at her as a model recently backed out due to his work schedule, piling more stress onto her. She was desperate for a new model.

TWO

More models meant she didn't have to rush everyone with as many clothing changes. It was difficult to find good models on such short notice.

The headache pounded Inga's head, and she grabbed her third cup of coffee and sipped. She should reduce her caffeine intake, but Saedo coffee was absolutely delicious. It was the best she had ever tried.

It came from some mystical vine that grew from a rock formation. A formation that baffled the villagers. They considered it a divine blessing from the Cosmos and took care of that area like a precious gift. From a single coffee vine, an extraordinary farm of coffee trees and vines was developed. It was one of Saedo's most profitable products to trade with neighboring provinces.

Grateful for the energy boost, she took one last sip before flipping through her list. Tasks seemed to breed like bunnies when she had an important event.

Inga popped a sweetened pain killer pill into her mouth and gulped it down with blue water. She didn't want the headache to be the focal point of her evening. She chose five various tops and bottoms, separating them into two anti-wrinkle garment bags. She zipped them up and brought them out to hang in her silver personal rider, a sleek four-seater automobile that moved with great speed without making a sound. She returned to lock the door to Stellium Couture, owned by the established designer Stelli, who hired Inga without hesitation.

Not only that, Stelli invited Inga to showcase her first collection. Gratitude filled Inga at the generous offer. There was no competition between them. They had different styles. Where Stelli's apparel sparked with neon colors, Inga's preference embraced simplicity. She preferred the rule: less was more. With the help of droid seamstresses and high-tech sewing machines that printed out the designs rather than sewing them, Inga had gotten about twenty outfits completed.

She sent her two assistants, Laney and Melba, an update on the priorities and drove off. She didn't know what she'd do without them. They gathered models, scheduled them, measured them, logged the information, followed up with vendors and so much more. Even they couldn't help locate a decent model replacement. She prayed to the Universe to send her someone suitable.

Her stomach growled. When did she last eat? For breakfast, she munched on a Saedo pyrus, which tasted like the pears on Earth, but these were purple and diamond-shaped. She had worked through lunch. Well, at least she was bringing an appetite to Emma's. Her sisters, Emma and Vanessa took cooking classes that benefited Inga and her other sisters exponentially. Inga and cooking weren't friends.

She glanced at the two suns as they neared the horizon, casting a warm glow on the land. Even though it was seven in the evening, there was still a lot of daylight around.

She parked her rider next to Sasha's upgraded personal rider, which could hover above the ground. Hers couldn't, but one day she'd purchase her own small spacecraft so she could fly and observe this beautiful land all by herself. She appreciated beauty: its history, its poetry, its symbolism. There was so much more to beauty than what meets the eye.

Why couldn't people look at her and see something beyond her physicality?

Releasing a sigh, Inga got out of her rider and retrieved the garment bags. A handsome star-being walked toward her, wearing rugged high-tech denim pants and a white shirt under a light gray jacket with unique textures. His brown hair, shaved on the sides, created a mohawk that could be styled into interesting shapes. This wasn't the kind of hairstyle that suited everyone. The edgy look was an emblem of non-conformity, and this man radiated that energy.

His sage-green eyes gave her a once over, then met hers. "Do you need help?"

Her stomach fluttered at the chiseled features. She had seen several stunning star-beings in Saedo, but no one that interested her. More like she didn't allow anyone to interest her because she had shut down that part of herself and tossed the key into the abyss. She was now focusing on her career. There was no room in her mind for anything else. With men, she'd encountered too many failures to even want to try again, but she could control her career endeavors.

Because she worked in the beauty industry, she knew outstanding artwork when she saw it, and this green man was like an Art Nouveau painting, most notably the Gustav Klimt painting, *The Kiss*. It was a combination of mysticism, eclecticism, and longing beauty that gripped you from out of nowhere.

There was something about this star-being that made her want to understand the mystery flowing from him. A subtle hint was enough to tease Inga. She liked details because details matter. They were the important pieces that made the whole composition.

"Are you okay?" he asked, yanking her back to the moment. The glimmer in his eyes and the satisfied grin told her he was used to this kind of attention.

Her stomach growled again. Embarrassed, she shuffled the garments, trying to prevent them from falling, but they dropped to the ground anyway. "I'm fine. Apparently, I do need help."

He gathered them up in his muscular arms and raked a gaze down her body. Heat bloomed within her. "I like your outfit. It's simple, yet distinctive."

"Oh, thank you. This is just a basic outfit, nothing special." She couldn't get any simpler than denim jeans, a blouse, and gold earrings.

"You can determine a lot by what someone wears. How they move their bodies can show confidence or insecurity. Their word choices can show a lot too."

Was he judging her? A red flag waved in her mind.

"Did you take a class on studying behaviors or something?"

"I'm just good at reading people."

Well, if his perception was any 'good', he would know she wasn't in the mood to be read like a book or examined like a piece of clothing. She changed the subject before her headache increased.

"I'm Inga, what's your name?" She adjusted the strap from the shoulder bag that fell along with the garment bags.

"Osayik. Yes, I remember you." The greens of his eyes shifted, giving off a darker shade. Why couldn't she look away? "You're one of the seven Nelson sisters." The deep rumble in his throat sounded like temptation inviting her to some secret place.

That's dangerous territory, Inga. Stay clear.

She remembered his face, who wouldn't? Several images of Osayik surrounded by alluring females popped into her mind.

He was popular with the females. He was part of a group of soldiers that had rescued her and her sisters from the Ulkrin monsters who abducted them on New Year's Eve.

"Thank you for saving us back then. We're grateful for everything you've done."

Lines creased on his forehead as he considered her. She didn't miss the fact that she stood a head shorter than his six-foot plus build even with her heels on. He glanced down at her, and his expression was full of judgment, reminding her of the men from her past. She didn't know why or how he could judge her when he didn't even know her. But that had never stopped her ex-boyfriend's criticism or assumptions before.

Annoyance clawed at her as she waited for him to say something along the line of: *gratitude is the shawl that covers insecurities.*

He shrugged. "It's what we do. You're welcome."

Why did he look at her as if she wasn't capable of gratitude? Did he think she was thoughtless, that she had nothing constructive to offer?

She had thought and hoped that the male species on this planet were different. But she was wrong. Maybe it was just unfortunate luck that she was attracted to men who could see nothing beyond her physicality.

Inga was grateful for her high cheekbones, flawless skin, perfectly arched eyebrows, naturally full lips, and a toned body that made women jealous. Her mane of light brown hair with golden highlights was her favorite feature. It symbolized femininity more than anything else. She loved how it moved with the wind, flowing freely, not constricted by anything. It could alter her face with a simple change in style, and that held great power.

The men she dated preferred her lips and chest over her hair. Inga stayed rooted that there was a lot more to Inga Nelson than lips and chest. The first man who acknowledged love for her hair had potential. She blamed her sour mood for the ridiculous insistence.

Why would she care what others thought about her hair?

Feeling tattered for no logical reason, she stalked into the house, ignoring Osayik. The smell of excellent food welcomed her. The scent of home and family made her feel better.

"Hey, there you are!" Sasha rushed over, giving Inga a big hug.

The embrace squeezed some of her stress away. Inga drew back and looked at her older sister. "Love suits you." She tapped Sasha's cheek. "You wear it beautifully."

"Stop it." Sasha blushed.

Inga's stomach grumbled. "I need a snack. You have anything?"

Sasha offered a tray of pink appetizers. "Try these stuffed mushrooms. They're Emma's new dish. They're *so* good." She popped one into her mouth. "Did you bring the clothes?"

Inga chewed, swallowed, and moaned. "These are heavenly." Grabbing another mushroom, she whirled around and found Osayik standing with a straight posture, chatting with Maeson on the other side of the kitchen. The garment bags hung on a clothing rack along the wall. Emma must have gotten the rack ready for her.

Inga retrieved the bag, unzipped it, and pulled out a pair of light-washed denim with zippers decorating the back pockets. Unlike womenswear, where Inga could add rhinestones or embroidery to enhance the garment, her menswear collection called for subtlety. The males could have their bling, but those details and their locations were chosen carefully. Pockets, buttons, cuff links, and belts were some of the places that could be embellished, upgrading the styles to a new level.

"I'm not sure if Maeson would be comfortable with all those

zippers." Sasha chose the soft brown leather pants made from Saedo tree bark that had been recycled and formulated into functional ingenuity.

The recycling technology in Saedo continued to astound Inga. "That one has a quiet, sexy appeal."

"Perfect for my man."

Osayik exuded a mysterious sex appeal that captivated her for some damn reason. She understood why females were attracted to him. He emanated a sexuality that seeped into her skin. He lured without luring, and though she didn't like feeling powerless in that aspect, she allowed that emotion to wash over her tonight. She was too exhausted, and she wanted to conserve her energy for more important things on her mind.

A boom of laughter echoed in the air, and Inga glanced through the wide screen door that opened to the backyard. Osayik stood in a position that gave her a detailed view of him. He had taken his jacket off, revealing broad shoulders and muscular arms. The casual way he hooked his thumbs on the front loops of his denim made her stomach flip not once, but twice. His wide grin formed an adorable dimple that punctuated his sexuality.

Why hadn't she noticed the dimple?

Her sour mood probably blocked it from view. She didn't like that he had already formed an opinion of her. What could he conclude based on her clothing and word choice? Did he see her like all the female star-beings around him?

Why should she care what he thought of her? It wouldn't be news that he was exactly like those men from her past. Despite that, a strange part of her wanted to know. Was that hunger or exhaustion in her brain speaking? It didn't matter, she couldn't ask such a private question.

Horrified that she had digressed and forgotten her vow to focus on her career—even if it was only for a second—she cursed, forcing her gaze back to the clothes. "Let's go drag Maeson back inside to try these on."

Inga and Sasha strode out to a backyard flourishing with flowering shrubs. Emma glanced up from her herbal garden and smiled. "Dinner will be ready any second. I'm just plucking some colorful garnish to decorate my plate. Presentation is everything, right? You taught me that."

Inga warmed at the compliment. Emma was the oldest sister who took over parental responsibilities at a young age to care for her siblings when their parents passed. Emma had ensured they stayed together. She had taught Inga what it meant to sacrifice for love. For family.

"True, presentation is everything, but it could also be deceiving. But since I know you and Vanessa can cook, it doesn't matter how you display the meals, I'll eat it. Where's Vanessa and the others?"

"Busy tonight. We'll catch up with them another day."

"Inga, come look at this!" Sasha waved from where she stood with Maeson, Raeko, and Osayik.

Inga met Osayik's gaze. A quiet sizzle hummed between them. Or was that her imagination? Or was the sizzling her brain being fried from too much caffeine?

"Isn't this flower beautiful?" Sasha gestured to a lovely yellow bud with pretty white rocks surrounding the base of the stem. No other flower resembled or grew near it. "This looks exactly like the blue bud from my yard. Mine hasn't bloomed either. Raeko said this flower grew after he met Emma."

Raeko headed the rescue team that had saved Inga and her sisters from Ulkrin monsters. He bent down, plucked off a dried leaf, and moved the rocks around. "Emma was the one who discovered it while she planted new shrubberies." He rose and gestured a hand to the thriving yard. "This area had nothing but grass before. She transformed it. I don't have an eye for that kind of thing."

"A woman's touch makes everything better, right Maeson?" Sasha winked at him.

"Absolutely." Maeson pulled her in for a kiss.

"That's not what I meant." She rolled her eyes even as she leaned in for a second kiss.

There was a certain glow for those in love. Emma and Sasha both emanated that energy, and it made everyone around them feel the warmth too.

Sasha examined the bud closely. "I wonder if the flower has any significance to Saedo lore. I tried looking it up, but I couldn't find anything. I need to ask Grandma Ova. She'll know something."

Inga sensed Osayik's warmth close to her.

"It resembles a lot of unopened flowers. Maybe you'll know when it blooms." His voice sent chills down her body.

Why was she reacting to him like this?

Emma strode up to them with plants and flowers in hand. She turned to Maeson. "What are you going to wear for Inga?"

Sasha gasped. "Sorry, I got distracted. We need you inside right now. There are clothes waiting for you. There's a nice pair of leather pants that will make your butt look gorgeous."

Grinning, Maeson let Sasha drag him back into the house. "I thought it already was."

Raeko wrapped an arm around Emma. "Let me know if my ass looks good in Inga's designs, okay?" He leaned in and whispered something that made Emma blush.

Shaking her head, Inga followed them. "This isn't a butt contest."

Osayik chuckled, but didn't comment as he strode beside her. Why was he so quiet? And why was he walking so close to her? Her body reacted to him like a magnet. She slowed her steps to let him pass. Her eyes landed on his gorgeous ass, and she swore her organs shifted in celebration.

An idea occurred to her, but she wasn't sure if he'd be interested in working with her. After all, she was just a fashion designer who made clothing that helped determine whether someone was "confident" or "insecure." Did he see her as a confident woman? She remembered her clumsiness as she dropped the garment bags in front of him.

How did she perceive him? She had no answer for that yet.

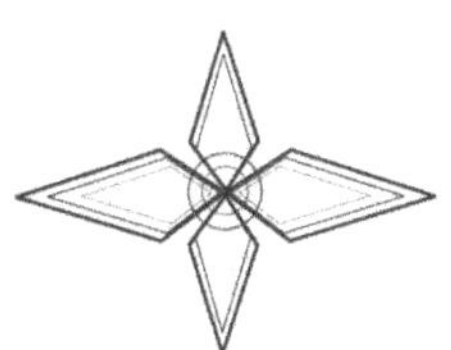

Sasha and Emma sat on the couch in the living room eyeing their men. With her arms crossed over her chest, Inga examined her two models. Raeko wore a vintage-wash denim pants made from high-tech fabric that was strategically ripped at the knees with whisker designs at the thighs. He had on a gray knit top that changed color with body heat. An asymmetrical brown leather jacket that could be converted into a longer jacket finished his look.

Maeson wore pants made of the high-tech leather that was soft as butter. It had brown striations from the natural tree bark properties. Inga paired the pants with an iridescent black top that could transform into a high-collared jacket.

"They look like they could be on the cover of Alien GQ. Someone should create a version for Saedo," said Sasha.

"What's that?" asked Osayik, as he sat on a stool and leaned back against the kitchen counter. His posture was casual, yet distinctive.

"It's a magazine on Earth," Emma said.

Osayik munched on Emma's lasagna and the pink mushrooms. Sasha had mentioned Maeson invited some of his brothers to join them this evening. Was Osayik one of them? If not, where were they?

Inga's stomach made a noise that got everyone's attention. "I'll eat once I know everything fits fine." She pointed to the hallway. "Okay, walk up and down here. Not too fast, though. A slow walk is best because people need to see the clothes. Strut, and if you're comfortable, add some attitude to the walk."

"What do you mean strut with an attitude?" Raeko formed a pissed-off expression and glared at Emma with so much attitude, she burst out laughing.

"Not that kind of attitude, love."

Maeson chuckled. "Haven't you seen any of Stelli's fashion shows on the screen?"

Raeko lifted an eyebrow. "No, and I don't plan to."

"Sasha made me watch it to get a gist of 'strutting' down the runway. You should take a peek. It'll help you define 'attitude.'"

Emma patted Raeko's shoulder. He had a natural reaction from someone who had never modeled before. The last thing Inga needed was for Raeko to lose hope and quit. "I can send you a video on how to walk. Just be yourself. There's no need for any attitude."

Raeko tried again, and his walk improved with a natural flair.

"Help me sell my designs, so I can have my own store one day," Inga said. "How do the clothes make you feel? Show that emotion when you're walking."

"Walk to this." Osayik tapped his gunmetal wristband and music boomed.

"Why are you walking like someone shot you in the leg?" Maeson teased his brother.

Raeko snorted. "Don't make me have to hurt you, and we'll see how you walk."

Unlike Raeko, Maeson was a natural at walking in the spotlight. Well, he was more prepared. "Don't hate. Some of us just have the skills."

Raeko wrapped a playful arm around Maeson's neck.

With hands on her hips, Emma said, "Guys, let's get serious. Inga doesn't have all day."

Maeson held up a hand. "Watch and learn."

Raeko mimicked his brother down the hallway, paused, shifted his weight to the other foot, and then swiveled, walking back.

Inga clapped and threw her arms around each of them. "You nailed it. Both of you! See? That wasn't so hard."

The music stopped and Maeson scratched his head. "To be honest, I don't really know what I'm doing. You *owe* me."

"How about free clothes? You get two tops and two bottoms of your choice when the show's done. Or I can give you credits to your favorite shop. Anything but asking me to cook. That's the bane of my existence."

"Inga can't cook. She almost burned down the house last time she tried. That was a few years ago. So we've banned her."

She rubbed her pinky finger on her right hand. That small scar had steered her away from the kitchen. "It's not my fault food prefers your touch. I don't have the patience for it."

"There's no such thing as 'can't' or 'won't.' You can do whatever you put your mind to," Osayik said, cleaning off his plate.

Who asked for his opinion? Inga sent him a haughty gaze, which he didn't see since he had left his seat to clear the counter.

Osayik walked out to the living room, holding his bubbly drink, and standing a couple of inches taller than Maeson.

Maeson gave him a once over and tapped his shoulder. "Do you still need a model for your show, Inga? If so, Osayik might able to help, right?"

Osayik choked on his drink. "What?"

"Inga needs help, so Raeko and I are helping her. But she needs another." Maeson turned to her.

"I need one more, but—"

"I don't strut. I prefer to stay out of the spotlight."

Yet, the spotlight is always on you.

Osayik narrowed his eyes at Maeson. "Is that why you invited me to dinner tonight?"

Maeson elbowed his brother. "I invited other soldiers too, but they were busy. You're a good friend who never refuses a delicious meal."

"Delicious meal, my ass. If I had known I was being set up, I would have stayed home."

"And do what? Be dessert for all those females who hover around you constantly?"

Osayik crossed his toned arms. "That's none of your business. I can't help they're attracted to my confidence."

Inga rolled her eyes at his massive ego.

"You seem to be in the spotlight all the time with Ameeya, Chandra, Lexxi and so many others. I can't keep up." Maeson slapped Osayik's back.

"I'm capable and I'll probably perform better than you, but wearing clothes and strutting around is just not my—"

"There's no such thing as 'can't' or 'won't.' You can do whatever you put your mind to."

Had she lost her mind? What prompted her to say that? The words escaped her mouth like they were waiting for the perfect opportunity. These were his words that had been swimming inside her brain. What was it about him that made her edgy and uncomfortable?

A sudden stream of red mist emerged from around his neck and shoulders as if he was responding to her mockery. The mist swirled toward her and snaked around her ankles. She expected a smart-ass retort from him, but he only gave her a crooked smile. One that tightened her core.

What the hell was wrong with her?

Sasha had mentioned something about the lore of Saedo mist, but she couldn't remember. At the time, she had been too focused on getting the show ready. Did Sasha say that star-beings produced their own mist color? Or did she say that about plants? Inga would ask her sister later.

She waited for Osayik to dismiss everything and leave.

Osayik leaned back against the kitchen counter and considered her with a challenging gaze. The intensity of the stare prickled her skin. How was it possible that a simple gesture from him could rile her body like that?

Amusement flickered in his eyes. "You're right. I *can* do whatever I put my mind to."

Everyone paused what they were doing and listened to her conversation with Osayik with keen interest.

Ignoring them, she crossed her arms, mocking him. "Let's see how capable you truly are."

A devilishly handsome smirk graced his face. A man shouldn't be allowed to have that kind of smile on that kind of face with that kind of body. Why was he so annoying and so stunning at the same time?

Why was he pushing her buttons?

She didn't like being pushed around. Courage soared through her. "I *dare* you to model for me."

A gasp erupted from her sisters. Chuckles from Raeko and Maeson filled the room.

A knowing grin splashed on Osayik's face. "You don't know what you're getting yourself into."

Inga didn't appreciate the mockery in his tone. She knew exactly what she was doing. He was the kind of man who thought he was better than everyone else. He probably thought she was incapable of accomplishing this fashion show. She'd prove him wrong. He'd see her competence, her proficiency, and her effectiveness. She was very effective at looping and twisting a tie knot until it could strangle someone.

Anger rose in her. "You don't know me."

He arched a fine eyebrow. "I think I do. I'll accept the challenge if you accept mine. But if you're frightened, stop now. No hard feelings."

Fear him? Oh, he had no idea. Irritation poked her. "I dare you to model two outfits for me."

Still leaning casually on the kitchen counter like nothing could agitate him, Osayik pursed his lips. "Only if you'll cook me a fine dinner from scratch. Not some meal you got from the store to warm up. I want the real deal."

The challenge stopped her for a second. She had expected him to want more free clothes or credits, but he wanted her to cook for him? Why? Did he want to *die?* Did he not hear about her skills, or lack of? She didn't understand him.

The smirk that slid onto his face gave his intentions away. He wanted to see her fail. He thought she was inadequate. Maybe she had encountered some resistance in the kitchen, but if she really tried and put in the extra effort, anything was possible.

Raeko whispered something to Emma, which earned him an elbow to his rib.

Inga was going to deliver her end of the bargain no matter what it took. She'd make something up. She had never been more inspired to prove anyone wrong than in this moment. He could have her meal and choke on it for all she cared.

"Deal." Inga stalked to her garment bag, pulled out a pair of gray leather pants and navy top, and tossed them at him. "We start now."

Osayik caught the items. "She doesn't mess around, does she?"

"Not my sister. Good Luck, Osayik." Emma shot Inga a smirk and returned to the kitchen.

"I can't wait to see what kind of meal you're going to make." Sasha grinned.

Right now, if Inga had to gather ingredients, they'd reflect her mood. Fiery peppers to burn his tongue, salt laced with laxatives to keep him up all night, a vegetable dish with itching properties, and a few pebbles to break that stupid grin on his face. An evil voice cackled in her mind.

Good god. Where did all those horrible thoughts come from? When did she become so cruel? What happened to the Inga she was used to? Had she worked herself to death? The death of her former self had birthed someone unrecognizable.

The need to pop his perfect bubble surged in her. What could she do to unravel him?

FOUR

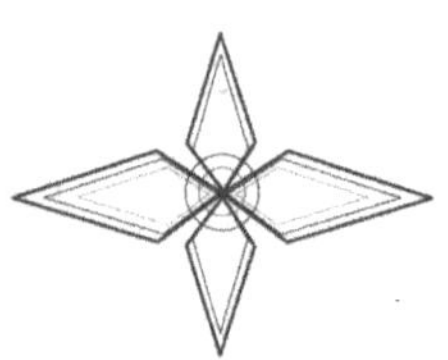

The next day, Inga rushed home with three garments needing her attention. She had to repair the intricate lace on two of them. High-tech equipment was efficient, but certain details required a set of hands from a living person to get the job done. If she had time, she'd attach the sequins on the dress that she'd be wearing on the day of the show.

When she arrived home, she checked the message on her smart bracelet. Emma had asked her to stop by and pick up dinner. Too late, Inga was already settled in her apartment and didn't feel like going back out.

She called Emma. "Sorry, I got your message late. I have a lot of work to get done, and I have plenty of food at home. Don't worry about me. Thanks, though."

"You should take care of yourself better. I can drop off the food for you."

"Don't be silly. I can take care of myself, and I do." Inga waved a hand at her sister from the virtual screen. "I won't starve. If you don't already know, I love to eat. Just because I don't cook doesn't mean I don't eat."

"Okay, but if you're craving some of Grandma Ova's soup, let me know. Sasha got the recipe, and I just made a huge pot."

Her stomach growled as if it could smell the herbal soup from miles away. But Inga didn't want to bother Emma. Besides, she had a lot of food in the coldbox, which was Saedo's version of the refrigerator. "I just want to finish these little things before I forget about them. You know how it is. Before any fashion show there's a bunch of little things I need to do."

"Yes, I know. I used to help you behind the scenes. Well, if you change your mind, let me know."

"Thanks, love you."

Inga changed into a cotton tee shirt and matching shorts. She twisted her hair into a bun and got to work. She laid the garments on the couch. On the dress form that was a replica of her own body, she put on the gown with a low v-neckline and a cinched waist that she'd be wearing to the show. The dress form allowed her to drape couture gowns in a way a flat pattern didn't. The monochromatic purple fabric inspired her to make this dress. Then she covered the dress with her Ingavex jacket. She turned on her computer, expanding the virtual screen so she could see her entire collection.

This jacket was her love in the making. It was a woman's best friend. She had been inspired to create it after a jogging incident that almost got her killed if it hadn't been for the Good Samaritan who helped her. This jacket could zap an attacker with a simple voice command. Voice was like a fingerprint, no two were alike. Voice vibration has an energetic stamp to it. Electricity ran around the top surface of the jacket in secured wires. A protective layer of the smart-vex fabric kept the wearer from being affected by its circuitry. A voltage adjuster hid inside the sleeve hem. A voice command could also adjust it.

Her doorbell rang. She glanced at her smart bracelet and saw it was eight in the evening. Who could it be? She strode over to the door, activated the screen on the wall, and her eyebrows furrowed at the unexpected guest.

She yanked it open. "Hi, what are you doing here?"

Osayik lifted a bag of food. "I was over at Raeko's house, and Emma mentioned you didn't stop by to get your food. I was on my way home, so I offered to drop it off."

"Oh." Inga didn't know what to say. Their interaction from yesterday hadn't been "friendly." It had been full of "challenges." He had gotten under her skin and she probably got under his. But the face that looked at her now didn't appear annoyed from the dare she had tossed at him. "You didn't have to do that. I told her I had food."

"Well, I'm here. So take it." He smiled, and that dimple sent a jolt to her core.

She grabbed the bag, and red mist from his hand swirled over to her hand. Did he see that? Probably not, because his eyes were fixated on hers. She was a mess. She should've looked at herself in the mirror before opening the door.

"Can I come in?" he asked.

Flustered, she said, "Yes, sorry. Come in."

Osayik entered, kicked off his shoes, and placed them next to hers. *Good perception*, she thought. She would have asked him to take off his shoes if he hadn't. She liked to keep her apartment free of dirt to prevent her designs from getting dirty. She worked too hard to have to redo everything if one of her designs acquired stains.

He stared at the dress form, the outfits on the couch, and the virtual screen displaying her collection. "You're still working?"

The surprise in his statement rubbed her the wrong way. She placed the food on the kitchen table and heaved out a breath. "I know you have an opinion of me. I don't know what the other females around you are like, but I'm a competent individual. Once I have a goal, I will do whatever it takes to achieve it. And my clothing, my looks—all of that jazz—don't determine my character."

He opened his mouth to reply, but Inga held up a hand. "Let me finish, please. You're not the first man to look at me and see something superficial. Yes, I love to dress up, make myself look pretty, but those things don't define me. It doesn't mean I'm incapable of being more. Of working hard. *Yes, I'm still working.* I have an important show coming up, and I will continue to work until the job's done." She sighed, tired of explaining herself.

"I didn't say you were incapable. I don't have an 'unappealing' opinion of you." His eyes intensified, searching for something she didn't know.

"You didn't need to. I saw it in your eyes. Maybe you're used to judging without knowing." She lifted a shoulder. "I put a lot of effort into things that matter to me. Some people choose not to see that. And frankly, I'm sick of it."

Osayik looked at her for a long moment. "You're right."

Inga prepared to retort, but his expression softened, so she didn't interrupt. "You're beautiful, confident, and daring. You know how to carry yourself well. I know a lot of female star-beings who are also beautiful, confident, and carry themselves well. There's nothing wrong with that, it's just who they are. But none of them has ever challenged me." He gently brushed a lock of disheveled hair from her face. "I wondered about you, the part of you that nobody knows about."

Her cheeks warmed, and she didn't have a reply to him.

He cursed and scratched the back of his head. "What I'm trying to say is that you made me curious about you. When I stood outside of Raeko's house, there was an energy that stopped me. It urged me to talk to you. I didn't understand it, and I tried to ignore it, but I couldn't. So for a moment, I was warring with myself. Who was this female who could stir me like this? I didn't even know her. So if my reaction seemed rude, I'm sorry. It wasn't my intention." Heat flashed in his eyes. "You'll know when something's intentional from me." He paused as if to emphasize that statement.

What was this energy he was referring to? *You'll know when something's intentional from me.* Was that a promise? Her body thought so.

"You leave me speechless."

A satisfying smile slid onto his face. "Maybe I like the fact that I can stir you. Do I?"

She wasn't going to answer that.

"I can be an ass, I'm not denying that. But I have respect for those who work hard for what they believe in because I work hard too."

She was wrong about his judgment of her. Had she fallen into her own trap of deception? She had constructed sturdy walls around her heart. Were those walls skewing her judgment of those around her?

"There's no need to apologize. Sometimes, I overreact and overanalyze." She changed the topic to satisfy her own curiosity. "You must enjoy the attention from all your female friends."

"There's nothing wrong with having a lot of friends." He eyed her. "You seem to stay away from the kind of attention that I get. Yet, you attract it anyway." It wasn't a question.

Had he been watching her? "What do you mean? I don't have crowds of men or male star-beings around me."

"You probably sent out a radar, telling them to stay away. Like everyone in Saedo, I notice you. You're distinguishable. Unlike everyone in Saedo, I'm disregarding that radar."

Why were her loins tightening? Why was her throat dry? Where was her vocabulary?

Inga, say something. Do something.

Sarcasm had always helped her. "So you like breaking rules?"

"Once I know the rules, I can bend them. But for now, I'll keep a safe distance."

What did that mean? She never considered herself a danger to anyone. A part of her knew what he was referring to. But did she want to acknowledge that he was interested in her?

A moment of silence passed, and all the air in her apartment vanished, making the space appear smaller, warmer. Making him appear more prominent. Everything about him elevated several notches. He was larger, towering over her. His green eyes sparked with glowing blue specks, hypnotizing her. His features were more refined, as if he was a painting she saw through a private spectacle. This unexpected guest in her apartment had thrown off her evening, twirling her to an unfamiliar place where her feet walked on air.

He should stop staring at her. Why was his gaze caressing her skin? How was that possible?

She forced herself to think about something else, *anything* else but him. He aroused her simply by standing next to her. She didn't want to excuse herself for a change of underwear. That would be ridiculous.

Desperate for distraction, Inga turned to the bag of food on the kitchen table, opened it, and peeked inside. She pulled out the container of soup and a box with a slice of chocolate cake. "Oh, my goodness. She didn't." Her eyes beamed. "Would you like some of Vanessa's truffle cake? I didn't know she was at Emma's."

He smiled. "I had some earlier."

Inga didn't want to eat while he stood there, and she'd forgotten her manners. "Do you want something to drink?" She dug into the soup and her stomach smiled.

Osayik shook his head and ambled over to the dress form.

Then he looked at the virtual screen, displaying her collection. "Your designs are impressive. This jacket is cool." He brushed the sleeve of her Ingavex jacket. "Can I help you with anything?"

Inga's hand paused, holding the spoon full of delicious soup from entering her mouth. "What?"

"I can help you. What do you need me to do?"

She blinked at the sudden offer. No man had offered to help her before. They weren't interested in her creative process, her accessories, her sequins or her "dull tasks" as Eric had said once. "You don't have to. I appreciate it though."

He whirled, meeting her eyes. "Do you think I'm nothing more than a handsome face?"

Arrogance much? He had a stunning face, an exceptional body, and an irresistible dimple. But his statement prompted a familiar question in her. How many times had she wondered if people could see more of her than her appearance?

"No, I think you're capable of many things." Some of which she preferred to keep to herself. "But I don't want to interrupt your evening."

"There's no interruption. I didn't have any plans."

Surely, he had more interesting things to do than help her with her tasks, right?

He stood with his hands in his pockets, reviewing the designs on the screen. "I'm actually interested in what you do. The creative process is interesting to me. How your mind works from a sketch to making it tangible is... magical."

Magical. Yes, that was exactly how she felt with every design. Maybe he could help her. She had plenty of stuff to do. *Let's see how fast you run, Dimple.*

She strode over and opened a file on a new virtual screen. "I need some graphics for my marketing campaign, can you help me with that? Can you add some animation to the images? I saw another business do that, and it was amazing. I also need help with choosing music. Can you mix something up? That would save me some credits because I won't need to hire a DJ. Basically, whatever I can do myself will save me credits."

She expected him to bolt from the long list of work. She waited for him to bolt.

He didn't.

"Okay. Does this mean I get to add a dessert to the meal you're going to make me?"

Shit. She almost forgot about the "fine dinner made from scratch" deal.

He beamed at her, knowing exactly what he was doing. It was another dare. She narrowed her eyes, but didn't retreat. "Sure. Don't blame me if you end up with a stomachache for a week."

He let out a laugh that brightened her home.

Something changed tonight. Maybe it was the fact that he hadn't formed an ill opinion of her, and that her own flaw of insecurity had created its judgment. She had some work to do on herself.

She pushed that thought away and focused on what he was doing. She gawked as he played with the graphics like he was a professional. "You're amazing."

"I know. Now go eat that soup before it gets cold. I've got this."

"And bossy."

He laughed again.

From the kitchen table, she reviewed the graphics splashed on the screen. How had her evening changed so drastically? There was now a man sitting comfortably on her couch making graphics for her fashion show.

Impressed with his creativity, she said, "These are incredible. What's your occupation in Saedo? Raeko and Maeson work with Chief Mozar, but Maeson also builds homes. What do you do if you don't mind me asking?"

"Most of the soldiers have multiple responsibilities. Like my brothers, I also work with the Chief. I negotiate trade agreements with the other provinces. Aside from that, I also help Maeson build homes when he needs it."

"Oh, so you love making deals."

"That depends."

"How old are you?"

"Two hundred and fifty solar cycles to your twenty-nine." He left it at that and continued working on the graphics.

How did he know her age? He probably asked Emma or Sasha. It baffled her how the star-beings on this planet had long life spans.

She studied his profile. Who knew he could fascinate her like this? She loved his fearless hairstyle. Would he let her play with his mohawk for the show? Her gaze wandered to his powerful shoulders, muscled arms, and long legs. God, he had a gorgeous form. An innovative design popped into her mind.

Could she make that for him? Would he wear it?

FIVE

The following day, Osayik stopped by her office at Stellium Couture, which surprised her and her assistants. Laney and Melba snuck glances at him, giggling and whispering among themselves.

"I appreciate your help, but don't you have work to do?" Inga checked the rack of steamed clothing.

"I do," he said, keeping his gaze on the computer that sat on the conference table in her office.

Why was he helping her? What did he want from her? Was his assistance a mockery that she couldn't accomplish anything on her own?

What if Osayik wanted to help simply because he wanted to? Was that answer too simple? *Yes*, answered her overanalytical mind. It was too good to be true.

Before he left yesterday, he finished the animated banner gracing her website that was displayed all over the Galacto Net throughout the galaxy.

Inga paused a moment to appreciate the magnitude of that achievement. Everyone in the Alarus Galaxy would view her collection. In her wildest dreams, she'd never imagined that was even a possibility. But now, everything seemed possible.

She was living and working with star-beings. Not to mention her powerful attraction to this green man who was helping her without her having to ask. Beneath his stunning looks, he possessed a creative talent that she appreciated and respected.

Inga's eyes scoured his body. Osayik wore iridescent gray denim pants with a black top that had shiny elbow patches that looked like flexible metal. She admired his edgy sense of style. Was that why he was interested in her creative process? The men she dated before had no interest. They didn't care how something was constructed or what went into it. They only wanted to see the finished product, which was what most consumers cared about anyway.

But as a creator of any kind of art, it mattered significantly to her. There was a story to that piece of artwork. And those who appreciated the story saw more than what was on the surface.

Did Osayik see more to her?

Inga stared at him. "Why are you here?"

He stopped working and faced her. "Because I want to help you. Because I find the work interesting." He rolled the chair closer, making her body tingle. "Because you're the first female to dare me, remember? The challenge annoyed me at first, but now, I find it irresistible." His eyes scanned her body, and her legs wobbled.

She crossed her arms, hoping that motion would somehow strengthen her legs and because she needed to do something while he looked at her like he could see through her dress.

A smirk grew on his face; he was enjoying himself. "I love challenges, and you're the most captivating challenge to cross my path. I will unravel you. You're like an undiscovered galaxy, and I'm still trying to figure out what to do about you. Does that answer your question?"

Her, a galaxy? Inga didn't have a reply to that. He was a man with many gorgeous women around him, and she was a woman who didn't trust that kind of man. Temptation was the stars that lured with illusions, and the spark didn't always reveal beauty.

When she found her senses again, she said, "You confuse me."

"That's the beginning of a beautiful relationship." Certainty etched in his words.

Confidence asserted power and knowledge, and she found it difficult to resist him. She returned to her desk, sat on her chair, and tried to focus on her work. If she remained by his side, her heart would have crawled out of her chest and into his arms.

She was not ready for that.

SIX

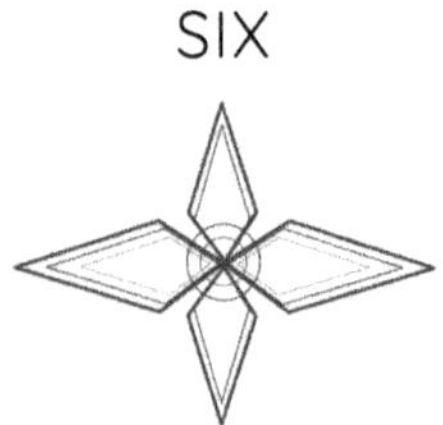

The next evening, Osayik came over to her apartment and worked on the music selection. She appreciated the work he did, but his continued assistance baffled her.

"You don't have to keep helping me. I can do this. Or I can hire someone to do this for me."

He flicked her a glance. "You have enough on your plate. It won't take me long to compose this."

"You think I can't handle it?"

Surprise washed over his face. "No. I just want to help you. That's all."

"No extra demands attached to your assistance?" Suspicion coated her voice.

A hand went to his chin, thinking. "Now that you mention it, that's not a bad idea. I'll let you know when I have new demands."

She stared at him while he ignored her and continued working. She didn't want to waste any more time and got back to her own work.

Not long after, Osayik completed her music selection. With

his help, she was able to rearrange her budget, allowing her to purchase more fabric for the next collection.

A problem floated across her mind.

What should she cook for him? He was contributing more than their deal called for. She was going to need help with this dinner endeavor.

Inga blamed a childhood accident for her dislike of cooking or anything to do with fire. She had spent a day with a friend pretending to play cooking. Jessica had stolen matches from her older brother. The pretense turned into a fire that earned Inga a burn on her finger, leaving a scar. Though she didn't fear fire anymore, she never developed a love for cooking because it reminded her of its potential. Somehow, she had channeled that healing toward her Ingavex design, where the jackets had high voltage that could scorch anyone. But that jacket also protected her.

She looked forward to cooking this time. She blinked at the shocking thought. When had she been excited to cook for anyone? She didn't even cook for herself. Did she like this alternative version of herself?

"Can I pay you for all the extra work you're doing?"

He skewered her with a look. "Don't offend me. I'm not helping you because I want credits. If I wanted them, there are plenty of things I could do."

"I didn't mean to—"

"I know." Osayik rose from the couch where he had been working on her computer. "Everything's all set. Your website, your music, your graphics are all done." He swiped the virtual screen, showing her what he accomplished.

Her heart rejoiced, seeing everything fall into place. Without thinking, she threw her arms around him. "Thank you."

He embraced her with his powerful arms. For a moment, she let herself fall into that comfort, allowing his firm body to support her. They stayed like that for a while, with his chin resting on her head. Being cradled by him sent a refreshing thrill through her systems. It made her feel safe in a way that liberated her.

Osayik drew back and looked at her with a seriousness she didn't understand. A "V" creased between his eyebrows. Was he still angry with her question?

"This embrace is payment enough."

"Are you still angry?"

"Let's put that subject to rest."

When he left, guilt pecked at her. Something changed in him that evening. Was he still bothered by her comment? She hadn't meant to offend him. She'd ask him the next day, but he never showed up. She shouldn't expect him to come over every day, but she had gotten used to him, used to his presence in her apartment. Somehow, her home felt empty without him, like a staple that had gone missing.

Yes, she missed him. She could acknowledge that. Did he miss her? She recalled her hot and cold attitude toward him. Any normal man would find that kind of behavior confusing. Hell, she confused herself.

Osayik had completed the difficult projects that would have taken her forever to figure out, so why should he come back? He was done. A part of her hoped he wanted to stop by just to see her. This yearning for him perplexed her. Something urged her to take a leap of faith.

She pushed the confusing thoughts aside and got ready for her virtual class. As she listened and watched Vanessa give her a lesson on vegetables, herbs, meat, cooking utensils, cooking temperatures, and so forth, she wondered what kind of meal she'd accomplish from this class.

His words inserted himself into her mind and gave her the unexpected boost she needed.

You can do whatever you put your mind to.

SEVEN

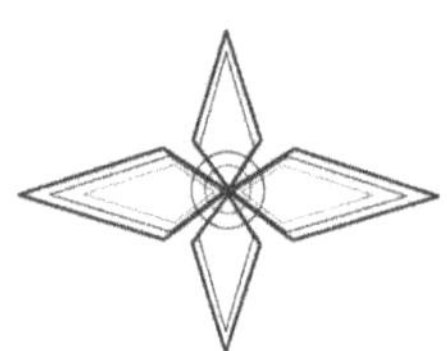

After everyone went home, Inga sat in her office and enjoyed the solitude to think clearly. It had been a few days since she last saw Osayik. She missed him more than she'd like to admit. Maybe he was busy with Chief Mozar and had traveled to another province.

Inga reviewed her checklist before she went home for the evening. She pulled up a virtual screen from her smart bracelet and inspected what needed a second pass.

Would it surprise Osayik if she sent him a message? What could she say? Would he assume she needed more help from him? After staring at her smart bracelet a few more minutes, she decided against it. What if he was in the middle of an important negotiation? She'd send him a message later.

She finalized the model lineup. She had five male and five female models ready. Osayik had completed the music and graphics. Lighting was all set as well. She glanced at the layout of the backyard where the show would take place. Four large tents made a seating area for the guests. Two on each side of a long rug that served as the runway, mimicking the appearance of a stone pathway. Round tables and comfortable chairs were all arranged. In one corner, a large banquet table allowed for foods and drinks, which Laney and Melba would take care of. Raeko's sister, Neesa, would provide the desserts because she worked at a pastry shop.

A loud crash sounded outside, and Inga jumped. She rushed out and found one tent had fallen. *Crap.* She rushed over, looking to see what she could do. She pushed at the frame, but she wasn't strong enough.

"What happened?" Osayik asked, standing next to her.

Her heart leaped at the sound of his voice. It thudded uncontrollably, not because he startled her, but because he was here. He wore a white shirt with a few undone buttons and rolled-up sleeves that showed off his powerful muscles. He paired the shirt with black leather pants, and the perfect image excited her.

"I don't know. I was working inside and heard a crash, so I came out to see."

Lines dug into his forehead as he walked around the tent. The absence of him from the past few days allowed her to look at her situation differently. Pressure from the challenge gnawed at her. At Emma's house, she knew he didn't want to model, yet she dared him anyway. She had put him on the spot in front of his brothers and her sisters.

Then again, he had retaliated with his own demands. She wanted nothing more than to prove that she could achieve anything she put her mind to. Since when had she yearned to please a man like this? His subtle hints and innuendos made her read between the lines. She was probably reading into the empty spaces of nothingness.

Regardless, the right thing to do was to give him the opportunity to back out. She could work with just four male models. She'd be fine with that.

A sliver of red fog appeared at her foot, snaking around. "If you want to back out of the deal, it's perfectly fine with me. I won't be disappointed. I can get Maeson or one of the other male models to wear the extra outfits. I know I cornered you at Emma's home, and that's not right."

Osayik approached her, standing way too close for comfort. "I would never accept a challenge if I didn't want it. No one corners me if I don't allow it." He tipped her chin up and green eyes searched her face.

Her body leaned into him, wanting more of this closeness. Heat pulsed between them. He swallowed and his Adam's apple bobbed. The veins on his neck throbbed, and her fingers itched to caress them. His quiet charm and raw masculinity lured her like a magical spell with no antidote.

"I need to retrieve the tools." His voice rumbled like a trapped animal.

The emptiness that followed left her yearning for his proximity again. Osayik headed to the storage room. Something grew between them in the last few days. She could feel it. Despite her doubts and insecurities, he made her want again. She had to get him out of her system. One night to know what it would feel like. One touch to put her curiosities and desires to rest.

What would it take for his controlled charm to break free? What lay beyond that charisma?

He returned with a bag of tools. Nothing on his face showed the sexual tension that transpired moments ago. How could he switch on and off like that?

He scanned her body, and she swore it sighed.

"You planning to do manual labor with that pretty outfit on?"

She wore a knee-length skirt with a bell sleeve top and pointed heels. "I considered it before you came. What are you doing here, anyway?"

Why are you disrupting my evening, my thoughts?

He rocked back on his heels. "I thought I'd swing by to see you."

The honesty surprised and elated her. "Why?"

A grinned stretched on his face. "To see if you could fix a jacket for me. There's a rip, and I don't know what to do about it."

"Sure. Where is it?" Disappointment stabbed her.

"It's in my sports rider. But let's take care of this tent for you first." He offered her a crooked smile. "I'll fix this for you, if you fix my jacket for me. How's that trade?"

"Aren't you tired of deals, compromises, and challenges?"

He was the challenge that could offer her triumph or defeat. If she took this leap of faith to be with him and fell flat on her face, would she have the strength to gather herself up again? She wouldn't know if she didn't try.

"Not when it comes to you. I like agreements where I benefit."

"Two outfits and a one-of-a-kind meal sound pretty beneficial."

He grinned, but didn't reply. He had planted enough intentions in her mind. Intentions that reflected her own. Was he waiting for her to make a move? What was she still afraid of?

She needed time. "I'll help you with it." She gestured to the tent. "It took three star-beings to set it up this morning. I don't want it crashing down on you."

Inga assisted by passing the tools to him. Apparently, whatever held the tent to the ground had gotten loose.

He added some huge sandbags to help secure the posts. "Animal footprints ran across that dirt over there." He gestured to a section of dirt and flowers that the landscaper had just arranged. "Everything else looks fine." He reached for her face.

The touch sent a rush through her body. Did he feel it too? If he did, he didn't show it.

"You have a stain on your cheek. The markings of hard labor." The smile brought out the adorable dimple on his face.

"You should back out now before I give you more work to do."

His hand wound around her neck, and something flashed in his eyes. Then his lips were on hers, nibbling. It was a gentle exploration that made her yearn for more. He drew back, his eyes darker than before. "I'm not backing out of anything, Inga. I've just sampled you, and I like the taste of you. I like how your body reacts to mine. I still feel this desire to know you. If anything, it's stronger every day. I want more of you when you're ready."

I'm ready now. But her throat was too dry to make coherent sentences out loud.

"Do you dare let me taste you?" His lips hovered over hers, and she opened for him. His tongue slid in, and she moaned from the sensation shooting through her. He offered her a hint of lemon and spices that warmed her belly.

"I've wanted this kiss for a while." His fingers threaded into her hair. "I've wanted to know what it feels like to have your gorgeous hair around my fingers. So soft, so seductive."

She was lost in his words. Did he just kiss her head too?

"I dared myself to kiss you tonight," he muttered against her ear.

Desire spiked in her. "And what were the results?"

"A victor who wants more." His thumb brushed across her lips, and he released her from his grip.

Doubts surfaced again, but this time, they only whispered. What did he want from her besides the obvious? Need, confusion, and a bunch of other emotions whirled inside her.

She ignored the jumbled thoughts and focused on something with a clear path. "Let me wash my face, and I can repair your jacket. Do you mind if we go to my place? I need to eat first."

"Only if you feed me too."

EIGHT

At her apartment, Inga took out some leftovers she bought from the local market. Stir-fried noodles with vegetables and striped fowless, which was similar to chicken on Earth.

Osayik sat across from her, watching as she prepped the meals. "Prepped" meant heating it up and nothing more. She didn't have time for anything more.

Inga tried to shake off his gaze. Tried and failed. The heat blazed a trail down her back, up her arms, around her neck, and expanded everywhere. Why did he make her nervous? Or was she nervous because she was anxious about the fashion show?

She turned and met his eyes. "Something amusing?"

"I like how efficient you are. You move with ease even in those heels."

Inga glanced down. "See? When I'm hungry, I forget every-thing. No matter how much I love heels, I don't wear them when I cook. Not practical at all. I like my home clean so my gowns can stay clean." She traded her shoes for soft indoor slippers.

"Are you a practical person?" He rose from the chair and walked up to her. So close. Again, energy sizzled between them, and it had nothing to do with the meals she just took out of the burner.

Without her heels, she was a lot shorter than Osayik. She glanced up and met his green eyes. Damn, they were gorgeous. A starburst of electric blue speckled in his irises.

"There are times for fantasy and times for practicality. Fantasy is where I go when I create. But practicality gets things done."

Why did her voice come out like she was seducing him?

He smiled and that dimple charmed her again. Her fingers brushed across it. "You have the most adorable dimple—"

Osayik crushed his mouth to hers, nipping, tasting, and then devouring. Inga didn't protest. She opened her mouth to him. He took it, and his tongue showed her how much he wanted her. This was both fantasy and practicality fused into one. After their kiss from earlier, she thought about kissing him again. This golden opportunity was the perfect time to make sure their kiss was as incredible as she remembered it.

Her arms wound around his neck, and her fingers dug into his hair. She moaned, and he pulled back, looking at her. His chest heaved, and his eyes intensified to a dark green, reminding her of a deep, dark forest filled with fairytales. His changing eye color mesmerized her.

Inga removed his jacket and undershirt. "My practical mind wants to see your body."

She wanted to dive into the man beneath the surface. That part of him had been calling her. For tonight, she'd allow herself to feel all the wonder.

Grinning, he stood in her kitchen, letting her strip him. Her heart raced with excitement and anticipation. Her hands adored his smooth, green skin. It reminded her of rocks that had been perfected and smoothed from erosion. Her fingers wandered to the slope of his wide shoulders, the dips of his pectoral muscles, the curve of his biceps, and the firmness of his abdomen. The composition of shadows and light enchanted her. His physique rendered him an impeccable landscape.

She sighed, or was that a growl? Since when did she growl?

"My turn," Osayik said, his voice now husky, seeping with need.

Knowing that she did that to him aroused her. He removed her loose top in one urgent swoop. But then he took his time, studying her breasts under the light purple see-through bra. Her nipples hardened from his gaze. When his fingers played with them, she gasped, arching for more.

Osayik took a nipple into his mouth, sucking through the thin fabric. Inga cried out in pleasure. Hot and frantic, her hands gripped his hair. Heat exploded in her, and she found herself on the kitchen floor. The marble floor cooled her back, a pleasant contrast to the fire bursting from her core. He tossed her bra aside and removed his pants.

He pressed his arousal against her. Need came like an animal. Their hands searched, demanded, and conquered. They couldn't get enough of each other. His body quivered against hers, as if he was fighting some violent urge. The same urge reflected in hers, and she wanted to release him from that caged yearning.

She wanted to uncage them both. She unlocked the latch by yanking his face back to her. She kissed him with a fierceness that surprised her. The powerful kiss left her mind spiraling.

"I've wanted you for so long," he moaned.

"Take whatever you want." Because she was taking what she wanted. She nipped at his bottom lip and met his tongue in a crazy dance, making him growl. God, she loved his reaction.

They rolled all over the floor, marking it with gasps, moans, and more growls. This was mating. This was primal need. She offered, and he took. He offered, and she didn't refuse. Her body shuddered from the untamed sensation, from wanting more.

"You're so wild." When his dimple appeared again, she kissed it. "I love this dimple. I can kiss it all day."

"I've got dimples in other areas too."

Inga laughed as he buried his head in the crevice of her shoulder, dropping kisses that tingled her body. He took her to a fantasy where she floated across a floral field of bliss. His woodsy and earthy scent promised new beginnings. It placed her on the mountainside, where she watched the sunrise and inhaled the fragrance the land offered. His hands roamed and claimed. He growled when his hand found her center and its wetness.

Osayik broke from the kiss, and a possessive smirk formed on his lips. He ripped her underwear away, and she arched against his palm. She moved with his hand's rhythm, then his fingers dove into her, taking on a new cadence. Pleasure shot through her, and his name escaped her lips.

"Say my name again." He breathed into her ear. "Mine."

"Osayik..."

"I want my name to be the only name coming from your mouth."

His fingers continued their decadent assault as he kissed his way down her body. Inga's hand sprawled on the floor, searching for something to grip, to hold on to as she rode this dangerous wave of pleasure. Her eyes followed his tantalizing kisses down her abdomen and inner thighs.

His gaze was so intense, she felt its fever in her blood, scorching every inch of her skin.

Osayik pressed his lips to her center and kissed. "I want to remember this scent of you. So intoxicating." Another kiss. "The taste of you. So sweet." Another kiss.

Holy shit. She couldn't hold it any longer. He sensed it,

grinned, and his mouth devoured her. Her thighs quivered as a massive wave of ecstasy rolled over her, tossing her into oblivion.

She didn't have to wait for the orgasm to ebb. He positioned his arousal at her entrance, and the look on his face told her she had unleased the beast in him. He plunged into her with no finesse, only primordial need. He moved with a speed and urgency that made her want to give and give. She reveled in that desire even as another orgasm traveled through her. He roared with pleasure like an animal that had found its freedom.

Osayik collapsed next to her, pulling her in close. "My first time on the kitchen floor." Her heart thumped against his chest.

"Mine too."

"This is my *favorite* kitchen floor."

Inga chuckled.

He kissed her hand, her fingers, and studied the pinkie with the scar. "What happened here?"

She shared her childhood trauma, and he kissed her finger seductively. "Then I should worship every meal you make."

He adored her pinkie in a way that aroused her again.

His body shifted and turned to her. "I forgot to—"

"It's okay. I've been taking these herbal vitamins that also serve as a contraceptive. You're good." She also had a bottle of Safe-Sex in her bedroom, but she didn't want to disrupt the moment by having him retrieve it.

"I am, aren't I? Want to tell me about it?" His thumb skimmed her chin.

That arrogance charmed her even as she rolled her eyes. Inga didn't know what to think of this evening. Instead of dinner, they feasted on each other. The feast satisfied her curiosity. It told her she wanted more of him. As the thought wandered in her mind, her heart skipped. She didn't want to acknowledge it because that would complicate things.

She wasn't ready for complications. Something casual and

fun suited her fine. She sat up, gave his firm butt a playful squeeze. "I'm famished. Let's go eat."

He popped up on his elbow. "No need to go anywhere. I'm right here. Eat away."

Delight erupted from Inga. She couldn't remember anyone ever making her laugh this much. He'd grown hard again. She studied the length and size of him. She gripped him, and he throbbed in her hand. "I should go to bed. I have a long day tomorrow..."

Osayik sucked in a breath when she kissed him. "I still need to repair that jacket of yours."

"No need to... That was just an excuse to see you..." A moan escaped him. "I... I ripped the seams..."

The stroking stopped. "Oh." Her eyebrows rose. "Well, ulterior motives cannot go unpunished."

She gave him what he deserved: a second release of her name from his mouth.

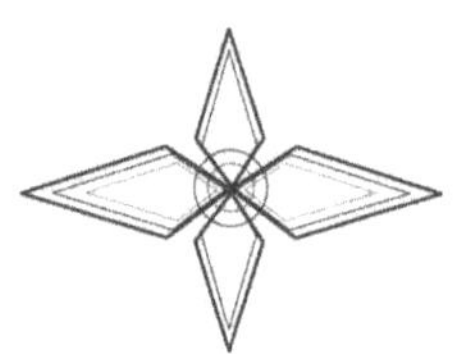

The next afternoon, the models showed up for the walk-through. They were all star-beings with various shades of green skin. Some had texture, while others were smooth like Osayik's. He stayed the night with her and left early this morning for some meeting. She couldn't stop thinking of him.

Last night, he had enjoyed himself, and so did she. His face remained in her head all morning as she worked. She should be tired. Where did this boost of energy come from? Smirking, she replayed last night's exceptional sex in her mind. She could get used to this strange joy bursting inside of her, giving her hope. Did he feel the same way?

As the day progressed, work consumed her. Osayik and the other models practiced their walks backstage while she gave interviews to the local and galactic media. She smiled and waved twice when she caught him looking at her.

When it was time for the practice walk-through, Inga stood on the end of the runway and studied her models. Her eyes followed Osayik as he strode down the path with the other models. He had a swagger that beckoned attention. His gaze met hers, and all the sensations from last night flooded her system. He winked at her, and a stream of pink and red mist lingered around her. She waved a hand over them. She had witnessed magical and mystical things in Saedo that couldn't be explained. She often saw white mist coming from the trees, plants, and ground. But she'd never seen colorful vapors coming from any star-beings until recently. She just paid no attention until him.

Perhaps it was an auspicious sign, kind of like finding a four-leaf clover or something like that. She'd have to ask Sasha later.

Osayik had shifted her consciousness. She was now aware of many things that had never occurred to her before. For example, she was more mindful of surrounding energies. Before living in Saedo, she didn't sense energy. When she was near Osayik, that awareness heightened. It was as if her body acknowledged him, recognized him, and wanted to converse with him in its own way. It sounded strange and surreal, but that was the truth.

She couldn't deny her powerful feelings for him. Their initial encounter had started off on the wrong foot with misunderstandings. But she was learning to trust again. In the short time they've known each other, he had tapped into a part of her heart that was extremely cautious of others. That part *wanted* to let him in, but another part warned her. At the moment, she didn't know what to do.

The female models gaped at Osayik. He was a treat for the eyes, and any female in their right mind would want him. Jealousy rose in her.

That was one reason why she hesitated to take the leap. She didn't want to be with a man who was swarmed with females, with temptations. She couldn't trust a man like that. That kind of man burned her before. A handsome face didn't always reflect handsome intentions. Yet, somehow, Osayik drew her in.

The music stopped, and Inga snapped back to reality as the

models went on break. She could get in a few more hours of work before they returned for the final walk-through with hair and makeup, followed by a photoshoot.

Inside her office, Osayik wrapped his fingers around her chin and kissed her. She moaned, and he drew back and smiled. "I love that sound."

She should focus on work, but she couldn't resist the taste of him.

"I need to run out. I'm meeting my brothers about the Ulkrin creatures."

One of them had attacked Sasha and Maeson not too long ago. Sasha helped Maeson kill one creature with her hairdresser scissors. Were there more of them around? These were creatures that belonged to the terrifying Ulkrin star-beings that had abducted her and her sisters.

"Okay, be careful. I'll see you soon."

He smiled. "I love that you're concerned about me. I'll be okay, it's just a meeting. I'll be back for the last rehearsal."

The hours flew by, and Inga, Laney, and Melba had all the shoes, handbags, jewelry, and other accessories all organized and labeled. Each model had his or her own rack and knew the order in which they'd come out onto the runway. Relief settled when the final walk-through proved a success.

After Laney and Melba had everything prepared, she sent them home so they could get some rest for tomorrow's show.

Inga spent the rest of her evening finishing the Ingavex jacket for Osayik. This jacket was a gift, something made from her heart. It was the male version of her own Ingavex jacket. She couldn't wait for him to try it on.

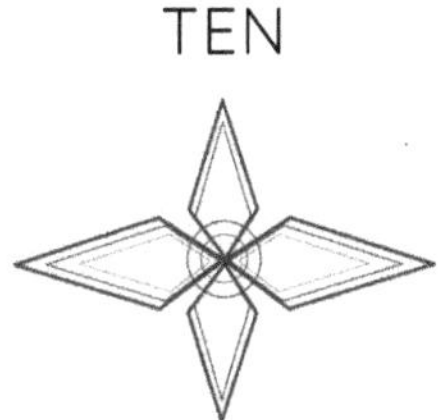

Inga expected a good turnout with mostly Saedo villagers, but her designer friend and boss, Stelli, notified her that more than half of the attendees were from different provinces and planets within the Alarus Galaxy. Her heart thudded with anticipation and excitement.

Osayik's graphic design skills and website creation had placed her fashion show on the top search on the Galacto Net.

All the hard work came to this moment when everyone got to see the entire collection together. Nerves pecked at her, but she calmed them with a deep breathing exercise she had learned from yoga. Gratitude for all those who worked with her, and because of her, spiked in her heart. Osayik played a huge part in making today possible. She'd never forget that.

Inga entered the hair parlor where Sasha and her coworkers from the Hair Spectrum were working on hair and makeup for the models. Sasha gelled Osayik's mohawk into an abstract lizard whose legs hugged the side of his head and a tail dangled on his back. Electric blue dye highlighted his brown hair.

"Wow, Sasha. This is great." Osayik shifted his head, examining his hair from various angles.

Inga led Osayik back into her office. "I have something for you."

He twirled a lock of her hair in his fingers. "Does it have anything to do with this?" He kissed her, and her body shivered. That sensation removed the scattered nerves regarding the show.

She smiled. "No." She took out a gift box and placed it into his arms. "I made it for you."

Beaming, he opened the box and pulled out a black jacket that mimicked her Ingavex one. He removed the jacket he was wearing and slipped on the new one. "This is so... me." He flipped up the asymmetrical collar and looked at himself in the long mirror against the wall. He walked up to her. "You made this for me?"

She nodded. "It's a one-of-a-kind jacket. I have the female version of it. It's part of my Ingavex collection that I haven't shared with anyone yet. You're the first."

"I've seen you work on your jacket. The way you forget about everything when you focus on it. That love for it stemmed from your *corra*. I've wondered what you were going to do with it. It's a masterpiece, and I'm honored you made one for me." Osayik didn't know what his compliments did to her.

He stared at her for a while and something serious splashed across his face. He wrapped both arms around her. "This is the most thoughtful gift anyone has ever given me. You gave me a piece of your corra. Thank you."

She gave him a piece of her heart without even realizing it.

"Watch what it can do." Inga demonstrated the functionality of the jacket where it could zap and kill an attacker. "This can help you during your rescue missions."

"This is extraordinary. Not only is it stylish, it's functional. It's a gadget jacket. Why aren't you showing this off today? This is a fabulous artwork." He beamed and pride filled her.

His dimple appeared, and with that simple gesture, her heart swung open. Excitement gripped her as she realized she was falling in love with him. The emotion overwhelmed her, but it also anchored her to the present moment. Inga stopped doubting herself. She wanted him.

"You should promote this *today*. It's too much of a novelty to hide. I want everyone to see that my woman is admirable and phenomenal."

My woman.

His belief in her was too much. Tears welled in her eyes, but she pushed them down. She didn't want to ruin her makeup right before the show.

Inga shrugged. "I don't know how people will react to it. Maybe they won't like it. It was a fun and private project just for me. And when I met you, I made a second one."

"What inspired you to design this jacket?"

She told him about the assault she experienced during a jog alone. He hissed and inquired if the attacker was now dead or locked up. It warmed her, and his approval of her creation sent her heart soaring.

"I love what goes on inside your mind. This is an innovative design that reacts to personalized voice command. If you can produce more of these, I assure you, everyone will place orders. Chief Mozar will want an exclusive version for all the soldiers. You're right, this will help us in combat. Other planets would want it too. I can show them to my Norakian friends from planet Terrakado."

"Okay, we'll save the best for last. You end the show with it."

"No, we do it together. Show them the male and female styles. Show them your corra. Your work is your corra." His hand rested on her lower back. "I've seen how hard you work, and I admire your dedication and creativity. You're like an undiscovered gem to me, and I'm never letting you go."

Inga thought her heart couldn't swell any more, but it did. He understood her. He had vision and creativity, and that made him perfect for her. The wish she had tossed out into the Universe echoed back.

I deserve a man who sees and understands my heart. A man who values me as the gem to his soul and not a gem on his ring.

Tears broke free, and he wiped them with his thumb.

"I never thought I'd meet anyone better than me until I met you." He grinned and brushed a knuckle down her cheek. "Underneath the beauty, you're smart, diligent, creative, thoughtful, and so much more than me."

Inga placed a finger to her lips. "Shhh... Do you hear that sound?"

Perplexed, he tried to listen. "No. What is it?"

Her eyes beamed. "Is that your ego deflating?"

He roared with laughter, and a serious expression came after. "I'd give you the limelight, love."

She embraced him. *Love.* Was that the powerful emotion blossoming inside her heart?

"If anyone tries to steal you from me," he said. "I'm going to roast him with my jacket."

Smiling, she touched up her makeup. "Be careful with it. I added higher voltage on your jacket." She showed him where to activate the energy and where to adjust it. Her smart bracelet buzzed, notifying her it was time for the show to start. "Let's go."

Nerves came alive again, and she inhaled several deep breaths. Today, she bared her soul to the world—no, to the galaxy. Some would hate it, some would love it. But she didn't care either way. She had the most precious art beside her: Osayik.

Music boomed and the lights dimmed inside the tent. The

flat stones on the runway illuminated a soft glow. Though it was daylight, the two suns hid behind dark clouds.

From the backroom, virtual monitors from various angles showed the models strutting, posing, smiling, and working their magic. Raeko and Maeson did a wonderful job. They'd adopted a swagger that was uniquely theirs. Maybe Osayik inspired them. Raeko and Maeson stopped and glanced toward their significant others in the crowd. A roaring cheer erupted from the table where all her sisters sat with Chief Mozar and his stylish wife, Ivian.

The eclectic audience ranged from star-beings with massively wild hair dressed in neon colors to muted styles with holographic properties. Star-beings, cyborgs, and other fantastical creatures attended her show. Some had two heads, others had several tails. For her next collection, she'd incorporate the extra appendages to her design functionality. She wanted her designs to encompass as many beings as possible, leaving no one out. The audience clapped and checked off the styles from their ordering tablets.

Laney patted Inga on the shoulder. "The orders are coming in. So exciting!"

Inga's attention went to the monitor when Osayik came out and owned the runway. All eyes followed his casual walk. He paused several times to let the audience see the details of his ensemble. Several female star-beings shouted, "Lovely ass."

Hands off, he's mine.

Time flew by, and the models returned to the backroom. It was time for Inga to step out and greet the audience who came to support her. She slipped her Ingavex jacket over her purple gown. On a normal day, she wouldn't have worn these two pieces together, but right now, they worked. Techy material over soft satin made her look edgy and sensual.

From the backroom, she heard the loud cheer of the audience. Nerves gnawed at her, but Osayik clutched her hand and kissed it. "Don't be nervous. They love your collection." His simple touch and his conviction calmed the nerves.

With courage and confidence, Inga walked out from the back curtain and onto the stone path her collection had graced. Osayik ambled beside her down the runway. She paused at the end of the path, removed the jacket, and swung it over her back, revealing her purple couture dress with the v-neckline and the elegant drape. She glanced at the virtual screens as the gentle breeze made the light fabric sway, making her appear to be floating. She hand-painted the dress in certain areas to resemble a nebula and added random sequins that twinkled like stars. She felt like she was wearing part of the Universe. The audience ohhed and ahhed, and the noise made the sequins sparkle even more because of their noise sensors.

Osayik showed off his Ingavex jacket. He tapped his chest pocket—which was safe to touch—and voiced the command to activate the energy currents, sending colorful waves of energy rushing up and down the body and sleeves of the jacket. The audience erupted with delectable approval.

There were other designers in the Province of Saedo that showcased innovative fashion, but Inga's creations stemmed from her love of simplicity. Her jacket had clean lines that made the design contemporary and functional. Osayik flipped up the asymmetrical collar, and another flash of energy zapped down the sleeves. He lifted his arms, clasped the hems of his sleeves, and commanded the deactivation of the circuitry. Then he opened the jacket and revealed several pockets.

The audience rose from their seats with a standing ovation.

"Do the models come with the purchase of the jacket?" Someone shouted, causing a delightful uproar in the audience.

"What about the designer?" Another voice boomed.

"No," Osayik replied, wrapping an arm around Inga possessively.

After the show ended, Inga thanked everyone, including her siblings. The cleanup crew dismantled the tents and took care of tables and seating. Osayik stayed to chat with his brothers and friends who came to support him.

Inga returned to her office and plopped down on the chair, releasing a sigh. Pride settled in her. For a moment, she closed her eyes to wallow in the show's success. It was over. All that hard work ended quickly. But it was all worth it. She couldn't believe everyone's reaction to her collection, especially her Ingavex jackets. She had planned on variations of it. Pants, vests, boots, gloves, handbags were just some ideas floating in her mind.

She opened her eyes and went to change into a comfortable top and pair of pants. She kept the jacket on because she wanted to relish in her accomplishment for a while longer. It reminded her that dreams do come true, that as long as she stayed true to herself—and not be swayed by outside sources— she'd find her success.

Inga also knew that she wouldn't have found the courage to show off her Ingavex design if it hadn't been for Osayik. He saw her vision, he understood it, and he *encouraged* her. No man had ever done that for her.

She wanted to share her emotions with him. Tell him they should start a long-term relationship. He was the only man to see into her heart. She never imagined she'd find love with a star-being from another planet. The Universe had its own design, a lover tailored to suit her. She wanted to tell him, watch his reaction, and then invite him over for the most interesting meal of his lifetime.

Filled with hope, Inga grabbed her bag and left her office in search of her lover. She walked by the door and glanced out into the yard where the show had been. A small group of star-beings still hovered around the banquet table, probably enjoying the free cocktails and appetizers. She was about to step outside, but sounds from the front of Stellium Couture caught her ear. The store was closed because of the fashion show.

Who could be in the shop right now?

ELEVEN

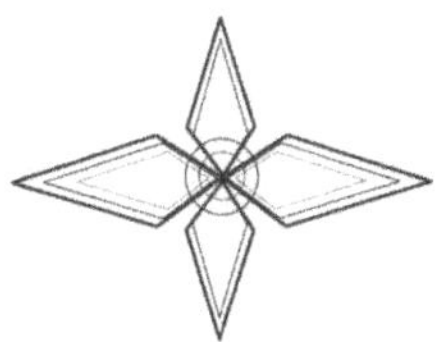

Inga strode by the large fitting area with two couches for customers to sit.

"I've wanted this for months..." A female voice trailed off.

"You've had too much to drink."

Inga entered the room and gasped because her heart stopped beating. A female star-being clung to Osayik as he placed her onto the couch.

"Kiss me." The female grabbed at his face.

Inga's heart released a sound of a dying balloon. She didn't know love and hope could deflate from her like that, slow and painful. She clutched her chest as pain and betrayal knifed into her heart. She'd been wrong about him, wrong about herself. She should have known better. The male species were all the same. Why did she let herself believe Osayik could be different?

She backed away and bumped into a rack of clothing. It rattled and Osayik turned, meeting her eyes. Shock splashed across his face as the female puked onto the floor. He cursed and pulled the female back onto the couch.

Inga whirled and stalked out of the shop. She gathered

whatever was left of herself, shoved it into her bag and headed out to her personal rider, wanting to go home.

Voices called her, but she ignored them. She strode past two soldiers who said, "Great show, Inga."

She didn't reply and continued on. She had encased herself in a protective shield, not allowing in anymore exterior distractions. More star-beings passed her, but she didn't register their faces or what they said to her.

She just needed to get home. Needed a quiet place where she could fall apart.

A combination of sadness and rage consumed her. Sadness because her heart had just experienced a massive eruption, ripping away the pretty image of their relationship. Rage because she blamed herself for believing in something that wasn't real. Deception was a monster that existed on all planets.

Despite what had occurred, her heart had felt alive during her time with him. She had felt love. For what it was worth, it gave her an opportunity to *feel* that emotion in all its facets.

A broken heart hurt like hell. The brokenness speared her deeply. Why did love have to hurt this much?

As she drove, she wallowed in the quietness and solitude. A comfortable place to remove the protective barrier. Tears rolled down her eyes like an unwelcome flood. She couldn't stop the torrent that blurred her vision.

A large rock smashed into the middle of the road about fifty feet from her personal rider. Inga slammed on her brakes, and the automatic emergency brakes also kicked in.

What the hell?

Her rider stopped inches away from a boulder that came out of nowhere. From the corner of her eye, a heinous creature between a wolf and a bear with bulging red eyes appeared. It licked its long tongue as it glared at her. It howled, and two more creatures arrived at the back of her rider.

Panic surged as she searched for a way out. She couldn't drive forward, and she couldn't go backward unless she went through the creatures. But they would topple the car and drag her out in no time. She debated running into the woods, but how far would she get before they caught up to her? Staying inside the personal rider was the safest route for now.

Were these the same creatures that had attacked Sasha and Maeson?

Oh God, please help me. Inga sent a message to her sisters and pressed the emergency alert for help.

Fear lodged in her throat as the three beasts prowled toward her. They pushed the rider back and forth. One jumped onto the roof, beating it down. *Shit, shit, shit!*

Inga flinched when one of them exploded on the windshield. Flashbacks of the abduction overwhelmed her. Relief swelled when Osayik's face appeared nearby. She shoved all the anger and disappointment aside to deal with the threat before them. With a blaster in hand, he fired at the two remaining creatures. They charged and swiped their claws at him. One beast jumped on him, pushing him to the ground.

"Osayik!"

A sizzling sound hissed in the air, followed by a wail that chilled her bones. Osayik kicked the beast off of him. Smoke steamed from the creature's carcass. Electrical currents illuminated from his Ingavex jacket. *Holy hell.* It worked. Pride overwhelmed her, and the realization that she could get out of her personal rider sparked.

Two beasts snarled and jumped at Osayik. He blasted them, and blood oozed from their bodies. But they kept coming and howling as if they were calling for help. Her fears were confirmed when eerie howls echoed in response to the call.

Inga didn't know how helpful she could be, but staying

inside her rider while more beasts attacked Osayik was not the answer. If she was going to die, she'd go down fighting.

Inga exited her personal rider just as five more beasts leaped out of the woods. Osayik shouted, "Stay inside!"

She didn't listen. She didn't take orders from him. She could make her own assessment. But then again, her assessment of him had been wrong. *Don't think about that right now, Inga.*

The largest creature in the pack swerved its claw at Osayik. Blood marked his face, and her heart lurched. An indescribable fear squeezed her chest. The fear wasn't regarding her own life, but for his. She grabbed a rock from the ground and whipped it at the beast. The rock smacked into its head. The creature whirled, facing her with fangs that glinted like knives.

The beast snarled. "You killed my children, and I will kill you all."

It could talk? Inga blinked at the unexpected dialogue. Was this mother beast referring to the offspring that Sasha and Maeson had killed? Or was she referring to the dead bodies on the ground?

Osayik sent a series of blasts at it, but it didn't affect the creature.

The mother beast glared at Inga. *Come here, you bitch.* She tapped her chest pocket, voiced her command, and clenched her fist, preparing to defend herself. The creature leaped at her, its mouth clamping down on the arm she had lifted in defense. Electricity singed and sizzled. The creature convulsed as Inga wrapped her other arm around its neck, pulling its body into her own. She squeezed the hem of her jacket several times, increasing the voltage.

The smell of burned flesh sent bile up her throat, but she pushed it down. The cries from the mother beast infuriated her offspring. Three glared at Inga as she released their dead mother with flesh falling from her body like overcooked meat. She deactivated her jacket as the heat from the surface was making her sweat.

Osayik fought off four creatures as sirens echoed. His brothers arrived and fired at the rest of the creatures while Osayik shrugged off a burnt carcass. The circuitry on his Ingavex diminished as he rushed over to her. Fear sprawled across his face and aged him. Devastation replaced his handsomeness. He yanked her body to him and held. She thought she saw his eyes glisten, but it was probably her own, blurring out everything.

"Are you okay?" he asked as he brought her over to a safer location, allowing the emergency crew to collect the dead creatures.

"I'm fine, and you?" Her fingers touched the wound along his jaw.

"Just a minor scratch." His eyes pinned her. "It's not what it seems."

She took a closer look at his injury. "Okay, we'll put a bandage on it."

"No, not that." He swiveled her face to meet his gaze. "There's nothing between me and Ameeya. She's Arkon's sister, one of my brothers. She had too many cocktails, and I took her into the shop so she wouldn't make a fool out of herself. Arkon had been on his way to retrieve her. He and Jarzell walked by you earlier, but you didn't pay attention to them."

Inga recalled the soldiers, but she couldn't get the image of what she saw out of her mind. "She seemed close to you."

"She was interested in me several solar cycles ago, but I only see her as a sister. She knows that." He placed a gentle hand on each side of her shoulder. "Do you trust me?"

Could she trust her heart once again? Had she overreacted? Anyone walking into a scenario like that would respond the same way she did, right? Moments before that event, she had wanted to tell him it was time they start a long-term relationship. That kind of commitment required trust and honesty.

She had intended to fight those beasts for him, even if that meant giving up her own life. The answer was clear as day. Sincerity and anxiety warred on his face as he waited for her reply.

"I went to look for you earlier because I had something important to tell you."

"Tell me now."

"We make an impressive pair. Like these jackets. It's time we start something serious."

The anxiety that had been on his face vanished, replaced by the largest grin she'd ever seen. His dimple deepened. "I've always been serious about you. All this time, you were just teasing and taunting me?"

"I assumed you were treating me like all your female friends."

He shook his head. "I don't kiss my friends, and I don't stay late at their house helping them make their dreams come true. I don't dream about them, or rip my jacket just so I could have an excuse to see them. And I certainly don't sleep with them."

"I guess you are crazy about me." She smiled.

"Love does that to you. I want you." He kissed her. "The day I brought food over to you was the day I knew you'd be mine. You showed me what dedication and devotion look like. I admire your passion. Unlike everyone else, you see something more in me. I let my creative side out when I'm with you." He took her hand. "Promise me one thing."

"What is it?"

Sadness flickered in his eyes. "I want to be the first person you call when you're in trouble. I was already on my way to your place when I received the emergency alert on my wristband. I'm one of the soldiers, so I get all these urgent calls. I was waiting for you to contact me personally, but you didn't."

She had considered contacting him, but she was still reeling with anger. "I didn't know if you'd come, or that you'd care."

He closed his eyes for a moment, as if settling an internal war. When he opened them, love filled his eyes. "I care, Inga. I care so much that I would give my life for you. Please don't do that again. Don't run off. If I make a mistake, talk to me. That's what relationships are; to talk, to communicate. What we have is love, and that's the strongest bond between two souls. Let nothing get in our way, okay?"

A lump formed in her throat. She couldn't reply, so she just nodded and embraced him.

He took her to the emergency autobus, which was like a long ambulance, so the medics could examine her. "Let them check you quickly, and we can go back to your place." He leaned in and whispered. "We can continue our conversation over dinner. I believe someone owes me a home-cooked meal." His voice skated down her spine and a quiet hum rippled out to her entire body.

She shivered. "I think I overcooked the mother beast."

He laughed. "Now I'm scared of your cooking."

"If you still have an appetite, I have everything prepped."

His eyes sparkled with suspicion. "You're heating something up?"

Let him believe that. "You'll have to find out."

TWELVE

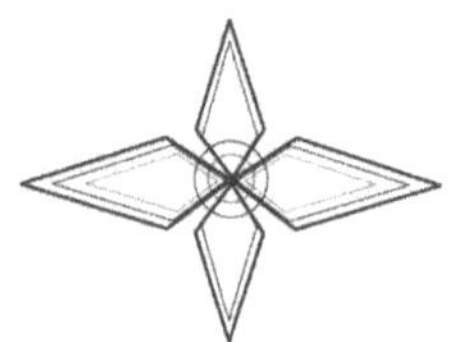

Hours later, Inga and Osayik arrived home. They would've gotten home earlier, but Chief Mozar arrived at the scene and wanted an update. The Ulkrin creatures had appeared in the provinces of Saedo and Finntoro, which was their neighbor.

"It shocked me when the mother beast spoke." Inga took out a container from the coldbox.

"The mother was more developed than her offspring. More dangerous. These creatures probably knocked down your fashion tent the other day. I'm attending a meeting in Finntoro next week with my brothers to discuss a plan. We have to figure out a safe way to deal with the Province of Agarrek. That's where the Ulkrins and their creatures are from."

"I'm glad you're getting more help from your neighbors. Do you think these attacks are because you rescued us from them?"

"It could be, but we've rescued many humans and starbeings. These Ulkrins are known for mayhem and destruction. They've been causing trouble in other provinces too, not just in Saedo." He pulled her in for a long kiss. "I don't want to talk about anything else for the rest of the evening except you and food."

"Sounds good to me. Why don't you have a seat and relax? Dinner will be ready soon." Inga sorted out the food she had prepped the previous night.

Osayik didn't sit. Instead, he hovered around her, watching her every move. "Do you know what you're doing? I don't want you losing a finger over this. We can call this deal off. I already have you, so I need nothing else."

"I do. What kind of person do you think I am? A deal is a deal. You helped me, and I will deliver my part. Besides, I'm excited to cook."

"*You are?*" His shocked tone and adorable expression earned him two kisses, one on his lips, the other on his dimple.

"What can I say? Love makes me do crazy things. You've inspired me to take a cooking class from my sister, Vanessa. So you're my experiment."

"When did you find the time to learn?"

She shrugged. "I made time. I delegated a few tasks to my assistants. Vanessa taught me through the virtual screen. I just had to watch and follow the directions. I could do that."

She turned to retrieve a plate, and the pot near her window caught her attention. The pot with the dead plant she had removed was now growing with a red flower bud. How did it get there? She hadn't put any seeds in it.

Osayik followed her. "What's the matter?"

"Look at this flower. What does it remind you of?" Something magical sparked in her heart.

Osayik shrugged. "A flower?"

She rolled her eyes at the typical answer.

In that moment, red mist emerged from the unopened bud and swirled around Inga and Osayik.

"Do you see what I'm seeing?" Inga waved a hand over the mist.

Osayik furrowed his eyebrows. "You see the red mist too?"

"Yes, I've been seeing it recently. I've been wanting to ask Sasha about it, but I keep forgetting. What does it mean?"

His eyes warmed. "We're starmates. You're my forever mate. It's a Saedo lore."

Inga thought back, and Sasha did mention something about that.

"What does the lore say?"

"When you see someone's mist color, it means you're their forever mate," he said. "I'm not surprised you see the color of my mist. Now I understand why I had that strong feeling for you during our first encounter in front of Raeko's house. The mist energy gave me a hint."

Fascinated, she asked, "Do you see any other colors? I mostly see white mist around others. Sometimes I see hints of color coming from the plants and trees."

"Nature produces colorful mist. The white mists are normal vapors that everyone can see."

"I wonder what this all means." She studied the flower. "This looks like the same flower in Emma's garden; hers is yellow. Sasha mentioned she has a blue version, and we're looking at a red flower with an unopened bud. This isn't a coincidence."

"It's not. We should ask Grandma Ova." He flicked her a glance. "It's like a love sprout."

She chuckled at his perspective. "I like the idea that love gave birth to this bud."

Something inexplicable was happening in Saedo. She could feel something swirling, but she didn't know what it was. What did this flower mean? She looked outside her window, and a storm was brewing with dark clouds. The Universe was a mystery, working its magic with so many twists and turns. All they could do was trust it, even during the dark times. *Especially during the dark times.*

Staring into his handsome face, who would have thought her wish made all those months ago, would come true and change her life so completely. She'd wished for someone who saw her heart. And here he was. Her career was taking off, and she had a man who believed in her talents, not her appearance. She had to be the most fortunate woman in the Universe. *Thank you.*

The beep to her burner sounded, and she retrieved the meal. She placed a lovely dish in front of him.

He looked at it with interest. "What is it?"

"It's grilled yellow pisciss with a citrus sauce. The first time I tasted this fish, I was in heaven. I sauteed Saedo onions and blue kale from Grandma Ova's garden." She slid over a round dish with star sprinkles floating around a heart-shaped purple crepe. "This is your dessert. My version of a cosmic crepe."

He wolfed down his meal and rubbed his flat stomach. "That was the best dinner I've ever eaten. I want us to cook for each other every day. My place is a lot bigger than yours. You can have a large studio there if you move in with me. I *dare* you to live with me, cook with me, and sleep with me every night. What do you say?"

She was going to laugh, but his expression was serious. She hadn't even been to his house yet.

He must have read her mind. "We can discuss all of that later. I have pictures to show you, and I'm sure you have decorating ideas." He pulled the dessert plate closer. "Right now, all I care about is decorating you."

"What are you talking about?"

Osayik clasped her hand. A mischievous smirk grew on his face. "I *dare* you to join me on a decadent adventure in bed. I dare you to let me eat this lovely crepe off your body, in *very* specific places."

Inga sucked in a breath and gave him exactly what he

wanted. "Only if you let me eat it off your body in *very* specific places."

"Deal."

That evening, the lovers created the most innovative love recipe that could inspire an edible fashion collection.

AN ALIEN STORM

SOLDIERS OF SAEDO 4

USA TODAY BESTSELLING AUTHOR

CALLA ZAE

"There's something different about you… Something untamed. Something mysterious. It's driving me crazy."

Battered and bruised from a previous relationship, Vanessa now prefers a quiet life as a chef on a new planet. But then a captivating star-being storms into her life and whips up a whirlwind of emotions that makes her heart yearn for things she has long forgotten.

Arkon, a skilled soldier who prefers numbers, charts, and anything with absoluteness is attracted to Vanessa. But she favors no rules and lures him out of his comfort zone. Having been scorned once, he fears she will burn him.

Is their union a recipe for love or destruction?

CONTENTS

ONE

Vanessa clutched her stomach as she sat inside Sasha's state-of-the-art home. She curled on a couch made of high-tech fabric that changed scenic views at random. Despite the peaceful landscapes, the erratic nerves remained and settled at the center of her gut, radiating out to her entire body. Her stomach tightened, and an uncomfortable sensation she hadn't felt before squirmed through her, and she shuddered from the tingles.

"You okay there?" Sasha asked, offering a cup of herbal tea with a layer of stars sparkling over the liquid. The dream plant was supposed to induce a good night's sleep, which Vanessa desperately needed.

Living in the Province of Saedo on planet Celeron had opened Vanessa's eyes to an abundance of plants that enabled her to create the most interesting culinary dishes she could ever imagine.

Vanessa took the warm cup, leaning in to inhale the sweet steam. "Thank you. I don't know what's going on with my stomach lately." Was it a stomach issue or something else? She didn't want to worry her six siblings, so she kept the details to herself for now. "Maybe I've been experimenting with too much food at work, and the combination isn't working out well for my stomach?"

"The Happy Belly has been busy with all the dishes you've created. Abba must be excited for all the business." Inga sat down beside her and crossed her legs.

Vanessa used her culinary skills to spice up the menu with some human flair. The Saedo villagers responded well, and that delighted Abba, the owner. Her profits had tripled from Vanessa's creations.

Vanessa learned that certain ingredients could create chemical imbalances, so maybe that was why her stomach was upset. However, intuition told her differently. She sipped the tea and the sparkling steam tingled her tongue. For the past three days, she'd been dreaming about her ex-husband, Travis. She didn't know why he'd come back into her thoughts now. Their relationship had ended over a year ago. But then again, the ghost of an abusive relationship followed her no matter where she went. Even on a new planet.

He wasn't here, was he? The thought chilled her, and she shivered.

"Are you sure you're not coming down with something?" Inga wrapped an arm around Vanessa.

Inga had just moved into Osayik's house last week, and the loving energy radiated from the couple wherever they went. Just over a week ago, Inga and Osayik battled Ulkrin creatures including a mother beast that spoke the universal language, which Vanessa also understood from the language translator inside her ear. She could read the universal language after a doctor activated the language codex within her brain via a beam of energy. The human brain was a magical wonder that hadn't been fully discovered yet.

What other threats were coming to Saedo? This odd churning in her gut warned her to be careful, or was it just discomfort from food aversion? Vanessa was a chef and food was her specialty, so she should be used to all kinds of food by now. But she was on a new planet. She convinced herself that was the reason for the stomach issues.

Inga leaned in and ran her fingers down a lock of Vanessa's red hair. "You're the only one with red hair. Are you sure you're our sister?"

All her siblings had inherited the brown except her. Somehow, she came out different from the rest of the family. Her mom mentioned Vanessa was blessed with the fire from one of her great-great-grandmothers, who was a priestess from back in the day. She didn't know if it was true or just something the family made up to make her feel better. Vanessa didn't care, she embraced her fire... until her damn husband snuffed it out.

Her silence earned a tug on her hair.

"Only a real sister could deal with you." Vanessa elbowed Inga and answered the other question. "I don't think I'm coming down with anything. Extra sleep would probably help."

"Take a few days off from work," Sasha suggested. "That fire in you is coming back. Saedo is truly helping us become our best selves."

There was no need to mention that Travis had invaded her dreams. His name would infuriate them, remind them all of what he had done to her. Her body remembered and wanted to shudder, but she willed herself to be strong and not give him any more power.

Her sisters didn't need to worry about her now. She was fine. She just needed to rest. That was all.

Vanessa glanced at the time on her smart pendant, dangling from the gold chain. "Where is everybody?"

For tonight, the seven sisters planned a girls' night out at Sasha's huge house that her lover, Maeson, had built. Grandma Ova agreed to stop by for a discussion about Saedo lore.

"Rita won't be able to make it. She's helping with the renovations at the Village Library. Emma, Isabella, and Nina already can't make it either. So it's just Sasha, me, and you. It was a last-minute idea, anyway." Inga made herself a fruit bowl. "Thanks for hosting us, Sasha. Your massive house is the only one that can host all of us at once, and your backyard has the best view of the stars."

"Anything for my sisters. Besides, I'm curious to know what Grandma has to share about Saedo lore. She should be here any minute." Sasha checked her smart ring. "She only lives up the street."

"She's probably bringing a pot of her herbal soup for us," Vanessa said. No one in Saedo could resist Grandma Ova's soup, which was a blend of herbs and vegetables from her abundant gardens. She prayed a bowl of that soup would settle her stomach.

At first, Vanessa thought about cancelling to go home and sleep, but curiosity won out. Saedo lore intrigued her. Emma, Sasha, and Inga had all inspired a rare flower bud to grow after they met their starmates, their forever mates. Each flower reflected the color of their lover's mist. No one else could see it but them.

Would she inspire a flower to grow? Would she ever find her forever mate? Or was she too flawed, too wounded to attract that? She had tossed out her wish to the Universe on that fateful New Year's Eve night when she and her sisters were abducted by the horrible Ulkrins and rescued by the soldiers of Saedo.

I deserve a man who loves me regardless of my wounds.

Though Vanessa's idea of happily ever after had disappeared after Travis, a part of her yearned for the impossible. It was normal to want what you couldn't have, right? This opportunity to delve into Saedo lore allowed her to believe in magic again. When she was younger, she loved getting tarot card readings even though she couldn't tell if they were true. But they gave her hope, and hope saved her sanity.

The doorbell chimed, and Sasha rushed over and opened the door.

"Hi, Grandma Ova! The gang's all here for you. Come on in. Here, let me take that." Sasha grabbed the large pot in the elderly woman's hands and placed it on the dining table. "Make yourself at home."

Grandma Ova's white hair gleamed silver against her light green skin. "I'm so happy to see all of you. I've been meaning to go down to the Village Center and meet everyone, but once my injured legs healed, there were too many administrative things I needed to catch up on." She embraced Inga and Vanessa.

From Sasha, Vanessa learned that Grandma Ova was one thousand and three hundred solar cycles old. But her vibrant eyes, smooth skin, and healthy white hair portrayed her as someone in their early sixties. She was told that time behaved differently on this planet, even though a solar cycle was similar to one year on Earth. Most of all, it was the energy that made the lifestyle different. She learned that Earth vibrated on a third dimensional matrix as opposed to planet Celeron, which existed on an eighth dimensional matrix. The higher vibrations affected how the bodies and cells reacted to aging. Vanessa didn't understand it all, but she concluded these star-beings lived a long life.

Would her lifespan be like theirs too?

After everyone had a bowl of soup, they gathered in the living room with a huge skylight. Vanessa's stomach settled a bit. Sasha slid the side door open, and a sweet breeze snuck in.

"What's that lovely scent?"

Grandma Ova smiled, pointing toward the pink grass field. The tips of the grass glittered like gems as they swayed. "When the suns go down for the evening, the spade of the grass opens and releases a sweet fragrance. During the day, they collect the rays of the sun and make this sweet substance that they share during the evening."

"What's all the glitter on it?" Vanessa inquired.

Grandma Ova's amber eyes warmed. "It's a sparkle they show off at night. They're like stars. The sweet fragrance has healing properties. So inhale it, it'll release tension in your muscles. I usually tell people to camp outside for a night near a field of pink grass to heal any muscle ailments."

The wonders of this planet continued to awe Vanessa. Nature was truly healing, and the villagers appreciated their land.

Grandma Ova sat in a wide armchair with two large pillows. "I understand you girls have questions for me."

Inga and Sasha were curled up on the wide couch, while Vanessa sat on the shaggy rug with a soft pillow in front of her.

"We'd love it if you could tell us anything about the significance of these flowers." Inga pressed her smart bracelet, pulling up a virtual screen that showed the three flower buds. The yellow bud from Emma's garden was still closed, but hers had more leaves sprouting around it. Sasha's blue bud and Inga's red bud hadn't opened either.

Grandma Ova placed a hand to her heart, which the star-beings referred to as corra. Tears welled in her eyes as she zoomed in on each image. "You don't understand how delighted I am to see this. These are blessings beyond my imagination."

Grandma Ova's hands trembled, and Sasha retrieved a cup of warm herbal tea and offered it. Grandma Ova took the cup, sipped, and looked at the sisters. "I knew something was different the day the soldiers brought you here. The energy shifted. I felt it in my bones. I love this land, and there's so much wonder and magic in it. It is sacred, and when this kind of shift happens, that tells me the land is ready for a change."

Vanessa stared at her, holding on to her every word, like a kid hypnotized by a fairytale.

Grandma Ova continued, "As you already know, each star-being here possesses their own special mist color that only they and their starmate can see. The mist chooses the mate from energy resonance. It knows what's best for each individual. Color is important as well. The magic is in the details, so pay attention to the flowers and the mist. They'll give little hints on what they need you to do."

The concept fascinated Vanessa, and she turned toward the skylight. Was that a shooting star she just saw? She blinked, and it was gone. It was probably an illusion. Magical things like that didn't happen to her.

"Each mist color represents a wave in the color spectrum." Grandma opened her arms for emphasis. "Each wave holds a certain energy, and each energy field has its own purpose. Some we can see, some we can't."

"It sounds complicated," Vanessa said. There was a point in time when she used to love dissecting the meanings behind meanings, but after her failed marriage, she stopped looking for the hidden meanings. However, right now, in this moment, something dormant sparked in her again. The desire to believe in magic sprouted in her.

Was that the reason for all the nerves?

"Everything is perspective, my dear. If you learn how to look through the right lenses, everything will have a divine meaning to it." Grandma Ova looked at her with keen interest.

"We were destined to be in Saedo," Sasha said. "It's bizarre, but everything seems to point that way."

"The Cosmos is extraordinary and powerful. It has plans for all of us—the planets, the inhabitants, all the worlds and dimensions. It's mind-blowing, and there's a beauty to witnessing what happens and trust that the outcome is for your benefit." She pointed to the images of the flower buds. "Love gave birth to these flowers for a reason. These are called blessiums. It's been eons since I've seen them. The last time they grew, they saved a star race from being destroyed."

Inga gasped. "What?"

"That sounds serious," Sasha muttered.

"It is," Grandma Ova said. "I know about the story because my friend and her family were the recipients of the flowers' blessings. There were three buds then as well, and this occurred in another province, so these flowers don't belong to a particular territory. They belong to the Cosmos, and they are here for a reason. Something is happening here in Saedo, and I have a feeling more flowers will emerge."

Vanessa's heart thudded for no reason. The powerful pounding made the nerves in her stomach appear like a whisper. "Do you think Saedo is in danger?"

Grandma Ova pressed her lips into a thin line. "I think something is trying to disrupt Saedo, and these flowers will help fight it." She looked at all the sisters and her gaze landed on Vanessa. "All of you are part of it. It was meant to be. You were meant to be here in this now moment."

A hint of fear and uncertainty flashed across Sasha and Inga's faces. The same emotion stirred in Vanessa.

Grandma Ova noticed it. "I don't mean to frighten you. I just wanted to tell you the truth. The truth can be scary, but the fear will dissipate once you understand it. Knowing ahead of time only prepares you. Love is the most potent energy in the Cosmos. It's a pure energy that transcends time and space. Love made these flowers, and that means we have the most powerful energy as our ally."

"What do you think is happening in Saedo?" Vanessa asked.

Grandma Ova lifted a shoulder. "I didn't pick up on

anything during my meditations. Sometimes I learn things from the land, and sometimes from the sky. Spirit is always guiding us. We must pay attention and listen. Right now, what I'm feeling is that we need to wait and watch." Her chin gestured to the night sky. "Have you noticed something odd in the sky this past week?"

"The dark clouds," Inga said. "They seemed strange because the suns are still shining while these dark clouds are hanging in the air. I mean, I understand weather is strange and you can have dark clouds on a sunny day, but they look... stiff, stagnant, and out of place to me."

Inga with her love for fashion and the arts would notice small details like that.

"Yes, you're right. Those clouds have a strange energy to them. I've been watching them too. They seem to disappear during certain times of the day and then reappear. For instance, right now, I don't see them, which is why we can see the stars clearly. Keep an eye on them. Maybe they're just normal clouds signifying an impending storm."

"I started seeing them a week ago, but there hasn't been a storm in Saedo yet. Is there something we should be doing?" Inga asked.

"No, the village weather forecast will alert us if the radars pick up something dangerous. Like I said, these are speculations based on my knowledge of things. I could be wrong."

Vanessa didn't believe that.

"I'm sharing this information with you because you have an interest in Saedo stories," Grandma Ova said. "And like all stories, there are lessons to be learned. You carry high vibrational energy, all of you. Saedo loves it, hence the rare flowers, but something isn't used to this energy."

Or doesn't like it. Vanessa had no idea where that thought came from.

"I say we keep tossing these high vibrations in its face." Sasha made a sprinkling gesture.

Inga pounded a clenched fish to her palm. "That's right. Anyone or anything that wants to destroy love deserves to be crushed like garlic. Right, Vanessa?"

"Smashed, chopped, and completely destroyed. Nothing messes with the Nelson sisters." Vanessa made a chopping motion with her hand.

Grandma Ova beamed. "That's exactly what I'm talking about. You raise the vibration from your joy and intention. I think you've heard enough about Saedo lore for tonight. I have to get going. I need to wake up early and prepare a few things for the two assistants I hired to help me with my gardens."

After Grandma Ova left for the evening, Sasha and Maeson went to bed. Inga took one of the guest rooms. Vanessa could hear her chatting with her love, Osayik, who was on a business trip with Chief Mozar. Vanessa chose the comfortable sectional so she could gaze up at the night sky. She pressed the button on the wall, and the skylight opened. A sea of stars mesmerized her.

As Vanessa immersed herself in the wonder of it all, the nerves in her stomach resurfaced like a wave of remembrance, making her shudder. What was happening to her body?

She prayed for a restful night because she needed the energy to get through work tomorrow.

TWO

After a restless night, Vanessa yearned for a day off. But she couldn't do that to Abba. Abba hired Vanessa to work with her at the Happy Belly restaurant when she settled in the Main Village, which was about the size of a large suburb. The Province of Saedo was comprised of several villages, and Vanessa and her sisters resided in the main one. They worked in the Village Center, which was like the downtown area of any city. It was packed with shops and activities.

Happy Belly had three family parties scheduled for today, and Vanessa's assistance, along with two other star-being chefs, was vital to the day's success. She loved her work; it kept her mind busy, so she didn't have to think about the dream from last night. Why was Travis reappearing in her mind? She had no feelings for him other than disappointment. She should hate him for the scars he left on her body, for the trauma that seeped into her bones. But all she felt was disappointment and pity. Was that wrong of her?

Travis was a lost soul who could never understand love or any kind of positive affection. It took her a long time to see that.

She remembered how she'd fallen head over heels for his charm, but that was just a front for the monster within.

The burn scar that ran along her arm twitched as if it remembered what the skillet had done. The muscle on her shoulder throbbed as it relived the moment he shoved her against the bookcase.

She closed her eyes, squeezing away those dreadful memories. *Go away! Leave me alone.*

Vanessa opened her eyes as a stream of sweat slid from her forehead down the side of her face. It dripped onto her uniform which consisted of a peach top and black pants. She wiped another bead of sweat on her sleeve as she dropped into the chair in the backroom.

"You look beat. Take a break. We've got this." Abba prepared a plate of food for the customers waiting in front of the restaurant. She had three eyes, purple hair, dark green skin, and a warm smile that made everyone feel welcome. Her mother watched her young children while she worked at the restaurant. Her husband left her last solar cycle for another star-being with a bigger bust.

Vanessa blew out a breath. "I didn't sleep too well last night."

"It's been crazy busy, and I'm not complaining, but you've been on your feet for six hours without a break. I don't want you passing out on me. I need my best chef recharged so she can continue to help me." The third eye on the side of her forehead winked, while the other two focused on the garnish. "D-1 and D-2 can hold the fort back here."

The humanoid droids stopped loading the Aquajet—a massive dishwasher—with dirty plates and cutlery. They both whirled toward her. "Take a break, Vanessa. We don't want you passing out. We like your presence here."

She smiled at the male and female droids that looked like

brown-skinned star-beings. D-1 was a female with short green hair and D-2 a bald male. Both were programmed to lift heavy things, reach for boxes in high places, clean the floors, wash the dishes, cut the vegetables, and help with anything that their software provided.

Vanessa wished she had one of these droids when she was on Earth. She could program it to help her with whatever she needed. It would save her time. But then again, convenience would probably make her lazy.

"I suppose I can take a break. I can always rely on you both." It still amazed her that she was living, working, and talking to star-beings and droids on another planet. Just months ago, she was living on Earth unsure of what she wanted. Now, she was in Saedo mending her heart and soul, finding her way to who she was before the trauma. These star-beings showed her more kindness than a man who once vowed to love her.

She rose from the chair and glanced outside. Some fresh air would clear her mind and energize her. "Do you need anything from the garden? I'm going to take a short break outside."

Abba looked into her basket. "Some herbs and maybe a few jomatoes. The salads are selling fast this week. Can you get me a combination of colors? Thanks."

"Will do."

Vanessa entered the bathroom and splashed cold water on her face, washing away the sweat. The cold water refreshed her, giving her a boost of energy. Dark circles hung heavy under her eyes. She should have worn some makeup before getting to work, but she had been too tired. Her braid had come undone, and the messy red hair stuck out like a bird's nest.

After fixing her braid, she grabbed a basket and strode out to the back door and into the huge yard that also served as a garden for the restaurant. Farther back lay a wide ditch with a small stream that separated the yard from the woods.

She headed over to the jomatoe bush, which was similar to grape or cherry tomatoes on Earth. But these jomatoes grew in clumps of threes or fours, and they came in various colors. Some even had dots that made them look like ladybugs.

Nature healed in many ways. She inhaled a big breath, held it in her lungs, and released it. Her body lightened a bit, but the nerves lingered at the pit of her belly, causing a minor cramp and tightness in her chest that often occurred from worrying too much. But she wasn't concerned about anything right now. So why were they bothering her? She inhaled another breath, and though the muscles relaxed, energy zapped her. Something hissed like static electricity.

What was this strange sensation?

The unease reminded her of times her body coiled with tension in anticipation of what Travis would find wrong with her that day. Were these nerves warning her about something? Was she developing some kind of syndrome? That was the last thing she needed. What the hell was going on with her? *I need sleep.* Tonight, she'd go home, shower, and go straight to bed.

She held a purple jomatoe in her hand. "It's not too much to ask, right?" She dropped it into the basket. "I just want a good night's sleep. That's not a difficult thing to ask. Everyone needs rest, even you."

If someone were to listen to her talk to her vegetables, they'd consider her insane. She didn't care. Plants were living things too. Just because they couldn't speak didn't mean they weren't alive.

"Sometimes, I wish I could be like you." She glanced down at the pink jomatoe. "Your life is simple, and you exist for one purpose only. You're food to the birds, animals, and the customers who come to Happy Belly. You don't have a dark past you're trying to erase. You don't have nightmares. You just exist—"

"I'm sure it has nightmares too, especially when a giant mouth with big teeth is about to bite into it. Wouldn't that scare you?" a voice sounded from behind her.

She whirled and gasped as a green star-being climbed up from the ditch about twenty feet from her. In one hand, he held a tablet, and in the other, a scanning device that blinked. He surveyed the area, pointed the device at the soil, and glanced back to the tablet. Then he clicked the device off.

He strode up to her. "Sorry I startled you. I didn't mean to eavesdrop. I was working near the ditch and heard a voice."

She recognized him as one of the soldiers who had rescued her and her sisters. The soldiers of Saedo were the elite police force of the province. Besides working with Chief Mozar on government business, most of them had other occupations and interests. Her sisters' lovers contributed to the villages with building construction, cybersecurity on the Galacto Net, which was like a massive internet for the galaxy, city planning, and so much more. They were multitalented, and it intrigued her how they embraced their responsibilities without complaint. The men she'd encountered in her life didn't have the same exuberance as these star-beings who worked so well together. Maybe she never had the opportunity to meet the right man.

"It's okay." She shrugged as a new wave of nerves escalated in her stomach. This sensation differed from the cramping and chest tightening. The excitement reminded her of nerves that emerged when she started a new job or did something thrilling. "I talk to the plants a lot. It's nothing new. I'm Vanessa. You're friends with Raeko, Maeson, and Osayik, right?"

"Yes, they're my brothers. I'm Arkon. We've missed each other a few times at Raeko's house. I've had your pies. They're delicious."

"Oh, thank you."

She did miss a few parties at Emma and Raeko's house.

Emma had fallen in love with Raeko during the rescue mission, and now they were living their happily ever after. Grandma Ova's words popped into her mind.

You were meant to be here in this now moment.

Arkon smiled, and a warmth zapped her skin, skating down her spine. She willed her body to calm. The energy around them slowed, and the gentle breeze that caressed her skin moments ago froze in time. Even the plants stopped swaying, or was that her imagination?

He was a gorgeous green man who stood well over six feet tall with broad shoulders formed from hours in the gym. He wore a short-sleeve black knit top that showed off his taut muscles and high-tech denim pants that defined his strong thighs and legs. He had high cheek bones, a square jaw, and deep-set eyes that pulled her in. His brown hair was tied into a short tail with a leather strap. A sexy mouth with fine lips curved, and for a moment, she wondered what it would feel like to kiss them.

What? Vanessa blinked at the audacity of her fantasies.

Sunlight glittered in his eyes, making his irises appear copper. She should stop staring at him. She should stop being rude. But her brain and her body had other plans that included wild images of him in the nude. The shock of it startled her. When was the last time her body reacted to a man like this? She couldn't remember.

She willed her mind to the present moment and changed the topic. "What were you doing down at the ditch?"

"I'm investigating something for the city. There are unidentifiable holes along the ditch that follow the stream. I'm trying to figure out what's causing them. Have you seen anything out of the ordinary here?" He gestured to the yard.

"No, I don't think so, just the usual plants, birds, and animals. Sometimes I go down to the ditch during my break and watch the birds play in the stream. I haven't noticed anything strange, but I'll keep an eye out for you."

Arkon tapped something on the tablet, and his shiny brass wristband blinked with data codes. His fingers worked fast. When he was done, he looked at her. "Please do. That'd be great. I'll give you my identification."

She clutched her smart pendant and touched it to his wristband, syncing the information.

"Great. Thank you." He smiled and reached a hand toward her, and she flinched with an arm bracing to defend herself.

Arkon retracted his hand. "I'm sorry. I was just going to remove the dried leaf that's stuck in your hair. I wasn't—"

Shame and embarrassment heated her face. "It's okay. It's been a long day. I'm not myself today."

Why did she allow Travis to sneak into her life even on this planet? She refused to give him any power over her. That time was over. It pissed her off that, somehow, his presence still lingered and affected her life. How could she get rid of him? How could she make herself forget the trauma?

The concerned look on Arkon's face beckoned for information. How could she explain this to him?

She didn't know him. She didn't need to tell him anything. That brought her some relief.

His eyes steeled, but his voice was calm. "How did you get the scar on your arm?"

"It's a wound from a long time ago."

"You didn't answer my question."

I don't need to.

He stared at her, and more questions swam in his eyes. She could guess his internal war. The desire to know why she thought he was going to hit her and how she had gotten the scar. But he should understand he was in no position to pry answers out of her. It was none of his business, and she preferred it that way. The past was best left in the past. She didn't want to talk about it.

"Some things aren't meant to be discussed with strangers," Vanessa said as nerves tumbled in her stomach again.

His lips thinned, and he nodded without comment.

"I've got to get back to work." She tightened her grip on the basket of jomatoes. "Like I said, I'll keep an eye out for anything unusual for you."

"Thank you."

With basket in tow, she turned and headed to the door. She knew he was watching her. His gaze singed her back, and her body tingled from the sensation that lingered long after she was inside.

Was her body's reaction a side effect of embarrassment, of him seeing her flaw? Or was it something more?

THREE

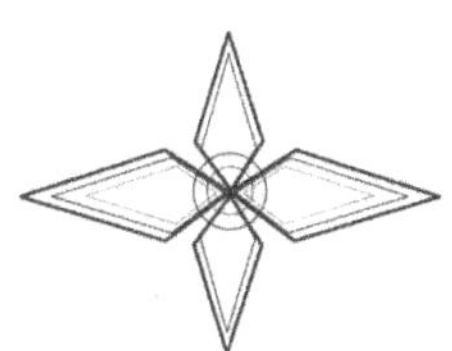

The next day, hungry customers swamped Happy Belly, wanting to try Vanessa's new dish, the Nelson meat pie with a Saedo twist. It was her version of a shepherd's pie. She released it two days ago, and orders kept coming in for pick-ups and deliveries in addition to sit-in dining.

Abba beamed as she checked her daily profits. "I don't normally review numbers in detail like this, but the Nelson meat pies have been such a big hit. Thank you."

"Thank *you* for giving me a job." Vanessa gave Abba a one-arm hug. The villagers had accepted her and her sisters with open arms, giving all of them opportunities to make a decent living.

"Best decision I've ever made. I'm going into my office to make some calls. I'll be back." Abba strode down the hallway to her office.

The front doorbell chimed as more customers stepped in. Vanessa wouldn't have noticed or bothered to look, but an energy slammed into her like it wanted her attention. She glanced up from the counter and noticed Arkon taking a seat facing the back garden.

What was he doing back here? Did he find what was causing those holes in the ditch?

He met her eyes and waved. Vanessa remembered the strange exchange from yesterday. Embarrassment still lingered, so she let Klori, the sage-skinned waitress with curly yellow hair, serve him. Vanessa continued with her inventory list and balanced the numbers on the virtual screen. Numbers and Vanessa weren't on friendly terms. They were too rigid, too analytical, too strict. She preferred something with more flexibility, more creativity. She could never work at a bank or anything that required meticulous concentration. With food, if she were a bit off, it could taste good. With numbers, if she were off by a few digits, chaos would erupt.

Klori stepped up to the counter. "Vanessa, do you know that sexy star-being over there? He keeps looking your way, trying to get your attention, but you're glued to the screen here." She jerked her chin at Arkon. "He's working on something while he's having lunch. He ordered your pie and asked if you could stop by when you get a chance."

Vanessa wasn't trying to avoid him, was she? Who was she kidding? She didn't want him to ask about her scar again. Not only that, there was something about him that made her want to kiss him amongst other decadent things. The wild Vanessa—the one who was shoved into a corner by violence—was finding the courage to get out of that corner. Arkon lured her without having a clue. Did she want to give another man that power? The wanting, the needing, and the curiosity all tangled together in a wild turbulence in her mind. When she looked at him, desire sparked in her.

Was it just repressed sexual energy? Or was it her hormones acting up? She wasn't due for her menstrual cycle for another two months. The herbal pills she'd gotten from Grandma Ova also served as a contraceptive that allowed her body to skip a few cycles.

She learned a while ago that hiding was cowardice. Facing her issues head-on was how to resolve them. She was no coward. It took her a while to understand this, and that was when she finally filed for divorce from Travis. The problems had glared at her from the beginning, but love was blind. When he chased her with a knife and threatened to kill her and her sisters, the blindfold came off. She felt so stupid for being under that dark spell.

No more hiding.

When the order for the Nelson meat pie came, she brought it over to Arkon. From his brass wristband, he pulled up two small screens in front of him while he sipped a fruit shake.

"You're a busy man." Vanessa set down the plate decorated with edible flowers.

He smiled and sniffed. "I've heard rave reviews about this pie." He took a fork, dove in, and made a sound that sent a jolt to her core. "I think I need to order two more of them for dinner."

Vanessa laughed, and the awkwardness that had been there yesterday vanished. "Klori said you had some questions for me?"

"Yes. I was just wondering if you've seen anything strange by the ditch."

"No, I haven't been back out there." She studied his screens. Numbers, charts, graphs, and neat summaries splashed on two screens. "You like numbers? You like to analyze things with an absolute answer?"

He pinned her with an inquisitive look. "I like to know exactly where things fall. I don't like to leave things to chance. I make my own solution based on facts. Sometimes, I make an educated guess based on data I've collected."

What did you collect about me?

"I'm the opposite. I don't like things with one definite answer.

I like limitless things, things that could have many possibilities. Kind of like my recipes. I can create something from anything. There's no one way of doing it, and I can have many solutions."

His lips twisted as he seemed to consider her words. "That's a compelling perspective. I've always been good with data and research. I know where those details will lead me, and I can anticipate the outcome. I tried to do things differently a long time ago, and that failed miserably. You're the creative type, so you wouldn't like numbers. I don't have a creative bone in me." He paused and studied her. "We are different."

"We're opposite each other."

"No, we're polarities."

Vanessa arched an eyebrow. She hadn't heard that explanation before.

"In simple terms, we exhibit energies that complement each other. Together, they complete each other. Like inhaling and exhaling, night and day. They are 'opposites,' yet they complete the entire process."

"That's an interesting way of looking at it." The longer she stood near him, the more her body warmed. "Well, you enjoy your meal. I've got to get back to work. I'll be sure to let you know if I see something in the ditch."

Did something happen last night to make him think she saw something in the ditch today? He didn't seem concerned. Then it occurred to her. Did he come to Happy Belly just to talk to her? No, that couldn't be it. Could it? It had been so long since any man showed interest in her. The truth was that she hadn't been open to dating then. But now, she wanted to know. It had been so long that she'd forgotten how it worked.

Arkon turned heads with the female star-beings. He could date any star-being in Saedo. Was he with anyone? That thought didn't even cross her mind until now.

Vanessa entered the back room and assisted the food orders with Klori and Bashlin, the waitress with the long, dark hair.

Her heart raced as Arkon's face popped into her vision. Why couldn't she push him out of her mind? This powerful attraction gripped her senseless. She hardly knew him. Why would a man like him want anything to do with a simple human female like her? She had a darkness that still haunted her. Being with her meant he had to deal with those monsters too. Who would want the extra baggage?

Despite all those thoughts, his exquisite face and mesmerizing copper eyes did strange things to her stomach. A different set of nerves churned, and for a moment, a spark of hope brought a smile to her face. There was nothing wrong with imagination. She could have a private story unfolding in her mind about him. No one had to know.

Time flew by as more customers arrived and kept Vanessa on her toes.

"I'll see you tomorrow." Klori waved at Vanessa, who was opening a bag of plant-based napkins.

"Already?" Vanessa checked her smart pendant and blinked. Five hours passed by in a blink. She glanced over where Arkon had sat, but he wasn't there. Of course, he wasn't there. Did she think he'd sit there all day waiting to talk to her? He had come in for lunch, and that was it. Would he come back tomorrow?

A twinge of disappointment settled in. It was better that way. She didn't need Arkon to complicate her perfect lifestyle. She worked, went home, experimented on her secret recipe collection, and went to bed. One day, she'd have her own restaurant with the freedom to create whatever she pleased. Happy Belly allowed her the liberty to explore, but it wasn't her restaurant. Vanessa wanted something that represented every aspect of her.

At a glance, her life sounded boring, but she was content. She didn't have to worry about the verbal abuse that came from a wrong word choice, or from the incorrect way she greeted anyone. *Incompetent bitch. Stupid slut.* These were names Travis used to call her in addition to the smacking and punching just because he had a bad day.

She adored her simple life now. Though she would love to connect to a man again, she was afraid. What if he ended up the same as Travis? Her body quaked from that thought.

Stop thinking. Stop analyzing. She had one thing in common with Arkon: she overanalyzed things that should be left alone.

Vanessa blew out a breath as she focused on refilling the napkin rack behind the counter for the takeout orders.

"Long day?" His voice startled her.

Her heart jumped with joy. "Hi. Are you here to pick up an order? I didn't see a pending order on the screen." She searched the screen again.

"No order. I'm here for you. Do you have a minute?" Copper eyes looked at her, and her legs lost their balance.

Vanessa assumed he wanted to ask more questions about the ditch or share some information about his investigation.

"Sure." She gestured for him to follow her through the side door onto the private patio filled with pots of herbs and vegetables.

"I didn't know there was a little private patio out here." Arkon walked up to the iron fence and rose on his toes to peer over the tall bushes separating the area from the rest of the garden.

"It's only for employees, so consider yourself lucky. I usually come out here to retrieve herbs instead of having to go into the big garden."

She chose a handheld water pitcher and watered the plants.

She could have activated the irrigation system, powered by the sunlight stored in the discs on the top of the roof and the tubes on the fence, but she needed to do something with her hands.

Arkon's presence overwhelmed her, made her nervous. She plucked some dry leaves from the pot of pink cilantro. Her skin tingled, and when she looked up, his stare seemed more intense. She'd almost forgotten why they were out there.

"What did you want to ask me? If you're wondering if I had a chance to visit the ditch, my answer is no."

A wide smile stretched across his face, making him so handsome she wondered if the cosmic gods were having a good day when he was born. It should be illegal for someone to look that good.

"Are you busy tomorrow evening? I'd like to take you out to dinner."

Shock froze her in the spot, and a lump lodged in her throat. Her grip on the pitcher tightened while she struggled for words. Why couldn't she speak? It had been so long since someone asked her on a date. Her brain scattered, leaving her clueless.

What should she say? She wasn't prepared for this. He only met her yesterday. Was that enough time to want to date somebody? Unsure of what to do, she placed the pitcher down and noticed the scar on her arm. At that moment, the scar grew bigger than what it was. It zapped the joy and hope from her. The memory of how it had gotten there dulled the moment, and she retreated back to her corner.

"I'm busy tomorrow." The words came out flat. This wasn't the reply Vanessa wanted to give, but she was afraid of his question about her scar. Eventually, he'd ask again.

What did he see in her, anyway?

"I understand. The restaurant has been busy. Your meat pie is the talk of the village." Arkon moved closer, standing only inches from her. A musky scent seduced her nose, her body.

She shivered, and he noticed. "But I'll be back until you say yes."

Vanessa swallowed. "Why?"

"Why not?" A crooked smile formed on his face. "I like what I see, and it makes logical sense to go after it." His gaze skimmed her face and down her body.

Vanessa, do not melt into the floor.

The copper in his eyes sparked. Was that even possible? She couldn't take her eyes away from his. "I like how I make you nervous, and I especially love how you affect me."

"What do you mean?"

"My body has never reacted to a female the way it reacts to you." He glanced down at his high-tech denim pants.

A large bulge pushed against it. She should have looked away, but she didn't. His reaction gave her power.

"My eyes have never intensified like this. I feel the energy coming from them because of you. Why you? I'm going to find out, Vanessa."

Say it again. Her name sounded precious on his lips. She'd never been precious to anyone but her parents. That was a different kind of affection. The kind he just teased her with was something she'd only dreamed of.

Could she have that?

She saw herself at the center of his eyes. A gold rim glowed around the light amber. Specks of copper glittered in his irises. They looked like gems promising wicked things. Wild things that the previous Vanessa had once loved.

"Can all star-beings do that with their eyes?"

"Maybe." He lifted a shoulder. "But you did this to me. I just reacted." He ran his fingers down her cheek. Not only did she not flinch, she welcomed it. "I had no control over my body's reaction to you. Believe me when I say that I've never reacted this way to anyone in my two hundred and forty-five solar cycles on this planet. This is beyond simple attraction. It's something more, but I won't rush you. Take all the time you need. I'll be around."

He was a lot older than her, but then again, these star-beings had long life spans and didn't look their age. Time was tricky here.

"I'm only twenty-eight," she muttered.

"I know."

How did he know? He probably asked her sister or one of his brothers.

"I'm an investigator for Saedo, so I have my ways of obtaining information."

Was she that obvious to read?

"I've taken up too much of your time today. I should get going. I meant what I said: take all the time you need. But I'll be back. That's a promise. It's an absoluteness. There's no other answer but that, Vanessa."

When he left, a wisp of purple mist lingered and circled in front of her like a secret performance saved just for her. Her hand trembled as she waved her fingers through it. It dispersed, leaving her in awe.

Her heartrate increased because the purple mist greeted her. Arkon's color was purple, and it had come to give her a sign.

Did she believe in fate? It was hard not to. Standing alone outside with the plants and the sky as her audience, she prayed for guidance. If Arkon knew about her past, about her weaknesses and flaws, would he still want her?

Did she have the courage to tell him the truth? Did she want to? Joy and fear collided and left her more confused than she'd ever been.

FOUR

For the next few days, Arkon didn't show up at the restaurant. Disappointment pricked at her. Every time the doorbell chimed, she glanced up, hoping it was him. She even scanned the orders on the virtual screen, but none came in with his name. Every time he didn't show up increased her longing and anticipation. This yearning for him pushed her further out of her cave.

Stop being ridiculous, Vanessa.

This wasn't some high school crush. She was a woman who knew the power of the heart went beyond the surface of physical attraction. Arkon enticed her "wild" side to escape from the dark corner she had found comfort in for so long. She wanted to do all these depraved things with him.

Being near him sparked her imagination in untamed ways. She sucked in a breath at the provocative images of what he could do to her. Her body shivered as she envisioned him kissing her. Arkon brought on an alluring set of sexual nerves that delighted her instead of the stomach cramps, zapping her with electricity. Somehow, thinking of Arkon made her forget the uncomfortable nerves. Was he the distraction she needed? Was he the remedy for her healing?

Travis had shamed this creative side of her, and because of Arkon, she wanted to step out of that cave. Her heart soared at that revelation. It was one step closer to healing herself. And if things didn't work out between them—even though nothing had really started yet—she was thankful that he opened that door for her.

Would he appreciate her wildness? Or would he disgrace her? Regardless, Vanessa vowed to never let a man humiliate, degrade, or dishonor her ever again. She made this pledge the day she left Travis, filed for divorce, signed up at the shooting range, and attended therapy, which she no longer needed. Cooking became her therapy. The creative possibilities were endless, and that abundance allowed her the freedom to do whatever she wanted. Cooking became the temple that saved her.

Arkon ignited an internal storm in her that illuminated what she had been missing all these years. The past few days of longing had pushed her former self further out of hiding. Desire and the need to explore lured her out of the cave.

The more she became her true self, the less the nerves tumbled in her stomach. Were these nerves an internal storm that warned of what was to come? Or were they foreshadowing the clearing of the old? Wasn't that the purpose of a storm? To clean and clear out the old energy? Things that were stuck that no longer served her? Didn't the sun shine with calm weather after a powerful rainstorm?

Vanessa shook her head. She'd been analyzing too much. Arkon would appreciate that.

Damn it, where is he?

She checked her smart pendant, but no messages appeared from him. Had it been a dream that he was outside in the private patio having a discussion with her? Did she imagine the stream of purple mist?

Vanessa let out a breath and gave her mind a rest. She focused on her work, which to her surprise wasn't busy like the previous days. She glanced outside, and the dark clouds loomed in the sky, signifying a rainstorm. This would be her first storm in Saedo.

Abba emerged from the back room. "Business is slow today. I need to get home to help my mother. She's not feeling well and the kids are driving her crazy. I'm going to send Bashlin home and deactivate D-1 and D-2. Klori can stay to help you—unless you want to go home early?"

"I'll be fine. If business doesn't pick up in another hour or two, I'll let Klori go home too. I'll lock up myself."

"Keep an eye on the storm and close early if you have to. I don't want you getting stuck out here. Send me a message when you leave."

She'd driven in a rainstorm before, but not in Saedo. It couldn't be that different, but she didn't want Abba to worry. "I will."

Thirty minutes later, not a single customer came through the system.

"It's dead today." Klori checked her bracelet and pulled up a screen of the weather forecast. "Looks like a lot of rain and wind approaching."

"You can go home. I'll be right behind you. I'll do one walk-through and lock everything up."

"You sure you don't want me to stay?"

"I'll be fine. I'm just going to wait for the Launderjet to finish and then I'll head out. We need clean tablecloths and towels this week."

After Klori left, Vanessa locked the door and went downstairs to check on the Launderjet, which was an innovative washer and dryer using solar light to clean. It also had a section for folding. She took the finished pile of folded tablecloths and divided them up. She tucked half into a drawer and took the other half upstairs.

Something hissed or whispered in the basement. She glanced around but didn't see anything. It was hard to tell with the folding noises from the Launderjet.

She took one step toward the staircase, and her equilibrium wavered. She gripped the railing to stabilize herself. Was it dehydration? Dizziness often occurred when she didn't drink enough liquid during the day.

Vanessa inhaled a breath, found her balance, and strode back upstairs. She placed the tablecloths inside a closet. Then something crashed into the front of the store, shattering glass everywhere. She ducked below the counter to avoid the flying glass shards. The wind howled, and for a moment, it sounded like eerie words. It must have been her imagination because the wind didn't talk. Outside, lighting slashed like blue blades across the sky.

Holy shit.

Could she make it to her personal rider and drive it home? She received her answer when a tree uprooted and flew across the street. Panic rose in her. She couldn't get home. The only thing she could do was stay put until the storm died.

She sent Abba a message but wasn't sure if the message would go through with this massive storm. When she last checked on the forecast, no one mentioned this danger. Was this a hurricane? A tornado?

"Vanessa! Are you in there?"

Her heart leaped when her name cut through the howling wind. She gripped the counter and peered over. Arkon rushed through the opening of the broken glass. "Vanessa!"

"I'm here." She barreled into him.

His arms tightened around her. "We can't be up here. We

need to take cover in case the roof flies off. Is there a basement here?"

She nodded, gripped his hand, and led him down the stairs. He locked the door, followed her down the steps, and surveyed the basement.

"What are you looking for?" Vanessa asked.

"Are there any windows or a door to the outside?"

Vanessa brought him to door that led up to the garden. A small window by the side was covered by a fallen tree. Arkon tugged at the door, testing its security.

"What kind of storm is this? I checked the forecast earlier, and it didn't appear urgent."

Arkon gripped her shoulder, turned her around, and examined her. "Are you okay?"

"I think so. Just spooked."

"This is an unusual storm. We haven't experienced anything like it before."

The unsettling nerves returned. "What do you mean?"

"The clouds we saw on the radar didn't signify a dangerous storm. But what came was different... Engineered."

"What?" Vanessa's mind spiraled at the insane possibility. "Is that possible? Like, could someone actually create a storm on purpose?"

"With the right equipment, I don't see why not. It's all energy. You mix the energies together and you either get something harmonious or destruction. Our experts are looking into it right now." He moved some boxes aside, making a pathway to the couch against the wall. Then he pulled her down to sit beside him.

Vanessa jumped when a loud noise crashed upstairs. Arkon wrapped an arm around her. His hand rubbed her arm, chasing the chill away.

Her heart sank, knowing Happy Belly was being destroyed

and there was nothing she could do about it. "Abba's going to be crushed. This place is her soul."

"I know. But she can rebuild it. Right now, the most important thing is that she's safe with her family."

Did Abba get home safely? Vanessa didn't even know. She checked her smart pendant, but no reply from Abba came through about her closing up. Vanessa prayed her sisters were safe too. She sent a message to all her siblings, informing them she was all right.

"Are messages going through?"

"Most of the radar is being disrupted. Whatever is causing the storm has infiltrated Saedo's security." He looked at his wristband. "I'm on the government net, which has a stronger connection to the Galacto Net, but even that's spotty."

"Can you let Raeko, Maeson, or Osayik know that I'm okay? I don't want my sisters to worry about me."

"I already did." He smiled. "When the first of the lightning struck, I was with Osayik. I told him I'd swing by the restaurant. No one could have prepared for this, and I assumed you were still working."

A thought occurred to her. "Were you working on something the past few days?"

The corners of his lips tilted up. "Why? Did you miss me?"

"Maybe."

The smile grew bigger. "I missed you more than you know. New data arrived, and I had to go with my team to seal up some of the worm tunnels in the ground. We found a dead squirmur that got stuck trying to reenter the hole. Poisonous secretions damaged the soil where it died. We had to clean that up."

Her image of a worm was probably not what he was describing. Her stomach knotted. "What's a squirmur? It's not a small worm like the ones on Earth?"

"No, these are huge, and they're not native to Saedo. We

don't know how they got here. Who brought them here, and why? These were things I was working on the past few days. I wanted to stop by to see you, but these squirmurs are threatening the land with their poison. I had to help my team. I meant what I said before: I'll give you time. Just don't make me wait too long. I'm not the most patient—"

Vanessa held her fingers to his lips. "Do you hear that?"

The wind howled an angry sound and repeated itself several times.

Arkon's brows furrowed, and his face tensed upon recognition of the words.

This is our land now. You must leave.

The wind wailed its angry demands as Vanessa tightened her grip on Arkon's hand.

"Tell me you heard that eerie voice." A chill rushed down her body.

"I did." He removed his hand from hers, pulled up a virtual screen from his wristband, and typed a message. "I need to alert my brothers and Chief Mozar about this discovery."

She yearned for the warmth and comfort of his hand but understood the urgency of the situation. "The wind talks. Is that normal for Saedo?"

"Natural wind doesn't speak, at least to my knowledge. But there's nothing natural about this sudden storm. It's either dark magic or someone created it. My gut tells me the latter."

"Why would someone do that?"

"I don't know, but I'm going to find out." The stern voice carried a promise she respected and believed. "There's going to be a lot of damage. I hope everyone found shelter."

Feeling the need to do something, she asked, "Do you want some coffee or tea? There's a backup Coffeewhizz down here in case the one upstairs breaks down. I can turn it on with the solar crystals." One of the best technologies in Saedo was the solar crystals. They absorbed the sunlight used to charge equipment. Abba had invested in a few large crystals.

"Coffee would be great, thanks." Arkon took a seat at a desk next to the couch and pulled up two large virtual screens from his wristband. "I don't know if my messages will get through to anyone right now, but someone will receive this information eventually. They'll have better visuals from the satellites and start some kind of investigation."

Vanessa turned on the Coffeewhizz and made two cups of coffee. She brought the little white cups over and placed them on the side table near the desk.

"Thank you." Arkon sipped and returned to his screens.

At that moment, the lights dimmed in the basement, and Arkon cursed. "Flekken!"

The power grid around the restaurant was probably damaged and activated the stored solar energy in the basement. She never imagined having to use the emergency lights.

As she sat on the couch with the warm cup of coffee between her hands, Vanessa evaluated the situation. She should be freaking out right now, but a strange calm overcame her. She didn't understand what was happening to her. The sudden nerves and now the sudden calmness. What prompted them?

Needing to do something, she activated the restaurant's second computer with a button on the wall. A screen splashed in front of her. Since she had time, she could finish the new menu brewing in her imagination. Would a menu with meals that symbolized hope, perseverance, and survival attract people? She was drawn to those virtues because they were aspects of her life. A breakfast menu that boosted the customer's mood, a lunch assortment that urged them to keep going, and a dinner menu that ended with contentment in their stomach. There was nothing wrong with a happy gut.

Vanessa wasn't sure how Abba or the others would react to such a strange menu. It was even strange to her. Could she pull it off with just unique names? An inner voice urged her along, and she was beginning to listen to her intuition. As she typed up her ingredients and recipes for her experiments, she got lost in the pleasure of creation. She found strength and hope by doing what she loved. Whenever she felt wounded or anxious, she went inside herself and remembered all those things that gave her joy. From that inner temple, she nurtured her gifts and turned the wounds into strengths. While she worked, she forgot about the storm outside, about the fact that she was hiding in the basement, and about the handsome star-being sitting at a desk a few feet from her.

"What are you working on?" Arkon's voice yanked her back into the moment.

She didn't know why, but embarrassment flushed her cheeks. She quickly swiped to a new screen that showed a list of items she had to restock for the restaurant.

"Nothing important, just helping Abba with the administrative stuff."

Arkon only nodded. He probably knew she wasn't telling the whole truth, but he didn't call her out on it, nor did he press on. She appreciated that more than he knew. With Travis, she had no privacy, even in her own mind. Travis had shoved fear into every corner of her body and soul.

Arkon stood too close to her, and sexual energy sizzled between them. The chill she felt earlier vanished, replaced by a pulsing heat that bounced around the basement. Did he finish his work? Why was he staring at her like that?

"Is something on my face?" Vanessa wiped her cheek.

He smiled and her heart flipped. "There's nothing there except beauty." His fingers skimmed down the side of her cheek, along her jawline, and settled at her chin. "This face has been in my mind for days and nights."

Why couldn't she muster up the words to say something? She didn't even know her lips had parted until he traced his fingers along them. The energy between them throbbed, and she lost track of her senses.

She swore it wasn't her brain that urged her to lick his index finger. He gasped at the shock of her seductive act. Vanessa blinked at what she had done and reveled in that spontaneous thrill. That excitement tore away the shield around herself, and the wild Vanessa broke free.

"That was hot, and I want more of it," he said in a hoarse voice.

"Then kiss me." Vanessa rose from the chair and climbed on him. She *climbed* him like a wild animal gripping for dear life. What the hell was wrong with her? No man had ever provoked her this much. Arkon yanked at her senses, making her heart sing.

With Arkon, she felt free to be herself. Her heart thudded at this liberation that was long overdue.

"I want you," Vanessa whispered.

Arkon smirked. "I'm all yours." He crushed his mouth to hers, and she opened for him. His tongue slid in and met hers. Sensations ricocheted through her body like little zaps of lightning, waking up all her nerve endings.

Heat exploded in her core as his mouth devoured hers. Her brain absconded somewhere. She couldn't think. Emotions and desire battled inside her. Arkon woke up a storm within her, and now she let it roar through her with passion and need. She was the storm, and he was the cause of it.

When he backed her against the wall, the coolness toned down the fire in her blood.

"Oh, the things I want to do to you." Arkon veered back to

look at her. His hand slid under her uniform top and found her breast. Mischief danced on his lips. "Do you like me touching you?"

"Yes…"

"Have you thought of me the past few days?"

"Yes…"

"Did those thoughts involve me seducing you? Touching you here." He teased her nipple through the bra. "And tasting you here." His teeth nipped the crevice of her neck.

"Yes…"

Oh, God. Where was her speech?

"Do you want more of me?"

"More." She sighed. "I can't think. I can't even talk with your hands on me."

His copper eyes beamed. "I love hearing that word from your mouth. 'Yes' and 'more' are words I want to hear from you." The huskiness of his voice aroused her. "I love that I can move you like this. I want you melting from my touch. I want you begging me for more."

He seduced her in the most delicious ways.

She soaked her panties, and no shame washed over her. "I guess this is our date after all."

"The first of many. Hold on tight."

She didn't know what he meant. Her mind was still elsewhere, her back still flush against the wall. He took one of her hands and placed it against the bookshelf beside them. Her other hand gripped his strong shoulder for balance.

When she met his gaze, need sparked in those eyes, and she understood his desire. With one hand, he lifted her shirt and held it up. With the other hand, he unclasped the front hooks of her bra. Her breasts sprung free, and he captured a nipple into his mouth. She cried out with pleasure as he took and took.

She'd never been ravished like this. His mouth tantalized

her, and she couldn't look away. She loved the image of him loving her. She loved the way his mouth claimed and took what he wanted. She'd never felt more alive than in this moment.

Desire whipped through her, and she moaned, "More."

He gave what she asked. Her legs tightened around his waist as bliss coursed through her.

An unexpected wave of dizziness overcame her. She didn't understand it. It was more of an intrusion that cut into the beautiful act between them.

She stiffened, and Arkon drew away, looking at her with concern. "Did I hurt you?"

"No, no not at all." He set her on her feet, and she wobbled. "Something's not right." The nerves that had disappeared resurfaced in her stomach. But now, it was ten times more prominent. So prominent she knew something was about to happen. Her gut warned her.

Vanessa re-clasped her bra and collected herself by straightening her shirt. The floor shifted like water was beneath it, and she gripped Arkon's hand for balance.

He cursed and pulled her away from the spot and pointed to the floor. "Watch out for that."

Vanessa blinked and placed a hand to her forehead. "You see the floor moving too?"

Her dizziness reflected the imbalance of the ground. Was her body trying to give her clues all this time?

Arkon gripped his blaster and moved further away. "I see it." His jaw tightened. "I know what's moving underground." He stretched out a long arm protecting her. "Stay behind me."

"What is it?"

"Squirmurs."

SIX

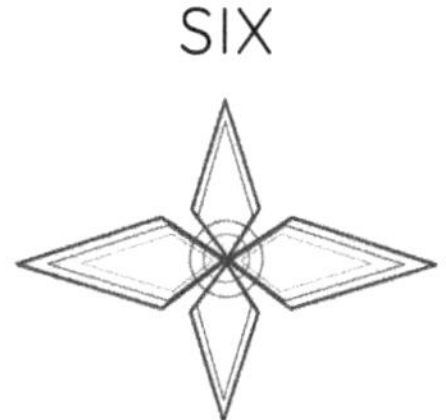

"The worm monsters that have been digging holes in the ditch? The ones you've been investigating?" Vanessa remembered Arkon mentioning that the squirmurs possessed poison. "Do you think they're infecting Saedo?"

"That's one way to conquer a place: infect it with your own poison, and then heal it after it's yours. It's a cruel way, but Ulkrins aren't loving beings."

"I thought it was my dizziness that made me see strange things." Each time the floor shifted, her stomach lurched. "This may sound weird, but I sense its movement." She recalled her imbalance yesterday. "I felt it yesterday too."

Arkon glanced at her. "We'll need to look into that later. I want to know how you can sense it. If it has some connection to you, then I need to keep you away from it. Keep you safe."

The firm voice and the intention seeped into her heart. No man ever wanted to protect her like that. For the first time in her in life, she felt treasured.

Ten feet away, the floor cracked, and a squirmur's head broke through the cement. Electricity hissed as the squirmur crawled up from the giant hole. It had six antennae around its head. She didn't see any eyes, only thick, segmented skin, which was the only thing that resembled the worms of Earth. It looked more like a giant mutant caterpillar. The monster made a strange sound that chilled her bones. It lurched toward Arkon.

Arkon blasted the squirmur, and the beam sliced a chunk of flesh from the flailing creature. But the injury didn't stop it from jerking toward him. Energy sizzled around its nasty body. Standing so close to it, Vanessa's skin prickled from its energy. Every time energy sparked from its body, a zing zapped her stomach.

A pair of eyes opened under thick skin, and Vanessa gagged in both disgust and surprise. The small eyes glanced around, searching. The bricks from the wall beside her crumbled and thudded to the ground. More squirmurs emerged.

Arkon cursed and yanked out a smaller gun from his jacket. The ball of light at the top of the gun flickered. "Do you know how to use a gun? Just aim and shoot."

Thanks to her dark past, she had experience at the shooting range and learned how to kill a dummy. Though these squirmurs weren't dummies, Vanessa could kill them without qualm. She hoped. She'd find out soon enough. Her hands trembled, but she willed calmness into them.

She grabbed the silver gun from his hand. "I got it."

His eyebrows furrowed with questions. "You can explain how you know what to do with a gun later. Right now, if that thing comes near you, aim and shoot. The gun shoots out energy beams, not bullets."

"Okay."

Another squirmur veered its head from the wall and thudded to the ground. Energy sizzled, illuminating the veins on its body. Again, the eyes on the creature scoured the area in slow motion.

Thunder boomed outside, and the circuitry on the squirmurs' bodies buzzed and radiated in response.

"Did you see that?" Vanessa asked Arkon.

"They're connected to the storm." He cursed and gripped her hand, heading toward the stairs as more squirmurs broke through the floor. Electricity crackled as a separate storm erupted in the basement. "We need to get out of this enclosed space. It's too dangerous."

Arkon shot several blasts at the squirmurs, and they wailed. Rows of sharp teeth glinted from the illumination. The nerves in Vanessa's stomach spiked as more circuitry increased nearby.

As a child, she had a sixth sense for things. She just knew things, felt them as if some invisible guide was beside her. But that ability had stopped when she married Travis and fear took over. Why was her intuition so keen again? She'd contemplate on it later. At the moment, she had to concentrate on staying alive.

Outside, hell greeted her. Dark clouds loomed and sagged, blanketing the area with a heaviness that sucked the life from the area. In the distance, a blue sky peeked through the gloomy contrast. Several squirmurs broke through the ground, angling their heads toward the sky. Arkon blasted a large squirmur that crawled at him from his left. The blasts demolished the squirmur, and its flesh splattered everywhere. One piece slapped against her thigh, and she kicked it off.

Vanessa aimed at one squirmur that busted through the ground twenty feet from where she stood. It opened its mouth as it moved toward her with swiftness. How could this nasty thing move so fast without legs? She aimed and shot out a laser beam into its mouth. It injured the squirmur, but not enough to subdue it. She fired again and again, until she cut the creature clear in two.

She'd never killed anything before. Okay, maybe she had

squashed a few mosquitoes trying to nibble on her, but this was different. When she signed up at the shooting range, her intention had been to protect herself from Travis and anyone who wanted to hurt her. At that time, she needed something to defend, not offend. But ending a life was ending a life, wasn't it? Though guilt gnawed at her, she reminded herself that this animal was a monster. And she had to kill it before it killed her or Arkon. Her action was in self-defense.

More wails erupted, and adrenaline coursed through her as she glanced over at Arkon, who fired at a monstrous squirmur. It wouldn't die. The antennae on its body stood erect as if they were downloading information from somewhere.

The squirmur whipped its body at Arkon, and his back slammed against a large tree trunk.

"Arkon! Are you all right?"

Arkon pushed himself away from the trunk and held up a hand. "Stay over there! Don't come over!"

The wind died down a bit, which was odd since the dark clouds hadn't changed. Vanessa assisted Arkon, firing at the massive squirmur that was twice the size of a tractor trailer. When the creature wailed, lightning shot down into its mouth and energized its body. Its eyes glowed, and Vanessa noticed a device in the space between its eyes.

"Something's going on with the thing's eyes."

Vanessa aimed and fired a beam at its head, but missed when the squirmur crawled out of the way. Did it understand her? Or was someone monitoring them? Monitoring her?

Arkon fired several blasts at the eyes on the massive beast, but it thrashed and the blasts landed on its body. A smaller squirmur popped up from a hole in the ground beside Arkon, and he shot it in the eye. The creature flailed and wailed as energy crackled from its body. A second later, it stopped moving. Not only that, the buzzing energy also died like a switch had been turned off. The darkness in the clouds subsided to a lighter gray. The lightning dimmed, and the thunder weakened.

Vanessa and Arkon exchanged a mutual glance. His expression reflected her suspicion that the squirmurs were somehow related to the storm. Killing them would kill the storm, no doubt.

Standing back-to-back, Vanessa and Arkon fired at the creatures. Vanessa didn't think about anything but destroying these horrendous monsters. It was why she was in Saedo. She dictated how she lived her life. This was her home now, and she would protect it and its citizens. Her new life would not be ruined by these damn worms. The circuitry on the squirmurs dimmed as if something drained them of energy. They took the opportunity and fired more blasts into the creatures.

She never imagined a day where she would hold an actual gun and be part of a real battle. It was beyond storytelling. Her partner in crime was the most stunning star-being, who minutes ago was pleasuring her in the most unforgettable ways. She wasn't finished with him yet. Hope sprouted in her soul because of him, and she wanted an opportunity to see where that seed would take her.

The sky brightened now that the eight squirmurs were dead; four of which had emerged from the restaurant. Two autobuses with flashing lights arrived. As they approached, she recognized the emergency autobuses, which were larger versions of police cruisers, and one fire longship, which was an upgraded fire engine with cutting edge equipment that could easily suppress the fire.

Parts of Happy Belly were ablaze, and Vanessa's heart quaked. Several soldiers jumped out of the autobuses and headed toward them. Dressed in black armor, Raeko and Maeson each gripped a large blaster in their hands.

Arkon signaled to them. "The eyes will kill them faster."

With that direction, Raeko, Maeson, and Arkon fired at the squirmurs beside Arkon.

Osayik hopped out of the fire longship and rushed over to Vanessa. He wore one of her sister's innovative fireproof jackets and pants. It was an idea Inga had come up with after her successful Ingavex collection debut a few weeks ago.

If Vanessa had one of the Ingavex jackets, would that help her kill the squirmurs? But that would require her to touch it, and she preferred killing the nasty things from a distance. Besides, she didn't know how the circuitry on the jacket would react to the circuitry in the worms. Would that create a deadly outcome for her? It was something she would have to tell Inga later.

"Are you okay?" Osayik asked with a blaster in hand.

"Yes. Kill the squirmurs in the eyes. They're creating this storm, or intensifying it."

"Those squirmurs are being controlled by a powerful satellite above the dark clouds. We destroyed it just now. Did you see any difference in the squirmurs?"

Vanessa thought back. "Yes, their circuitry did diminish."

"There's an energy source in this location that's birthing these nasty creatures. There are eggs and poisonous secretions in the soil. We need to eradicate them and clear out the poison. Stay in the longship. It'll be safe there. Call Inga and your other sisters to let them know you're safe."

Her body shuddered from the thought of a womb of eggs under her feet, under the restaurant.

Osayik waved over two soldiers who carried autopumps and activated a driverless fire-hoover. The machine hovered in the air rather than the fire-meanderer that scoured the land searching for victims. She had seen these robotic machines in action on the virtual screen when a fire erupted in one of the buildings near her apartment. They sent in these robots instead of live star-beings to search for any citizens that could have gotten stuck. This kind of invention could save so many firefighters on Earth.

Vanessa walked to the longship, but she didn't enter. She leaned against the sleek metal surface and kept her eyes on Arkon. With the blaster still in her hand, she prepared to shoot at any worms within her vicinity. The image of the weapon did something to her. She wasn't the same Vanessa from a year ago. The woman clutching this gun was a fighter, a survivor. She took matters into her own hands now.

Her attention stayed on Arkon as he and his brothers killed the last three squirmurs. Raeko aimed a massive blaster into the worm tunnel and fired out white energy bolts. The ground buzzed, and the zing of energy crawled up her leg. Her body vibrated from the powerful burst. Raeko repeated that action several times, until the squirmurs' wails stopped. He sprayed a blanket of white energy over the soil where the dead worms lay, probably disintegrating the poisonous residue.

The nerves inside Vanessa's stomach subsided as the dark clouds vanished, revealing a blue sky. Her body jerked as an invisible vacuum sucked the negative vibrations from her body. In that moment, Vanessa knew her intuition—the innate knowledge—that she could sense these foreign vibrations, both light and dark energies. So far, her body's reaction to everything was a signal that alerted her to trust her gut. When the negative vibrations left her body, it removed blockages from her mind too. This external and internal storm had stirred up a whirlwind of emotions for her. It removed the blockades that had trapped her true identity.

Her sixth sense had been blocked by fear and shame. Now it was back and heightened her intuition to a new level. Her surroundings affected her body. The uncomfortable nerves mimicked the thunderous storm, the calm representing the blue sky—the symbol hidden behind the dark clouds. Most of all, the sexual nerves signified her attraction to Arkon. No wonder she had stomach issues. A cauldron of various energies stirred within her, all wanting her attention.

Could her nightmares about Travis be part of the dark vibrations that left her body just now? Was this her body's way of releasing everything that didn't serve her? Intuition told her yes.

How should she deal with this ability? Which energy should she listen to first? This was a new level of sensory awareness she wasn't accustomed to. Vanessa prayed Grandma Ova could help her.

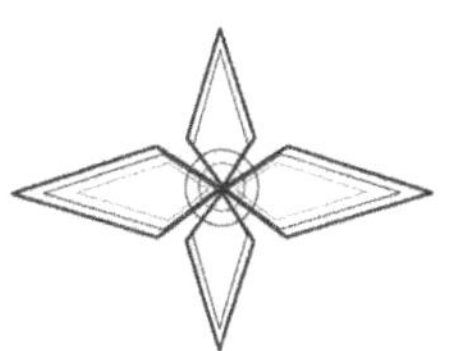

By the time Vanessa entered her apartment, it was around seven in the evening. Arkon stayed with his brothers to assist with the cleanup and discuss a plan to rebuild the area. Sixty percent of Happy Belly was destroyed, including the basement.

Abba was devastated, but she was grateful no one got hurt. She managed to find shelter with her family in their basement, so all was well with her. The Saedo government had a credit reserve to help their citizens. Not only that, the soldiers and any villagers who wanted to help Abba rebuild her restaurant could do so. With everyone's collaboration, Happy Belly could reopen in a month.

Vanessa jumped into the shower and washed off the day's filth. She let the three showerheads beat down on her face and body with warm water. With her eyes closed, images of squirmurs popped into her vision. She flipped her eyes open and shivered. Chills slithered down her body even though she was covered with steamy water.

Who had been watching them through the squirmurs' eyes? And why?

Her temples pounded, and she stopped thinking. She'd

exerted too much energy today. What her body needed was rest and sleep. She stepped out of her shower and plucked a long, fragrant leaf from the citric lotion plant and brushed it along her skin. The citrus smell offered a boost of energy. It reminded her of a clean lemon scent.

Dressed in her soft pajamas, Vanessa sat in her bed thinking. She skipped dinner because she didn't have an appetite. She leaned into her pillow and replayed the events of the day. She thought about Arkon and how he had come for her. So much had changed since that first day they chatted.

Heat bloomed in her center as she imagined the event in the basement before the squirmurs interrupted. She only wanted pleasant thoughts right before bed. Especially, when she needed to sleep. Nightmares would keep her awake, and she couldn't have that. Their kiss ignited a desire in her, welcoming the wild Vanessa to come forth and stake her claim. This was the Vanessa who believed in love and that anything was possible. One man had ripped that belief from her and used violence to threaten her life, keeping her in darkness. Now another man had reached out to her, offering her the freedom to be herself again.

Vanessa didn't even realize she was crying until a teardrop dripped onto her buzzing pendant. She collected herself before activating the video on the call from Sasha.

"Hey. You okay? Emma, Inga, Rita, Isabella, and Nina are all at my place. That was some wild storm out there. Do you want to come over?"

A girl's night out sounded lovely, but not tonight. "Other than extreme exhaustion, I'm okay. I'm about to fall asleep. How's everyone doing?"

"We're good. No one's hurt. Given the extent of the storm, I'm surprised there weren't more casualties."

She hadn't checked the village media. Her chest tightened, wondering about the aftermath. "How many casualties?"

"Maeson said only one star-being died, but he was already ill. Another star-being went after his pet and the strong gale swept him against a building. He's recovering now. Despite the danger, it seems like Saedo was blessed."

It could've have been a lot worse. Her stomach churned as if agreeing with her. When she used to read books on esoteric and new age stuff, she remembered that the mind was linked to the stomach. In college, her studies on eastern traditions stated that what happened in the mind was connected to the gut energetically, which was why when she was stressed, she got indigestion or heartburn, and her stomach inflated for no reason. Knowing this didn't really help decipher her current situation, but it allowed her a different perspective. There were various ways of looking at things.

Her stomach reacted to energy, and it was her job to filter through what was important at the moment.

"Maybe Saedo is blessed," Vanessa said. "We've witnessed a lot of magical things here. It wouldn't surprise me."

"There are a lot of damages to homes and businesses, but those can be replaced. You sure you don't want to come over and hang with your sisters?"

"Thanks, but after today's craziness, I just want to sleep. I'm going to check in on Abba tomorrow. Happy Belly will be closed for at least a month or so."

"I heard. I'm so sorry. Maeson and his brothers will be helping her rebuild. You rest up, and we'll chat soon."

Sasha blew her a kiss and disconnected.

For now, Vanessa was jobless. She didn't mind. She needed the time to learn about herself and this heightened ability. Her mind wandered back to Arkon. She had sensed his energy when he stood on the private patio. She didn't forget the purple mist that wrapped around her. If Saedo lore was true, then she was meant to be with him.

Arkon didn't know she saw his mist. Did it matter? She was attracted to him before she even saw the mist. But she didn't reveal anything because she was embarrassed about how she had reacted when he wanted to pluck the dried leaf from her hair, and she was cautious around handsome men who made her *want*.

She had wanted Travis back then. That desire blinded her and led her down a dark path. She had every right to be careful, every right to protect herself now. She traced the scar on her arm. Unlike before, she looked at the wound and felt no shame. This revelation intrigued her, and she had Arkon to thank for it. He had inspired her to see herself in a new light.

Her pendant buzzed again. She smiled when Arkon's face popped on the screen.

"Sorry, took me a while to get everything done. I wanted to contact you earlier. I was worried about you. Are you okay?"

"I'm fine. Getting ready for bed, actually. How are you doing? Are you home?"

He paused a moment, scrubbing a hand over his face. "I'm actually just outside your apartment."

"You are? Why?" *What a stupid question, Vanessa.*

He smiled. "I was worried and wanted to check on you. See if you needed anything. Is it okay if I come in?"

"Absolutely."

Vanessa clicked off and went to open the door for him. She thought *she* was exhausted. His worn eyes, slouched posture, and the bloodstains on his clothing made him look like he'd come back from war. Well, he did survive a dangerous battle.

"You don't look okay. Do you need something to eat, drink? How can I help you?"

"Can I shower here? I don't think I'll make it back to my

place. I have extra clothes that I always keep in my sports rider when I'm working. Sometimes an investigation can take you down a dirty path." He lifted a duffle bag and showed her.

"Of course. It's this way." She led him to her bathroom and offered him a fresh towel.

While he showered, Vanessa made some tea and warmed up Grandma Ova's herbal soup. Despite his exhaustion, he still worried about her enough to come and check on her. Warmth blossomed inside her.

Arkon strode out to the kitchen wearing a loose top and knit pants. They didn't look like sleepwear, but they weren't work attire either. The casual clothing brought on a different handsomeness. With his work shirt and high-tech denim, he always looked professional, ready for business. But this green man standing in her kitchen with his messy, towel-dried hair which wasn't tied back into a tail, looked approachable and sexy as hell.

He grinned when she didn't stop staring at him. "Like what you see?"

The previous Vanessa would have made some lame excuse or not replied at all. But she was now peeking out from her dark cave to explore. This adventurous Vanessa pursed her lips and said, "There's nothing wrong with admiring a beautiful man. It's like how I appreciate an enticing entrée when it's placed before me."

He strode up to where she sat on a stool at the kitchen island. "Oh, really? What kind of entrée am I, Vanessa?" His eyes darkened, displaying no signs of fatigue whatsoever.

She scanned his face. "That must have been some shower. You don't look exhausted anymore."

"You didn't answer my question. That was a lovely shower because I thought of you when I was lathering myself with your soap and shampoo." He leaned in and sniffed her neck. "I have your scent on me. I want to know what kind of entrée I am."

How did the evening change so quickly? Just moments ago, she was about to pass out. And now, she wanted to nibble him. What the hell was wrong with her? Arkon could invigorate her body the way no man had done before. He aroused her simply by looking at her.

She hadn't been with a man in a while, and this gorgeous star-being was testing her limits. The intensity in his eyes revealed he wanted her too. God help them. Sexual tension swirled in her apartment, and she prayed they could both rest tonight so they would have enough energy to tackle tomorrow's agenda.

She twisted her lips. "You're the kind of entrée that I won't share. The kind that's decadent, hypnotizing, irresistible..."

His eyes glittered with satisfaction as he inched closer and tipped up her chin. "Orgasmic." A wide grin stretched across his face. "That's what you were thinking. You were just too embarrassed to say it."

What was she going to do about him? He read her mind, read her body like they were his own.

"There's something different about you. I'm not sure what it is." He brushed her cheek with his knuckle. "Something untamed. Something mysterious. I love it. It's driving me crazy."

"It's a secret recipe. You can find out another time. You've had a rough day today, and I did—"

His lips were on hers, tasting and teasing. "I need a sample now." He took his time with the kiss, and she melted into him. Her back leaned against the kitchen island while his hard chest pressed against hers. She was deliciously trapped, with no desire to escape. He nudged her mouth open with his tongue. Upon contact with hers, he growled, deepening the kiss.

Her fingers dug into his shoulder, wanting more. But she

knew where they'd end up if she didn't stop now. She pressed a gentle hand to his chest and broke off the kiss.

"You captivate me like no other, Vanessa." He ran a thumb over her bottom lip.

"You enchant me like no other, Arkon."

He laughed. "If I didn't have a full day tomorrow where my brain is needed, then I'd have you right here on this kitchen island all night long." His expression turned serious. "I've never wanted anyone like this. What did you do to me?"

What did you *do to* me? But she couldn't muster the words. The more they chatted, the more the sexual tension increased.

She didn't speak, so he continued, "We have things to discuss. I want to know everything about you. I want to know how you learned how to shoot with my gun."

Her past came flooding back, but she didn't flinch. In fact, a calmness accompanied her. "Tomorrow, we'll talk." She reached for the bowl of herbal soup. "Eat this. It'll warm your stomach for tonight."

"Thank you." He considered her a moment before saying, "I'll sleep on the couch. It's wide and long enough for me. If I share your bed with you, we won't be sleeping tonight at all. And you look tired." He scooped up a spoonful and fed it to her. "I don't think you've eaten either. Open up. We can share this bowl of soup and then call it a night."

She eyed him at the unexpected gesture. Her lips opened before her brain even registered what she was doing. No man had ever fed her food, and she found the gesture extremely sexy.

EIGHT

Vanessa woke to a note on her nightstand. *Urgent meeting. We'll discuss your "secret" recipe tonight. See you soon.*

She blinked, sat up, and read the note again. What time did he leave for work? The time on her nightstand clock showed it was only six in the morning. She glanced out the bedroom window, and the two suns peeked above the horizon like egg yolks, one red and one orange. She stared at the beauty of it for a moment. The daily routine of waking up and getting ready didn't allow for introspection. She was living on another planet with her sisters and star-beings, who, months ago, hadn't existed in her mind.

Of all the places Vanessa could be, fate had placed her in Saedo. Was it a simple act of destiny, or was something else at work here? Did it matter? Overanalyzing was one of her problems, but didn't every woman do that? Sometimes it helped, but most times it complicated the matter even more.

For instance, last night, she enjoyed her flirtatious conversation with Arkon. She loved how he watched her lips take in the spoonful of soup. The way his chest rose and fell, trying to calm his breathing, revealed how much he wanted her. What were his previous mates like? Why wasn't he with anyone? More importantly, what kind of relationship did Vanessa want with him?

The thought of that kindled her heart. A committed relationship hadn't crossed her mind. But here she was thinking about it, *wanting* it, with Arkon. Did he want the same? Or was he only interested in something temporary? There was no doubt he wanted to sleep with her. She wanted the same, but physical intimacy often led to complicated things. Intimacy provoked attachment, commitment, and the desire for more. Was she ready for all that?

Stop thinking too much. You're going to give yourself a headache.

She listened to her inner voice. It knew her best and steered her back to reality. No point in driving herself crazy. She had a busy day ahead of her and needed her brain to function properly.

Despite that, she showered herself with joyful thoughts. The flirtatious conversation between them was something she relished. Where did she even come up with the idea for some damn "secret" recipe? She supposed she could invent something. An idea sparked in her and aroused her at the same time. Damn him.

Arkon lit the torch to her creativity, and now he was going to be its recipient. She wondered what she could do to disrupt his organized ways. His mind understood numbers and charts. What would happen if she introduced something that was the complete opposite of that? Would that intrigue or irritate him?

Before she could focus on her idea, she needed answers and guidance from Grandma Ova on a different matter. Danger lurked in Sacdo, and if she could help keep her new home safe, she'd do it.

"I wondered when you'd stop by to see me." Grandma Ova gestured for Vanessa to sit down on a white chair next to her. On a round table was a plate of pastries topped with floral petals, two mugs, and a pitcher filled with green liquid.

The back deck faced a flourishing herbal garden with fragrant flowers. A sweet scent snuck up her nose, and a small bird that resembled a goldfinch with six wings fluttered over to the table. It chirped a lovely song that made the flowers sway back and forth. Or was that her imagination? She didn't sense any strong breeze that could shift the herbal plants in this rhythmic way.

"Are the herbs reacting to the birdsong?"

Grandma Ova smiled and made chirping noises that drew the bird closer. She dropped a few seeds onto the table for the adorable yellow bird. "My plants love when these little felicitees grace them with their soothing melodies. With their six wings, they spread joy everywhere." She poured the green liquid into the mug and offered it to Vanessa. "This is a good way to start your day. It's a blend of my green lantern fruits and some healing herbs." She jerked her chin to a tree with purple leaves and green fruits dangling from it like lanterns.

Vanessa sipped the drink, and the sweet and sour taste reminded her of apple juice. She grabbed a fruit tart from the tray, bit in, and fell into heaven. "Oh, these are divine. What's in it? I could eat a dozen of these."

Grandma Ova chuckled. "The fillings are made from my calmberries." She pointed to a bowl with triangle-shaped purple berries. "They're not too sweet. They help calm and balance your nerves, help your body maintain equilibrium. When our bodies are out of balance, discomfort occurs."

The topic of nerves wasn't a coincidence. "Did you sense

something from me when we were at Sasha's house the other day?"

Grandma Ova tucked a lock of white hair behind her ears. The classic hairdo suited her face and was the result of Sasha's skilled handiwork. That reminded Vanessa, she needed a trim soon. The red mane was getting too long, too wild.

"I sensed your frequency that day. It was powerful, but I also knew you had no idea what was happening. I couldn't pry." She stared out at her garden. "There are certain things in life that need to be left to their own accord. I knew you'd come here. How? Intuition. Just like how you had a hunch to seek me out."

Vanessa nodded. "The nerves started about a couple of weeks ago. But they're stronger now. I sense all kinds of energies. Why am I feeling them now?"

Grandma Ova's eyes warmed. "First off, I want you to know there's nothing wrong with you. What you have is a gift from the divine. You've always had it, but it was dormant. Something kept it hidden, but it's waking up and nothing can hold it back now. You're ready to hone that skill."

"How do I know which feeling to listen to when I feel so many at the same time?"

"Experience. You learn to trust your gut. We all have this ability. Some are more in tune with it. I can't tell you how to read your emotions or senses. Your body, your gut will let you know." She patted her stomach. "Your stomach is very important. Your entire body is its own system. Some of us forget that. Your body will let you know the difference between a negative and positive energy, what is urgent and what is nonurgent. Energy can't really lie. It can mask itself for a while, but that gets tiring, and the true energy will eventually seep through. Your body will be able to read that. It'll take practice. Don't rush it."

Maybe her mom wasn't making things up about her great-

great-grandmother being a priestess. Maybe Vanessa inherited her gift.

"I've been sensing those squirmurs for the past two weeks. My stomach kept acting up, and I didn't know why."

"Those damn worms. I pray the soldiers will destroy every one of them."

"Why are they here? What's their purpose?"

Grandma's cheerful face turned somber. "They want to infect Saedo soil. Our province is blessed with fertile soil that can grow all kinds of vegetation. The energy in Saedo is exceptional."

"I think the squirmurs were doing more than just infecting the soil. Their eyes connected to the lightning in the sky."

"I have no doubt the Ulkrins are part of this. They've wanted this territory for too long. They need to be eradicated." Grandma Ova got up from her chair. "Come with me. I want to do a little experiment." She took Vanessa around the house to an area with more trees and bushes.

They approached a tree that had curly branches and blue leaves with orange veins. The shape of the leaf wasn't abnormal. It was almond-shaped, about four inches long. A hissing sound came from around her. She turned, looking for a bug or some animal.

"It's the tree." Grandma Ova pointed to a low branch hanging near Vanessa. "Touch it and see what happens."

What kind of test was this? Vanessa hesitated and furrowed her eyebrows. Suspicion rose in her, even though Grandma Ova had no reason to harm her.

Vanessa placed her hand on the veiny blue leaf. It hissed upon contact, and electricity beamed on its veins. "Shit!" She pulled her fingers away, fearing she'd get zapped. "What's going on?"

Grandma Ova smiled and reached for a leaf. Nothing

reacted with her contact. She plucked the leaf off the tree and twirled it around. "I was right. You have the counterpart of its frequency. There are polarities within everything. Male to female, light to dark, hot to cold. They are polarities."

Her conversation with Arkon about polarities flashed in her mind. *We exhibit energies that complement each other.*

Vanessa thought she knew some of what was going on with her body, but now?

"I don't understand at all."

"This tree. You have a frequency that resonates with it, therefore it reacted. You have its polarity. That's also a gift."

"Why me? I'm just a chef. I love to cook interesting dishes. What am I going to do with that gift of knowing and sensing?"

"Don't undervalue yourself, Vanessa. We all have a part to play in the Cosmos. It doesn't matter what your occupation is. What matters is in here." She tapped her chest. "Your corra. What's more important is how you use that gift. Will you use it to help or hurt someone?"

Vanessa twisted her lips, still trying to wrap her mind around the whole idea. Grandma Ova dropped the leaf into Vanessa's palm. "Get to know it. I'm certain it would love to know you. If you have any questions, I'm here. Or you can always call me."

The leaf warmed her hand, and the veins continued to illuminate. She pulled the small notebook out of her purse and placed it between two pages. Inside the notebook was a collection of ideas for recipes. She kept the book handy for when she needed to jot down ideas. She could pull up a virtual screen from her smart pendant, but there were some things she preferred the traditional way. She liked pen to paper.

Vanessa had one more thing to inquire before she went home. "I saw Arkon's purple mist. I didn't tell him yet."

Grandma Ova clasped her palms together, and her eyes beamed. "Oh, this is lovely to hear! It's a blessing, Vanessa."

"What if it doesn't work out?" Insecurity snuck in, but she couldn't help it.

Grandma Ova sighed. "You didn't tell Arkon because you wanted to see if he feels the same way without the purple mist swaying his emotions?"

It felt like a privilege to stand next to someone so wise.

"You know everything, don't you?" Vanessa smiled. She wanted to talk to someone about the purple mist. Someone who knew about its history. If she told her siblings, they'd tease her about it and wouldn't stop hounding her with questions.

"It comes with living a long time."

"I'm attracted to him," Vanessa said. "But I also want to be careful. I don't want to make... a mistake."

Grandma Ova embraced her. "As long as you listen to your corra, you won't. Your past is in your past. Use that lesson for this present moment." She brushed a hand down Vanessa's hair like a grandmother would do to her grandchild.

The gesture comforted Vanessa more than she thought. "Thank you for everything."

"You're welcome. Now, get going. I sense you have something exciting planned tonight?"

Heat flushed on Vanessa's cheeks. "I'm not sure what you're referring to."

Grandma Ova angled her head. "I remember those days. Don't be shy. Have fun. Show him the fearless you. Introduce him to things that are outside of 'numbers and charts.'"

Vanessa grinned. "I guess everyone knows him well."

"He needs a female who can show him a different way of evaluating and investigating. Drag him outside the box. Do it with finesse and he'll go willingly."

Grandma Ova wiggled her eyebrows.

Vanessa's shoulders shook from laughter. Sexual talk with someone who was older than her great-great-grandmother was more interesting than she could ever imagine. "I can't believe we're having this conversation."

Grandma Ova waved a hand. "There's nothing wrong with our conversation. We're two women having an intelligent discussion on sexual energy, which is a form of creative energy." She winked.

"Thank you for entertaining me." A thought popped into Vanessa's mind. "Maybe you could help me with this idea…"

When she shared it with Grandma Ova, the woman burst with laughter. "I thought I was innovative, but you? I love that creative mind of yours. Let's go inside. I'll show you how to make it work."

NINE

After spending another hour with Grandma Ova, Vanessa's mind sparked with a plethora of ideas. Not only did she have something exciting planned for Arkon, the menu she had been trying to create for her very own line of foods and snacks formed in her mind. Once she settled on the details for the innovative menu, she'd propose a collaboration with Abba. If Abba refused, then Vanessa would look for a venue to start her own restaurant. Excitement filled her, and she knew she was on the right track.

Grandma Ova's unique character added an amusing layer to Vanessa's day. She encouraged Vanessa to release any limiting beliefs that she wasn't good enough. Somehow, the wise star-being knew and lured the stories out of Vanessa. Vanessa shared her past and her intentions about Arkon.

Grandma Ova showed Vanessa her other gardens. The farming techniques opened Vanessa's mind to new possibilities she had never considered. If Earth had this mindset, then the human race could live longer and healthier lives. The star-beings in Saedo possessed ideas that enhanced their land, made it magical. Was this why other star races wanted to conquer them? Steal their treasured land? Why didn't those star races administer the same or similar methods to their own regions? She supposed that answer came down to the fact that it was easier to take over something already established than to start anew.

Lazy bastards.

She didn't want to waste any more energy on that thought. With enthusiasm, Vanessa rushed into her apartment with a bag of plants Grandma Ova prepared for her. Ideas on how to seduce Arkon pecked at her, each one wanting her attention. She dumped the plants onto her kitchen island and sorted them out.

She recalled the meal he ordered at the restaurant and concluded a man like him wanted meat. He had tried the Nelson meat pie along with a side salad. The old adage was that the best way to someone's heart was through the stomach.

On one hand, it might seem like she was indifferent to the fact that she had just fought squirmurs yesterday and the threat was still prominent. On the other hand, she didn't want fear looming over her head and stopping her from living. What was wrong with a little adventure to make the best of the moment? Absolutely nothing.

She pulled out her little notebook of recipes and set it aside in case she needed a reference. She didn't think so. What she planned was clear in her head.

She separated the herbs and vegetables she'd be using and replanted the others in her little indoor garden by the window. A chef needed all her ingredients handy when inspiration struck. From the pile on the counter, she grabbed a plant called hematiss. It had oval-shaped leaves with purple edges. The plant produced peapods that reminded her of soybeans, the difference being the purple color. Apparently, this hematiss plant imitated the flavor of blood in meat, including the texture. It could elevate her vegan dishes even more, and it also meant that fewer animals needed to die. She imagined what humans on Earth would think about this marvelous plant that also balanced the hemoglobin in the body. Vanessa thanked Grandma Ova for the short science lesson.

Tonight, Vanessa was going to experiment to her heart's desire. For the next few hours, she busied herself with chopping, blending, and searing a hematiss steak that mimicked the one on Earth. She tasted a sample and moaned.

"I like that sound coming from you."

Vanessa jumped at the voice inside her apartment. She whipped her head to Arkon, who leaned against the wall that separated the living room from the kitchen. His eyes glinted with curiosity while his thick arms crossed over his chest, studying her. He wore a white button-up shirt with the sleeves pushed up past his elbows and high-tech denim. Why did that casual outfit make him so seductive?

How long had he been standing there? "How did you get in? I didn't hear the doorbell. I didn't feel my pendant buzz either."

"The door wasn't locked."

She blew out a breath. "Must have forgotten to lock it when I rushed in." Her excitement to cook had blurred logic.

He stood beside her, and heat increased. "Why were you rushing?"

What should she say? *Oh, I'm just chopping up ideas on how to make you moan out my name. Or I'm creating something that'll make you ravish me.*

She decided to keep the surprise from him. "I was excited to cook you a meal." That was the truth.

"Oh really?" He peered over at the kitchen table where she had bowls and plates set up. "Whatever you're making smells delicious. When I came in and saw you immersed in your own world, I didn't want to interrupt you. I love watching you work. And now that I know you're making something for me, that's an extra treat." He rested a hand on her lower back. "It deserves a reward." His hand lowered and squeezed a butt cheek. "I couldn't wait to get out of my meeting to come see you. I've been thinking about you all day."

Desire pooled at her core. She placed the energetic knife down, fearing she might lose a finger with this sexual energy building between them. She swallowed, hoping to moisten her throat.

Arkon noticed and traced a finger along the throbbing vein on her neck. "I like how I make you lose focus."

She looked into those darkened eyes. "I'll be the one who makes you lose your concentration. Your sense of organization will scatter for me. *Because* of me."

Amusement flashed in his eyes as he considered her. "You've been scheming, haven't you? So calculating. I normally like knowing the solution ahead of time, but this intrigues the hell out of me. What do you have planned for me, beautiful?" He brushed away the hair that fell over her forehead. "Your hair is like you. So much fire, so much heat." His fingers tangled in her hair. "It drives me crazy."

Her heart thudded as intense energy swirled around them. A stream of purple mist emerged from behind him and snaked around her waist. She didn't point it out, and he didn't say anything. He was probably used to seeing his own mist color.

The mist ribboned around her, kissing the skin on her arm and hand. "You started the fire, and now you'll have to pay for it." She reveled in this freedom to tease without fear of repercussions, without the dreading that a man would put his hands on her.

"Why did it take so long for us to meet?" he asked.

She didn't have a chance to answer. His mouth covered hers, kissing her with desperation. "I can't wait for later. I want you now." He lifted her off her feet, placing her on the marble island. The stone cooled her inflamed body. He nudged her legs open and stood between them. His hand slid under the hem of her dress, moved up to her thigh, and cupped her breast. "I'm hungry. Let's cook something now." A mischievous smile slanted in a way that promised delicious things.

"Are you playing chef?" She challenged him, and the green of his skin darkened a shade. How come she didn't notice that before? "Your skin changes color?"

"Only when I'm exceptionally aroused. If I'm the chef, then that makes you my main course."

In seconds, her dress was on the floor, leaving her with only a sheer black lingerie set she had worn specifically for this evening. The bra barely covered her breasts, and the diamond-shape of the panties locked his eyes to that area. She bought this set a week ago to support Inga's new lingerie collection made from edible fabrics. The one she chose had a provocative flavor with an extra surprise.

His hands cupped her breasts, and she arched toward his touch. "You're so perfect." He had amazing hands with amazing thumbs that did amazing things to her. Her brain melted, and she blamed that for her repetitive words.

She wanted to see all of him. She tore off his shirt, and a button bounced off the wall. Did she really do that? This wildness in her had been repressed for too long. An eyebrow arched, and his gaze followed the button as it clinked to the floor and rolled somewhere.

He faced her with amusement in his eyes. "You're so ferocious. It's shocking and I love it."

Vanessa smiled at the adjective no one had ever used to describe her before. She had a ferocity to live up to now. She yanked the leather strap from his hair. The messy mane of brown hair fell just past his chin and framed his angular face perfectly.

The green of his skin fluctuated, and his brown eyes glowed copper, revealing the need coursing through him. The same desire scorched through her, but she wanted this moment to examine him, like a chef understanding her ingredients before she started her masterpiece. Her fingers traced the strong lines on his broad shoulders and caressed the curve of his bulging biceps. Her fingers traveled to the thick pectoral muscles and slid down to his firm abdomen. Each movement was a claim to a territory that now belonged to her. He was hers.

How could anyone be this impeccable? Her hand remained on his rock hard abs as she pondered using it as a chopping board to mince herbs.

"Your touch is tearing me apart," he said in a husky voice. He gripped her hips, pulling her closer.

Vanessa wrapped her legs around his waist like a snake ready to jump her target. He clamped his mouth over hers, and his tongue swept in and sent a jolt straight to her core. His playful tongue tantalized hers. The muscles in her loins tightened as an internal tornado spun her in a dizzying storm of pleasure. She couldn't think, couldn't breathe.

Arkon intensified the kiss as she clawed his shoulders and back, digging her nails into his flesh. Need coiled inside her as she wanted more. Subtlety did not exist at the moment. He offered feistiness, and she gave it right back. She moaned out a pleasure that she didn't recognize. Was that a purr from her?

He tasted like a savory blend of spices, so musky, so male. His scent of cedarwood with a hint of nutmeg tossed her into another whirlwind that rocked her body.

"I can't get enough of you." He lowered her to the counter, his mouth skimming the column of her neck.

Fire followed his every touch. She slipped into another world, and the room blurred, leaving only her and the raging need that begged for more. This was the intimacy she craved, the kind that hadn't been accessible to her until now. This green man worshipped her like she was some damn goddess. She quivered when his hand found her wet center, and his mouth claimed a nipple through the sheer edible bra.

At the taste, he lifted his head. "Sinful cocktail flavor? I'll take damnation if that means I can have you. I'm going to devour every inch of this bra."

He feasted on her breasts, one after the other, eating away the thin layer of fabric laced with an intoxicating blend of cocktails. As he savored, lights hissed and sparkled from the contact of lips to material. He let out a sound like a satisfied animal. The innovative construction of this bra deserved an applause, especially when Arkon growled, "More."

True to his words, he licked every inch of the edible cuppings. She watched him savor her, and a bolt of need slashed through her. She loved how his mouth mapped around her breasts, over and under. Her body responded to every kiss, lick, and bite, hips bucking against the bulge of him.

"You have no idea what you're doing to me. I'm burning inside." The copper in his eyes reflected her fire.

Her heart hammered knowing she lit the spark in him. She entered the wildfire storm with him, not fearing if she got scorched. Vanessa heard fabric rustle and the clank of his belt dropping to the floor. On her elbows, she studied the magnificence of him, gasping at his size. The glorious length of his manhood beckoned her.

Arkon leaned over, lowering her back onto the marble island. "I'm not done with my entrée yet." He spread her legs and palmed her tiny diamond-shape underwear that clung to her skin like magic. "What flavor is this?"

She couldn't find her voice to answer. When his mouth pressed into her secret place, she cried out his name and writhed from the onslaught of pleasure.

"Decadent chocolate. My kind of dessert." His hands lifted her buttocks, ravishing her like she was his meal.

Waves of pleasure whipped her from side to side. She gripped his hair, holding on as the tornado tore through her, rippling down her spine. "Arkon..."

A shuffle of clothes sounded as he retrieved the Safe-Sex Spray and covered himself. Curiosity had her reaching for his bulge. An interesting texture coated the surface. "This adds a unique sensation when I'm inside you."

Their eyes met, and he slipped into her. A moan escaped him as he dove deeper and deeper. The texture added a new layer of sensitivity that sent pleasure skyrocketing through her. She loved connecting with him this way. She sat up and wrapped her arms around his neck, dragging his mouth to hers. They moved in rhythm as he continued to thrust into her. Each thrust broke a barrier until all that was left was her bare soul and the truth of her heart.

At that acknowledgment, purple mist encircled them. The mist knew what was best for her before she did. Now, she confessed it to be true. Now, she *felt* its power.

His body tensed, and his heart hammered. Feeling power-ful, she intensified the kiss and pushed him further into his own monsoon. With a forceful thrust, he bellowed her name, and she'd never heard anything more delightful. His body convulsed as she wrapped her arms around him, embracing him. The tender gesture surprised even her. She clung to this sensation that overwhelmed her heart. Love glittered like stars, and she couldn't avoid it.

His strong arms cradled her as his chin rested on her head. "That was some course. The best recipe for an out-of-this world con-*coc*-tion." His manhood throbbed at the statement.

Laughter burst from her. "You have a dirty mind." When was the last time she had so much fun with a man?

"I'm like most males. I'm just honest about it." He pulled out of her, the contraceptive spray dissolving on his length. A sly smile curved on his lips. "But I think *your* mind is more creative than mine. I bet it's *messier* and *dirtier*. I see it in your eyes. Show me."

Arkon saw her true self, and that perception deserved a reward. Vanessa pushed her recipe notebook aside and reached for her bag. She dug out a container, picking out a translucent blue petal that reminded her of a rose. The petals were infused with the midori melon drink that Grandma Ova helped Vanessa mix. Grandma Ova had a trellis of these blue melons.

Still naked and baring everything to her, he eyed the petals. "What are those?"

"Something that's going to inspire you to look at things differently." She slid down from the kitchen island and held out a petal that had a massaging property. "You had your turn. Now it's *my* main course."

She gripped the length of him and placed one delicate petal over him. It wrapped and tightened around him like a second skin.

His breath hitched, and he let out a delightful curse. "Flekken! What are you doing to me?"

She smirked and pulled out the stool, nudging him down. He leaned into the back of the stool, watching her every move. He trembled as she placed the other five petals onto his length. His breathing increased, and lust filled his eyes.

On her knees, Vanessa gripped him. "It's going to massage and tingle and end with a cooling sensation."

"Flekken."

She displayed her creative skills and proved that her spontaneous culinary invention would be a bestselling novelty item.

TEN

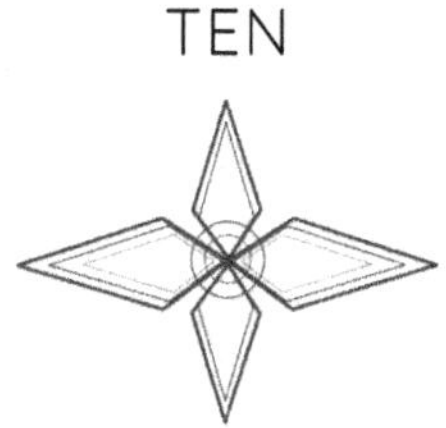

Hours later, Vanessa curled up on the couch with Arkon, fully clothed.

A smile beamed on his face. "You invented those... things? They're genius."

Pride swelled in her chest. "I did. You inspired me to explore my creativity. It doesn't have a name yet. I'm thinking once I save up enough credits, I can open my own restaurant, my own food boutique."

He looked at her. "Is that your dream?" He took her hand in his, and his gaze landed on the scar on her arm.

"Yes. I stopped dreaming after..." Her body stiffened. Was she ready to tell him?

"After?"

She inhaled a gulp of air and prepared to bare everything to him.

Arkon stared at the scar, and his thumb caressed the wound as if his movement could wipe it from her. "Did it have anything to do with this mark?"

Vanessa nodded. "Unfortunately, yes. For the longest time, I pushed my dreams aside. I had to work on myself first before I could go after those dreams again."

"No one has the power to take away your dreams. No one." His voice carried a lethal edge she hadn't seen in him. His eyes steeled. "Who needs to die for this? What's his name? Where is he? I can get a spaceship there and do what I need to do in no time."

His protectiveness shifted something in her. No man had ever wanted to protect her this way. "Don't waste your energy on him. I've put it all behind me. He's my ex-husband, and he's in prison for a long time. I wasn't the only one he abused."

Though his voice was calm, its thunder rippled through her. "What did he do to you? I want to know everything."

Arkon listened as Vanessa spilled the darkness from her past. "It all started with the verbal abuse when I didn't deliver dinner on his favorite plate with his favorite drink. The name calling wasn't enough for him, so he got physical. I remember the first time my lips bled from his attack. I was shocked and confused. How could someone who claimed to love me, hate me so much?"

Arkon's face tensed. Vanessa placed a gentle hand on his cheek, letting him know the horror no longer bothered her. The story flowed out of her like a river traveling toward the ocean and dumping all the unnecessary things at the delta to start anew. Arkon was her ocean, her new beginning. Revelation dawned on her. She was no longer haunted by Travis, her dark past because she found something brighter. She found Arkon.

With that thought in her heart, Vanessa continued. "I didn't want to believe that the abuse was really happening to me. Shame and guilt overwhelmed me. I thought everything was my fault. I turned to cooking as my salvation. It was something I loved before I met and married him, so I knew I was good at it. The process of making something from my heart saved me and kept me sane. I had hoped that he'd change one day. It wasn't until he took my favorite knife—the one I used to cook his dinner—and threatened me and my siblings that something snapped in me. It was as if that blade cut away the mental chord he had around me. I called the police, left him that day, and warned my siblings of his threats just in case he'd follow through on them. I filed for divorce. Then I signed up for the shooting range because I feared he'd come after me. I killed a little fear each time I shot into that dummy. After a while, I got good at it."

Arkon didn't interrupt and gave her enough time and space. When she finished, he released a heavy sigh, and his jaw clenched.

"I could kill him for what he did to you. There's no excuse for that kind of behavior."

"He's slowly dying behind bars. He's claustrophobic, so the punishment is fitting. He's suffering."

Arkon pinched the space between his brows. "I can live with that for now."

His concern for her brought back the wish she had tossed out into the Universe that fateful night. *I deserve a man who loves me regardless of my wounds.* Could Arkon be him?

Vanessa's heart thudded at that thought. Deep inside her, she knew. But did he feel the same way about her? She wasn't referring to the obvious physical attraction. Did he love her the way she loved him?

Her body shivered from that admission. There was no shame in loving someone, even if the person might not love you back. Could she deal with that? She wasn't sure, and she was afraid to ask. At this moment, her vulnerability was too high. She couldn't withstand that kind of blow to her heart, so Vanessa kept that emotion to herself for now.

"You know my darkest secret, but I don't know yours. I have

questions," Vanessa said. "What's your dream? Your worst fear?"

The question softened his expression. "I have a younger sister, Ameeya. My parents died in a spaceship accident a while ago. My dream is just starting to form now. Before that, I didn't have one." He looked at her. "But my fear is losing my corra."

He didn't answer her question, but she let it pass. She focused on other aspects of his response. No parents and a fear of losing his heart showed they shared some similarities. "I feel like I have so much to learn from you."

He flashed a wide smile. "I'm willing to teach you anything you want. In and out of bed." His eyes twinkled with mischief.

Purple mist emerged and floated around them. She waved a hand through the purple ribbons. "I've never seen purple mist until Saedo."

He flicked her a glance. "You see it too? You see my mist color?" The somber expression twisted her stomach. "When did you first see it?"

"When we were on the private patio."

"Do you know its significance? Why didn't you tell me sooner?"

"I heard about it, but I wasn't sure if it was true." Why did she feel like she did something wrong? "I didn't tell you because I didn't think it mattered. It's Saedo lore that could be true, or not."

The distrust in his eyes stabbed her heart. The indignation on his face and the muscle twitch on his jaw revealed someone who wouldn't listen to reason right now. Why was he angry at something so trivial? She realized she didn't know his past. Did he have monsters that gripped him the way hers did?

Nerves churned her stomach. The unease brought her mind back to the squirmurs. How was Saedo going to destroy these monsters?

Arkon's wristband buzzed, and he pulled up a video screen displaying Raeko. "Can you meet us at Derwood Creek? The radar just picked up a squirmur nest. We need to eradicate it."

Arkon got up from the couch, heading toward the door. "Why didn't we catch this earlier?"

"I don't know. Something's masking it from the radar. I'm rounding up as many soldiers as possible. The Guards of Finntoro will meet us at the border. They don't want any squirmurs invading their land. Make sure you have your armor. It could get ugly."

Vanessa's chest constricted from Raeko's words.

"I'll be there as soon as I can. I have my uniform in my rider. I'll change when I get there." Arkon disconnected and faced Vanessa with concern. "I have to go now. We'll talk when I return. Don't go out."

With that, he left her apartment, leaving her confused and crushed.

ELEVEN

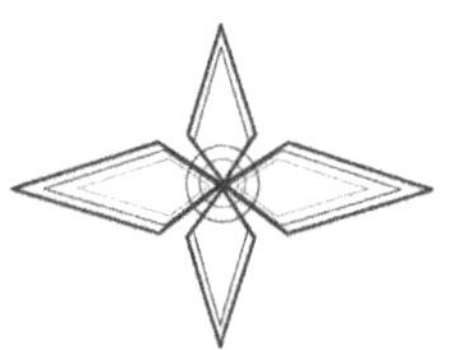

What exactly just happened between them? Why was he offended that she didn't tell him about the purple mist? Was that detail so important to him? What did she miss?

Sadness and disappointment washed over her, making her feel exposed. Feeling cold, she wrapped her arms around herself, protecting something she didn't know. She didn't see her relationship with Arkon lasting. Their communication was off. It was better to step back before things got more serious.

But things were already serious. She was already in love with him. It happened faster than she wanted. The heart worked in strange ways that she couldn't control. The icy way Arkon looked at her knifed her in the chest. The distrust and the disgust in his eyes pushed her away.

No man had the power to make her feel little again. She had been truthful all along, and if Arkon didn't see that, then he wasn't worth it. He didn't deserve her.

The more she thought about it, the angrier she grew. Anger cramped her stomach, like someone was twisting her intestines into knots. The unexpected pain grabbed her attention. Something awful was about to happen.

A hissing sound echoed in her apartment. With a hand to her stomach, she tried to locate the sound. It came from the notebook. She flipped it open to the blazing blue leaf Grandma Ova had gifted her. The veins on the leaf brightened to an electric blue. The leaf rose from the page and floated in front of her. Vanessa didn't sense any fear from it. If anything, its presence soothed the ache in her stomach. The buzzing of the leaf calmed her nerves.

How did she know that? She just did.

Her heart leaped when the leaf swayed back and forth as if a breeze was inside her apartment. It suspended itself in front of her face, and the leaf morphed into a single eye, greeting her.

"Holy shit." Instincts pushed her back a few steps from the floating eye. Was it real?

Logic told her to run from the freaky image, but something else held her in place. Again, Vanessa didn't sense fear, and the eye wasn't bloody or gory. Power radiated from it, asking her not to fear. Her mind understood the request.

She chose to listen to it.

An ancient wisdom entered her mind. The eye blinked, floated closer to where she stood, and images formed within the eye that created a little portal she could look into. Colors and abstract images jumbled together.

Don't fear us. We're here to help. You have energy that resonates with us, and that makes you important. He needs your help. Saedo needs your help.

A sincere truth rang with those words and settled in Vanessa's stomach. Within her stomach was a battle between nerves that shouted something was wrong and gentle nerves that calmed her. She reminded herself that these sensations were merely guiding her, making her aware of her environment.

The eye-leaf expanded like a movie screen. It showed Arkon fighting off squirmurs larger than the ones they fought earlier. A red squirmur with a bright beam on its forehead monitored on the side. Was this a snapshot of the future? Arkon wore the same outfit he had when he left her apartment minutes ago. He was all by himself. Where were his brothers? Why weren't they helping him?

Dark clouds emerged from the squirmurs, creating a storm around Arkon.

He needs you. Go to him.

Though her stomach twisted in knots, the calming energy enabled her to decide with a clear head.

First, she sent Arkon a message. "Are you okay? Where are you?"

While she waited for a reply, she retrieved the blaster he gave her the other day and changed into high-tech knit pants and a long-sleeve top. The dress she wore wouldn't help in battle. She never considered herself a fighter, but here she was, fighting for a man who changed her life.

No reply came from Arkon. Maybe he was too busy fighting off the squirmurs.

Vanessa didn't know if the eye-leaf could understand, but she asked anyway. "How can I help?"

You'll know what to do. Trust your intuition. The eye of the storm will show you.

One thing she learned with all this "magical" wisdom was that nothing was ever clear. Messages lay between the gray areas, the "this and that." Perhaps they didn't want to toy with her free will. If they told her exactly what to do, would that change the outcome? If they let her choose, then she made her decision all on her own.

Arkon needed her, and that truth surged in her heart. No matter what had happened between them, she loved him. There was nothing wrong with loving someone. If anything, Arkon inspired her to stand strong and acknowledge the survivor she was. She no longer feared her past. She reclaimed her dreams, and she reveled in the fact that she could explore her creativity in ways she never imagined. Arkon opened that door for her when he opened her heart.

Vanessa didn't have time to contemplate. The energy from the eye burst in her apartment, pulsing against her body as a portal opened. Not knowing where the portal would take her, Vanessa stepped forward. With Arkon's safety prominent in her mind, she entered the storm, figuratively and literally.

TWELVE

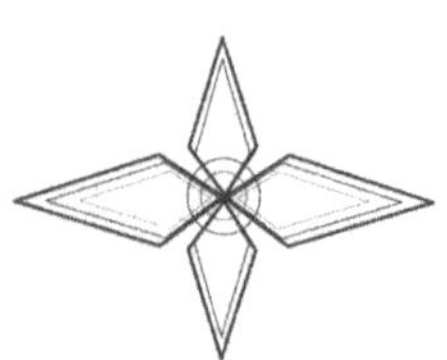

Inside the portal, total darkness and silence enveloped her, nudging her forward toward the gathering of twinkles that beckoned her. Intuition told her this silence was the space between worlds, between the inexplicable scopes of time.

As Vanessa approached the twinkles, the wind howled, and lightning slashed. *This is our land now. You must leave.* The words boomed louder than when she heard it the first time in the basement.

The tunnel of light splashed a screen that showed the danger before her. A squirmur leaped at Arkon, while another whipped its segmented body at him. He fell to the ground.

"Arkon!"

Vanessa fled through the portal, and the opening closed behind her. The blue leaf hung in the air, sizzling with energy. She gripped it, and the energy seeped into her skin, into her blood, into the marrow of her being. Her body shuddered and buzzed.

What the hell? Vanessa had questions, but she didn't have time to waste. She tucked the leaf into the front pocket of her pants and clutched the blaster tucked in the back of her waistband. She aimed the blaster at the squirmur and fired. Through the thunder and wind, Arkon didn't notice or hear her until the squirmur wailed from her blast.

Arkon whipped his attention to her and rushed over. "Vanessa! What are you doing here? How did you get here?"

Genuine concern flashed in his eyes instead of the distrust from earlier.

"I came to rescue you." *Like how you rescued me and my sisters.*

Despite the danger surrounding them, he smiled. "Be careful. These squirmurs aren't like the ones we battled. These are stronger, smarter."

The wind howled again like someone was blasting the words through the speakers.

On cue, the squirmurs thrashed their bodies and electricity glowed through their skin. Arkon fired at them, but only sent the electricity sparkling. Thunder lit up the sky, and that was when she saw his rider smashed against the tree. The broken road looked like an earthquake had occurred.

Ten squirmurs surrounded them, buzzing with electricity that matched the brilliant blue lightning in the sky. The red one, the one who had been eyeing them from the side, wailed a command. In that moment, Vanessa's body hissed.

Arkon gawked at her, and worry wedged in his forehead. "Are you okay?"

She glanced at her body, and electricity coursed through her, flashing like the squirmurs. The only difference was that hers was purple. Heat warmed her, but not in an uncomfortable way. In fact, confidence and power surged through her veins. Intuition kicked into gear, and she knew what to do.

As the squirmurs approached, Arkon stepped in front of her, protecting her. That simple movement confirmed he still cared for her, and whatever happened today, they'd resolve their personal issues.

She reached for him, but stopped, fearing her touch might electrocute him. A squirmur cried out as it twisted its fat body toward him. Vanessa moved around Arkon, and punched the worm right in the eyes. Her circuitry blasted into the squirmur's body. The force of the contact threw her away from the squirmur and she fell on her butt. Arkon ran over and assisted her up. Purple energy took over the electric blue of the worm. The worm exploded, and the spying device embedded behind its eyes flew out and thudded near Vanessa's foot.

"They're flekken watching us! I'm going to kill those damn Ulkrins!" Arkon blasted the device, and a loud hissing erupted in the sky.

The red squirmur cried out, and the bloody beam on its forehead brightened. A laser aimed at Arkon's chest, and a second one landed on her chest. Fear crippled her, and Arkon reached for her hand. A surge of purple mist grew from his body and hers. The squirmurs moved toward them, but the mist spun around and kept them at bay. Thunder roared and the wind increased, howling and whipping things around. A cyclone of twigs, leaves, rocks, and other debris spiraled around them.

The purple mist increased in size and density, taking over the cyclone that trapped them. The mist became its own storm, spinning and spinning. As it spun, it pushed the debris away, keeping Vanessa and Arkon at the center of the storm. The mist moved of its own volition. The wind and the lightning didn't affect it.

Something urged Vanessa to reach out and connect to the purple vapors. On contact, the purple electricity from her body joined the mist and illuminated the entire area. The red squirmur retreated from the burst of purple energy. It cried out as if calling for help. The squirmur's storm increased, lightning enlarged, and thunder screamed louder. Despite the chaos, Vanessa sensed a calmness.

You'll know what to do. Trust your intuition. The eye of the storm will show you.

The voice from the eye-leaf echoed in her head. Arkon blasted a squirmur that broke through the soil near her foot. She gripped his hand and squeezed. "We need to kill the red squirmur with our fused energies."

He didn't object; he didn't ask any questions. He just nodded, giving her his trust.

Vanessa wasn't sure what she was doing. All she knew was that she had to listen to this inner voice guiding her.

She reached into her pants pocket and pulled out the blue leaf. Energy sizzled from it. She held it out and looked at Arkon. "Together."

Both held an end part of the leaf, and purple energy vibrated from it, rippling out to the vicinity. Purple lightning with vapors surrounding it shot up into the sky and broke the squirmur's storm apart. They shifted her body toward the red squirmur that was crawling away, and with their intentions, a purple bolt of lightning lashed into the creature. Red flesh splattered everywhere. A device clanked by her foot.

Arkon kicked it aside. "We can dissect that for information."

Still holding onto the leaf, they each turned in different directions and targeted the various squirmurs. Their intentions sent blades of power toward the creatures. When they had obliterated all the squirmurs, they aimed the leaf toward the sky. A powerful spear with purple mist shot straight up. A thunderous explosion erupted in the sky. Another explosion followed elsewhere, then another like a domino effect. The explosions went on for another minute.

Vanessa turned to Arkon. "What's happening?"

"We just destroyed whatever brought the storm. The

Ulkrins are working with another star race to create a device that could send storms to other regions. Saedo is a treasured land. We have great resources, and they want Saedo. They won't stop until we stop them."

Vanessa glanced up at the night sky that was now cloudless with the moon glowing brightly. She picked the device up from the red squirmur and offered it to Arkon. "What happened on your way to your brothers?"

"The squirmurs blocked my path." His wristband buzzed.

Raeko appeared on the screen. "You okay? What happened? We were all worried."

While Arkon explained to his brothers, Vanessa glanced at the leaf in her palm. "Thank you for your guidance."

Thank you for listening, and thank you for trusting yourself. We'll see you soon.

Vanessa tucked the leaf back into her pocket, and Arkon came up beside her. "The emergency crew will be here soon to clean up and retrieve the device. We'll hitch a ride home. Is it okay if I spend the night at your place? We have some things to discuss."

She reached up and wiped the blood smear from his face. She didn't want any squirmur residue marring his handsome face. He clasped her hand and placed it over his heart.

A smile bloomed on his face. "Thank you for coming to my rescue. I didn't expect that at all. I wanted you safe at home, where nothing could harm you. And here you are, fighting beside me with a blaster and a blue leaf. No female has ever done that for me."

Vanessa didn't know what to say. She handed the blaster back to him.

"No, you keep it. You handled yourself well with it. All those classes you took paid off."

They sure did.

"That leaf is exceptional, and I want to hear all about it." Regret swam in his eyes. "I'm sorry for my behavior earlier. There are some things you don't know about me, and it's time that you do. After you hear what I have to say and decide to walk away from this relationship, I'll understand."

That idea suffocated her. What was he going to tell her? Was this a good time to let him know she loved him? Was there a good time for that kind of confession?

If he was going to her tell her something that broke her, then she should bare her heart now. A shattered heart had nothing to share.

"The leaf showed me you were in trouble, and I came because... because I've fallen for you." She met his eyes. "Despite what occurred between us, or what may happen later, you've opened my heart—my corra—in a way no man has done before."

He tipped her chin up. "Are you telling me you love me?"

Vanessa lifted a shoulder. "It sounds like it."

"I love the sound of that." He pulled her in for an embrace. "I feel the same. I know the emotion is still new between us, but it's so strong I can't ignore it. But just because it's new and hasn't had time to develop appropriately, doesn't mean it's not real. I've realized that things don't follow a linear pattern, and that no organization, no charts, could ever determine a specific outcome. I've learned to accept the idea that it's okay to not follow a straight line."

"Are you telling me I've inspired you to think outside the box?"

He smirked. "It sounds like it." He ran a thumb across her cheek. "All I ask is for you to keep an open mind about what I have to say."

He had no idea how wide her mind had opened.

THIRTEEN

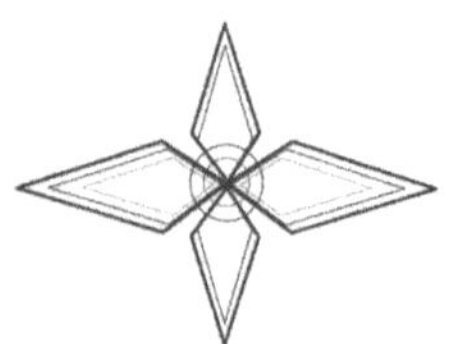

Vanessa woke up early the next day and made breakfast. She created her version of vegan sausages, meat cakes from the hematiss plant, and fruit pancakes. Arkon was still sleeping in her bedroom. When they got home last night, both of them were exhausted. After a shower together to wash away the filth of squirmurs, they passed out in her bed.

It had been a while since she last had a man in her bed. She loved waking up with Arkon's warmth. His presence felt right. Purple mist continued to swirl around her apartment, and she was getting used to it. She tucked the blue leaf in a special box by her bedside. Its energy had subsided, and that told her the threat was eliminated for now. The erratic nerves that had gnawed at her stomach also disappeared.

Thinking back, her body had been giving her signs about the danger all along. Though she didn't know exactly what it was, the discomfort was a signal to be extra cautious, to be aware of her surroundings, and to notice little symbols. Like her intuition, her body was giving her clues in its own way. She embraced her ability now and promised to practice more. Perhaps one day, she could communicate with the eye-leaf and even the mist. One important thing she learned in Saedo was that possibilities and magic were endless.

She steered her attention back to the task at hand and went to her indoor garden to cut some chives. A purple bloom had appeared between all the herbs. Or rather, the herbs appeared like protectors to the flower. This flower signified her union with her starmate. A blessium grew in her garden, but hers had two opened purple petals that appeared like two hands offering up something or receiving something.

Did that image mean anything? Probably, but she didn't have the brain power to dissect the symbolism.

"Well, hello there." Vanessa studied the flower. "It's good to see you."

Arkon wrapped an around her waist. "Are you talking to your plants again?"

Too focused on the flower, she didn't hear him walk up. His hair was tied back with the leather strap, and he smelled of her citrusy toothpaste.

"I'm talking to a flower. A purple flower that looks like it's breathing out purple mist."

Arkon stared at it and looked at her. "I guess the Saedo lore is true. We're starmates. We're meant to be together." With a hand on each shoulder, he swiveled her toward him. "Together, we're stronger. Just like last night, we destroyed those heinous creatures as a team."

The flower sighed and caught their attention. The purple mist emerged from the flower and formed an abstract shape. "It's a face."

"Looks more like an eye to me." Arkon angled his face, trying to gauge what shape the vapors made.

"Maybe it's both, part of the same thing." She stared up at him. "I want to research Saedo lore. I think we need to gather all the information to fight the Ulkrins. We stopped the squirmurs this time. But what else are they planning? We need to be prepared."

Arkon veered back and smiled. "You're right, and I love that you care for Saedo. Chief Mozar and my brothers are working out a plan. The Guards of Finntoro helped my brothers destroy the squirmurs' nest last night. Apparently, the Ulkrins stationed an energetic cloud around that area that masked the nest from our radar. Maybe their fake cloud malfunctioned and that allowed our radar to pick up the traces. It's hard to tell because we obliterated all of their energetic clouds and satellites last night from the explosion. Raeko mentioned he felt the soil ripple with energy."

"Did he ask you questions about it?"

"I gave him a brief explanation. I was too tired. He can get the long story from you if he wants to." He led her to the kitchen table and sniffed at the breakfast she made for him. "I could wake up every morning like this. We can discuss that after I tell you what I didn't get to say last night." He nudged her down on the seat and scooted his chair closer to her.

"Are you ready to share it? If you're not ready, I can wait. I'm not going anywhere."

"I've been ready, and I've been waiting for the perfect time to tell you. But then you surprised me about the purple mist, and I overreacted." He reached for her hand. "I used to have a mate. She told me she saw my mist, and I believed her. I didn't have any reason not to. We were together for five solar cycles. She inspired me to step out of my comfort zone. Do spontaneous things that didn't have an absolute answer. Then one day, she wanted to end things, telling me that she was in love with someone else. She confessed she never saw my purple mist. She knew about the lore connecting starmates, and everyone understood they were rare, so she created a lie to get it. I was too blinded by love to think otherwise."

Vanessa's heart ached for him. "I'm sorry to hear that. Love makes you do strange things, and I don't say that to excuse her actions. But love has its lessons for all of us, including me. I was blinded by love too. But none of that was my fault. If we're genuine in our feelings, then it's never our fault."

"I was afraid to step out of my comfort zone again when I met you. But my feelings for you were too powerful to ignore. I had no choice. Being with you taught me that possibilities are endless, and yes, there could be more than one answer to things."

Vanessa beamed with pride. "I'm learning that an absolute answer isn't so bad either. It depends on perspective. We're an absolute couple, and nothing can change that. One plus one is two. Me and you, forever."

"How did I end up with such a wise woman?" The copper in his eyes brightened, and she saw her reflection in them. "When you told me you saw my mist, the betrayal from the past resurfaced and punched me in the gut. The pain came back and I couldn't think clearly. I was falling for you too fast, and I couldn't understand it. Questions bombarded me. Were you telling me the truth? Why didn't you tell me sooner? What were you trying to achieve? A storm of emotions whipped inside me at the moment, and I needed space to think things through before I could talk to you."

Vanessa squeezed his hand. "I'm not like her. I didn't lie to you. I would never do that. Communication is important to me, it's the one thing that will make or break a relationship. I value what we share with each other." She looked him in the eye. "I didn't tell you because I was afraid. I was afraid you'd want me *because* of the lore. I wanted to be sure that you were attracted to me regardless of fate. I wanted to know you cared for me because you wanted to."

Arkon pursed his lips, thinking. "You didn't want the lore to influence my decision to be with you."

"Exactly."

"I respect that." He lifted her hand, flipped it over, and kissed her palm. "Remember you asked me what my dream was? I didn't give you a direct answer because I didn't want to frighten you. My dream is to be with you, to make a life with you." His hand rubbed the scar on her arm. "I love everything about you, from your scars, to your mind, to your creativity, and to your dirty culinary aspirations. Everything." His smile stretched for miles. "That novelty is going to be a bestseller. I just know it. I volunteer to be your test subject, your only test subject."

She laughed even as tears rolled down her cheek. Her wish to the Universe echoed in her mind. *I deserve a man who loves me regardless of my wounds.* She closed her eyes and acknowledged her appreciation. *Thank you.*

Arkon offered her a tissue. "I have an idea that could make us great business partners. I'm good with numbers, and you're fabulous with your culinary creativity. In fact, you're the most effective and dangerous chef I know." He leaned in closer. "You could essentially kill me with an overdose of pleasure, and I'd go willingly."

Smiling, Vanessa pushed him away. "I see what's *really* on your mind."

"I'm serious about the partnership. Your dream is to open your own restaurant. My dream is to be with you and make you happy. I have the credits for it. We can open it together."

The idea intrigued her, and she appreciated his support, but what if her restaurant failed? She didn't want him to invest in something that could end up being unsuccessful. "I don't want to take your hard-earned credits. I can save up. I mean, what if it doesn't work out?"

"You mean us or the business?"

"Both."

"Business is risky, and so is love. There's nothing wrong with investing in someone I love. Don't deny me that. This passion to help you is the one thing I'm absolutely sure about."

His words touched a sensitive cord that kept the tears flowing. Why was she so damn sensitive right now?

"Do you need me to make you a chart of the pros and cons? Because I will."

Vanessa took the second tissue from his hand. "How can I refuse this kind of love? I'd be a fool to do so."

"Excellent. After breakfast, we can visit Abba's restaurant. Did you know she decided to sell it? She wants to open a smaller restaurant down the street from her house to be closer to her family, and she doesn't need the current space anymore. Heard it from the property owner. It could be yours if you want that space."

Vanessa placed a hand on her heart. That was the perfect space with the large yard. Not to mention the memory where they met. "I love that space."

"Perfect then. We can take a look and decide on a name."

"How about 'Trust Your Gut?'"

He angled his head in consideration. "It's you—it's perfect."

Joy filled every part of her body. She had a man who loved and supported her. She never imagined finding him on another planet. But the Universe had its own plans, and she was grateful for them.

She leaned over the table and kissed him. "Just so you know, you've inspired my special culinary assortment called In the Mood novelties. They'll be special orders for adults only. I'm going to ask Inga to promote them with her edible lingerie collection. I think they'll do well together."

Arkon grinned. "Just so you know, I'm always *in the mood* for you, love. In fact, I'm free after breakfast."

Vanessa almost choked on her herbal drink. "Do you have books on Saedo history? I want to start my research."

"You want the ancient texts. The Village Library has a collection of sacred Saedo texts. We can stop by and ask your sister to make copies for you. The originals can't leave the library."

"Great, I'll contact Rita and let her know we'll swing by."

As the two lovers enjoyed their breakfast and immersed themselves in exciting conversations about their future, they didn't notice another petal opening from the purple flower. Or that a breath of purple mist emerged from it and twined its way through the window on a sacred mission. The mission to wake up the family that would assist in protecting Saedo and all its residents.

Thank you so much for reading! I hope you enjoyed Arkon and Vanessa's story. Read Rita and Jarzell's story in **An Alien Lore**.

Don't miss out on any new releases. Sign up for my newsletter!

http://callazae.com/newsletter/

Blurb

His heart is engulfed with the dark... but for her, it awakens with light.

Disheartened with relationships, Cathy Lu concentrates on her career. But the magic around the August Full Moon lures her to a stunning angel who illuminates her desires in a way that makes her wonder if everything is just an illusion.

As a seraph bound to blood, death, and responsibility, Daedriel has never had a long-term lover. But one kiss from Cathy unlocks everything for him, making him want the forever.

Can he keep her safe while evil swarms around them? Or should he keep her away from him, away from all the darkness that threatens him?

Excerpt

Cathy

Cathy Lu hammered a nail into the plank of wood on her back deck and thought about her ex-boyfriend—specifically his family jewels. How would he feel if she pounded him like this nail? Yes, it was a morbid thought, but as an ex-girlfriend who had been betrayed, she had every right to feel that way. Cheaters deserved a painful punishment, didn't they? They had to feel all the pain they'd bestowed on their significant other. That should be a law. So, she envisioned all the things that made her feel better. Wasn't that part of the healing process?

She pounded another nail into the wood and admired her work. She'd learned a few handy things during her two-year relationship with Gavin. He had promised to renovate her deck and the new studio she was adding to her house. But promises from a cheating man rusted over time. It made her wary of men's promises in general. Now, she depended on herself.

Cathy had kicked Gavin out of her home four months ago when she discovered several text messages and emails he'd been sending to two other women. She should have suspected something was up when he came home later than usual or when he had unexpected phone calls that took him into another room. She had been too trusting.

She considered herself an intelligent woman, but when she discovered the truth about Gavin, it made her feel stupid. Love had a way of distorting things, and she couldn't afford another loss like that. She was careful now. She had to be. Her heart had shattered, and she had hammered it back together. She sighed at the symbolism of hurting Gavin and also piecing herself together by hammering a single nail. Maybe that idea could make its way into her new greeting card collection.

Despite it all, she had moved on, mending herself one step at a time. Time spent alone gave her the retrospection and the clarity to focus on her company, Luminous Press. She had a small team of people who worked for her, making sure her journals, novelty books, greeting cards, and other miscellaneous products were delivered on time to their vendors. She and her mother, Celia, had started the company eight years ago, when she was twenty-five years old. Working with her mom had taught her how to be a successful businesswoman and a decent person who looked at things with compassion.

Be gentle to everyone. You never know what someone is going through. You can't measure someone else's pain from a personal scale.

Everything was different when it was personal, wasn't it? The measuring scale changed when you were the one experiencing the pain. It was all perspective. No one could ever understand that misery until they'd experienced it themselves. Standing on the outside made it difficult to see the storm from within.

Her mother's wise words echoed in her mind. If only her mom were still alive, she'd comfort Cathy, reminding her that not all men were the same.

Victor Perez knocked on the glass panel of her sliding door, opened it, and stepped out to the deck. "I'm all done for the day, Cathy. The two bathrooms, kitchen, and living room are all spotless now." He smiled and removed the apron, folding it into his hand.

Cathy rose to her feet and stretched her back. She appreciated his gesture even though she knew that his wife, Rosa, needed him more. Rosa and Victor had been cleaning Cathy's house for the last two years until she fell sick with a thyroid disorder that had gotten worse in the last few months. They had planned on early retirement, but life threw a curveball at them that readjusted their plans. So now, it was just Victor supporting his family. Their daughter, Lizzi, who was also Cathy's friend, lived in New York. She'd come home to visit and assist them whenever she could.

"Do you need me to help you with anything else before I head home?" Victor asked.

The weight of his wife's illness sagged on his face even with that adorable smile. The eyes and facial features revealed a lot of things that people didn't realize.

Cathy tapped the hammer against her hand. "I've got it handled. Thank you, though. Please send my best to Rosa. How's she doing?"

Victor sighed, and his shoulders drooped. "She's improving slowly. Her hair isn't falling out as much now with the new medication. We have a doctor's appointment next Friday to follow up. I'm praying for good news."

Cathy squeezed his arm. "Please keep me posted. Rosa's a strong woman. I'm sure she'll overcome this."

He nodded, giving her a warm smile. "Thank you."

"You don't have to come next week. I'll see you in two weeks," Cathy said and noticed the worry lines on his forehead. "Don't worry. The payment won't change. I figure you could use that time to be with Rosa. Besides, I live here alone. How much of a mess can I possibly make in a week?" She knew most people hired a cleaning service every two weeks, but she kept Victor and Rosa on once a week. She liked them and didn't mind supporting their business. They had been cleaning for her mom before Cathy hired them for her own house.

His eyes watered. "I don't know what to say."

"Say that you'll make the best of it. Life is short, Victor. Be with your family when you can."

After Victor left, Cathy resumed her work. She tried to take the same advice she gave to others, which was why she planned a three-week vacation to regroup. She hadn't taken a break in a long time, so this vacation was a treat. Her best friend, Sydney, the vice president of Luminous Press, could manage while Cathy was away.

Cathy planned on using this extra time to brainstorm the greeting card collections for the next few seasons. Designing the art for the greeting cards was one of the fun parts of her business. It activated a different area in her brain that wasn't crammed with numbers, profit margins, production, deliveries, and so on.

A bird squawked somewhere, and the unique sound broke through the silence. She rose from the deck and glanced toward the woods that drew her to this place. Beyond the trees was the gorgeous Prudent Lake. She had brought a tent out there a few times and slept under the moon and stars. She was due for another adventure soon, especially with the August Moon Festival next week.

When she was six years old, she looked out her bedroom window at the full moon and saw a gold rim around it. It glowed for a while, mesmerizing her. At that time, she had felt a warmth brush against her face when the rim glowed, but it could've been the imagination of a child believing in magic and fairytales. Because of that childhood experience, Cathy felt an odd friendship with it. The moon pulled at her in an inexplicable way.

With nature as her background, Cathy found the stability to move on after her mother's death a year ago. They used to come to Prudent Lake on vacation when she was little, so living here was somehow reliving the precious moments they'd shared together. She had no idea where her father had gone. He left when she was six, and that broke her mother.

Another squawk rang out, and she looked around, trying to see the bird or hawk that was making the lovely sound. She spotted nothing. She went into her kitchen, took out the bag of birdseed, and filled her bird feeder. "Enjoy your snacks."

She loved watching the birds gathered in her backyard like

it was their playground. The enchanting sounds of nature were the spa that relaxed her.

Her phone rang, and Sydney's name flashed on the screen. "Hey, I don't mean to interrupt your vacation, but I just wanted to remind you about the August Moon Festival next Friday in Boston. Are you going?"

The August Moon Festival was a special time of the year for her family and her heritage. In the past, she'd attend the event with her mother. But this year, Cathy wanted to do something personal, something without the crowd. She could celebrate the holiday right in her backyard.

"I'm going to pass. I'll just do something small at home."

"Are you sure?" Disappointment leaked from Sydney's voice. They had met in college and became fast friends.

Cathy appreciated Sydney's intelligence and foresight when it came to business. Outside of business, Sydney was the trusted friend every woman deserved. Without Sydney's support in both business and friendship, Cathy didn't know if Luminous Press would be as successful as it was.

"Yes, I'm not in the mood for crowds this year."

"Hang out with us girls," Sydney said. "We love talking shit about cheaters, and there's *a lot* of them. That means we'll have plenty of conversations and drinks."

Cathy laughed, appreciating her friend. "We'll hang out soon, I promise. I need to hire a contractor to finish my studio. I want to get it done before I return to work. And I'm brainstorming the new greeting card collection too."

"You're *supposed* to be on vacation," Sydney said with a disapproving tone.

"Yes, *Mom*. I know, I know. I don't mind it, though. The creative part is fun for me. You know that."

"I do, and that's why I'm not driving over there and dragging you away. Do you want me to bring you back any mooncakes, lanterns, food, or anything?"

"No, thanks. I already placed an order for the mooncakes. They're being shipped to me. Have fun, and don't forget to make your wish to the Moon Goddess. You never know. She could make your dreams come true."

"I'll be sure to make a long list for her. She should find something on there to give me," Sydney said.

"You are the queen of lists." Cathy could imagine the several pages of demands from Sydney.

"Hopefully, the Moon Goddess won't find me too high-maintenance. I only want intelligent, sexy, humorous, and thoughtful men to come to my door. I'll even settle for their snores and messiness." She let out an unladylike laugh. "Maybe we're doomed, Cathy. Maybe we're meant to be alone, which I don't mind now and then. But sometimes I miss that connection, you know? What happened to all the decent men who wanted gorgeous women with acute intelligence and creativity?"

"We're not doomed," Cathy reassured her best friend. "We're special, and special things are rare. 'Decent' men are rare too. We just have to wait for our turn. In the meantime, live life. Have fun. The right guy will come along. You're a fabulous catch, and you need someone who measures up to you. Don't ever lower your standards to be with someone."

Though Cathy offered words of encouragement to her friend, a part of her wondered if there was a decent man out there waiting for her. After her failed relationship, it was hard to believe in happily ever after.

"This is why Luminous Press is successful," Sydney said. "You always turn the bitter into beauty. We make fabulous journals and greeting cards that give people hope."

"Hope is the lantern that gives off light when you need it."

Cathy didn't know why these deep thoughts were spewing out of her so easily.

"Oh, I just thought of something!" Sydney said with excitement. "What do you think of these for Valentine's Day cards? *Do you want to be my lantern? I burn for you. Let me light you up! Let's illuminate the night together.*" She giggled. "They're cute and cheesy, but I have a weakness for that stuff."

"I think they're perfect." Cathy grinned into the phone, admiring the creativity of her friend. "I'll let you handle the next Valentine's Day Collection."

"Cute and cheesy, here I come."

Their conversation carried on a few more minutes before Sydney had to run to a meeting.

Cathy tucked her phone into the back pocket of her shorts, picked up the hammer from the deck, and dropped it into the pouch of her tool belt strapped around her waist. She strode over to the unfinished addition on the side of her house, which also shared the same deck. With hands on her hips, she envisioned the complete studio that would allow her more space to create.

Another squawk erupted nearby. Cathy glanced over to the tree next to her just in time to see a splash of glistening white feathers disappear into the woods.

What kind of bird was that? She loved discovering strange animals and rushed down the steps in the hope of catching the bird. Hoping it perched somewhere close for her to peek, Cathy made her way into the woods.

About ten feet in, she didn't see anything and headed back to her deck. As she walked, a strange sensation pulled at her. She wobbled a bit and blamed her imbalance on the lunch she missed. She got caught up with all the hammering. She glanced at her phone; it was already six in the evening. It was time for dinner. *Shit.*

She got back onto the deck and was about to enter her home to make a sandwich when she heard the squawk again. This time, it sounded further away, but the call echoed through the woods like gentle music that penetrated through the clutter of your mind, catching your attention. Not only that, she heard a loud swoosh of wings flapping somewhere. A powerful gust of wind carried an interesting scent to her nose. Was it citrus or sage? She wasn't sure, but she liked the aroma. It soothed her.

She waited a beat to see if she could hear it again, but silence reigned. Was it her imagination? Or was there some large bird out there? Perhaps it was someone's exotic pet that had gotten lost.

She'd investigate after she fed herself.

Read now! **Unlock the Angel**
www.callazae.com/books

ACKNOWLEDGMENTS

Thank you to Laurie, Carol, and Anna who helped my story shine. You are the shiny siSTARS in my galaxy. Thank you to my family who always give me everything I need to pursue my dreams. You are my entire Universe.

And thank you, dear readers, you give me a reason to keep writing. Without you, there's no one to appreciate the stardust within my creation. You have my utmost gratitude. Thank you, thank you, thank you.

ABOUT THE AUTHOR
CALLA ZAE

Calla Zae writes otherworldly romance. She loves delving into fantastical worlds where her imagination roams wild. Calla is also an artist who enjoys playing with colors, textures, and patterns. She has a love for mysticism, astrology, astronomy, Kdrama, Cdramas, true crime TV shows, romantic suspense novels, cats, and nature.

Calla lives in Massachusetts with her husband who keeps her grounded to Earth and two creative children who think she has her own secret planet. They're onto something...